JEALOUS OBSESSIONS

JEALOUS OBSESSIONS

From the Editors
Of *True Story* And
True Confessions

Published by True Renditions, LLC

True Renditions, LLC
105 E. 34th Street, Suite 141
New York, NY 10016

ISBN: 978-1-938877-66-7

Visit us on the web at www.truerenditionsllc.com.

Contents

JEALOUS OF
MY DAUGHTER
I want her husband and her life

"We'll get together on Monday and discuss the party," my son-in-law said. He squeezed my shoulder and ran down the steps to the car where my daughter was waiting in the passenger seat.

"Thanks again for dinner," Holly called from the open car window.

I waved good-bye to them and tried to ignore the shivers of desire running through my veins from Luke's touch. As their car disappeared down the street I closed the door behind me and leaned against it. What kind of mother thought about making love to her daughter's husband? What kind of mother looked at her daughter and son-in-law and had to fight waves of envy and swallow pangs of jealousy? Certainly not the kind of mother I thought I'd ever be.

Ashamed of the person I'd become, I moved away from the door and walked through the living room. As usual, my husband, Jerome, was sprawled in his recliner, deep asleep in front of the television. Gentle sounds of snoring escaped his lips, and his arms flopped over the sides of the chair. I picked up the remote control from the floor and flipped off the game that was playing on the television.

Another evening of stimulating conversation, I thought to myself as I wandered into the kitchen.

Thanks to Holly and Luke's help the dinner dishes were in the dishwasher and the counters were sparkling clean. A partially filled bottle of wine left over from dinner caught my attention. I pulled a glass from the cupboard, filled it, and went out to the patio to gather my thoughts. I had a lot on my mind, and most of it centered on Luke.

I plopped down on a chaise lounge and put up my feet. Jerome and I had a lovely backyard. Totally fenced in and lush with colorful flowers, it was a private haven from the busyness of the front yard with its traffic, lawn mower motors, and children's voices at play. Yet, Jerome and I never enjoyed it together. I couldn't remember the last time the two of us sat on the patio and talked. It was hard to remember when we'd really talked in any setting. That was one of the things that had drawn me to Luke. He was always ready to engage in conversation about everything in the world, from topics related to our family, to hot issues off the evening news.

I leaned my head against the cushion and closed my eyes. An image of Luke immediately appeared in my mind, stirring my senses.

1

Luke was the kind of man that demanded a woman's attention. He was tall with a hard, lean body from jogging daily. He had thick hair that I would love to run my hands through, and deep eyes with flecks of gold that came alive when he laughed. Besides his good looks, he had an outgoing personality with everyone he met. He showed a genuine interest in people and had a caring heart. Those qualities had probably helped him win the Teacher of the Year award last year.

Holly met Luke when he joined the staff at Southview High where she was an art teacher. She'd dated him for a couple of months before bringing him home to meet Jerome and me.

"There's something I have to tell you about Luke before you meet him," Holly had said as I fixed a special dinner for the four of us.

I couldn't imagine what Holly had to tell me. For weeks she'd been telling me how much she and Luke had in common, and how Luke was a nice person. What more could she say? I looked up from the cutting board and met her gaze.

"He's older than me," she blurted out.

Her comment took me by surprise, and I wasn't sure how to react. But I knew how to react when she said he was forty-one. Worry instantly filled my bones. Luke was thirteen years older than Holly, and only ten years younger than me. Such age differences weren't unheard of, but I'd always thought Holly would marry someone closer to her age.

When I warned Jerome before Luke arrived, his jaw dropped. "He's too old for her," Jerome said. "Holly may not notice the age difference now, but she will when they get older." Our gazes met and held, his eyes echoing my worry.

When we met Luke, he was everything Holly said he would be. He had a quick mind, a great sense of humor, and a helpful nature that was hard not to like. Jerome's and my worries about the age difference began to fade the more we got to know him. When they got married a few months later, my heart overflowed with happiness that Holly had found such a wonderful man to be her husband. They'd been married over a year now and still beamed like a newlywed couple.

I'd never thought of Luke as anything other than my son-in-law until a month ago when he and Holly came over for a barbeque. Usually Jerome manned the barbeque, but that day he was content to sit on a chaise and let Luke do the grilling. Luke and I worked elbow to elbow as we marinated the steaks, lit the grill, and served dinner. Holly was helping, too, but she spent most of her time preparing salads, slicing bread, and setting the table.

It was like I was viewing Luke though a different pair of eyes. Instead of seeing him as Holly's husband, I was seeing him as a man about my age—a man loaded with sexual chemistry. As we worked side-by-side preparing the steaks I was all too aware of the warmth of his body—it was like his body heat was radiating all around me and warming me from head to toe. Coupled with the heat of his body was the scent of his cologne—a soft spicy fragrance that made me want to touch him. I tried to ignore these sensations, but it was impossible. When we were done mixing the marinade, he looked down at me and smiled. My insides melted. I quickly found an excuse to step away for a moment so I could get away from him and quiet the desires running through my body that were frightening me.

I told myself I was just overwhelmed by his physical presence, and that I just hadn't thought of him as anything other than Holly's husband. But when we sat down to dinner I couldn't ignore the depth of our conversations and his attentiveness toward me. He wasn't flirting with me; he was just being himself. I was seeing him from a different perspective, and I was attracted to what I saw.

I thought my feelings toward Luke were a once in a lifetime occurrence, but the next time I was around him my eyes immediately noticed his tight-fitting jeans. I even felt awkward around him, like a schoolgirl with a crush on someone. My feelings took an even different turn when I saw Luke and Holly together. Luke paid attention to her; he gave her little love pats; and their behavior toward each other radiated love. I wanted a marriage like that. I wanted to feel openly desired by a man. I was envious of my daughter's marriage.

I took a sip of my wine. I knew why I was having these feelings toward Luke. My marriage was no longer alive. I hadn't wanted to admit it, but that had to be the reason I was attracted to Luke. I don't know what happened to my marriage to Jerome. We got along fine and didn't argue. There just wasn't any excitement anymore, or conversation. We used to talk all the time, while I worked in the kitchen, while we had meals, and as we lay in bed at night. We didn't ignore each other now, but we no longer had the deep conversations that I used to enjoy so much.

Life in the bedroom had slowed down, too. I remembered when Jerome could hardly keep his hands off of me. Now, my husband gave me quick kisses as he left for work and came home. When we went to bed at night, it was usually to sleep, not to make love or talk about our hopes and dreams. The more I thought about it, the more I realized that it was no wonder my body and mind came alive around Luke. I wasn't getting my basic needs met from my marriage.

But I wouldn't get carried away with my feelings and needs. I loved Holly, and I would never do anything to jeopardize her happiness. Besides, I wasn't the type of woman to have an affair and cheat on her husband. Jerome had a kind heart and was a loyal husband. I'd never want to hurt him. I loved Jerome. I didn't want a new husband;

I just wanted my husband and marriage back where they used to be. As unhappy as I was, I wasn't sure what I could do to breath life into my marriage. I did know that I had to quell my feelings toward Luke. Putting distance between Luke and me was the best way I knew to handle my feelings toward him. I would do everything I could to avoid being alone with him or doing things where we had a lot of physical proximity.

Unfortunately, today Luke had thrown a curve in my strategy to avoid him. He'd asked my help in planning a surprise party for Holly's thirtieth birthday. It was a last-minute idea and he only had two weeks to put everything in place. There was no way I could refuse to help. We were meeting for lunch on Monday to discuss his plans.

I got up from the chaise and walked back into the living room. Jerome was still sleeping in his chair. He did that a lot lately. I often thought it was because of his job. He was an engineer with the highway department and worked hard. But I knew in my heart that he wasn't working any harder than he used to. I didn't think he was sick—he'd just had a physical and was in tip-top shape. All I knew for sure was that he wasn't interested in me like he used to be and that my marriage felt dead.

The next day Jerome and I went to my sister Amy's house for dinner. Jerome immediately joined Amy's husband, Mitch, who was watching a game on television. The two men munched on potato chips, drank beer, and watched television while I helped Amy in the kitchen.

Although Amy was several years older than me, we'd always had a close relationship. We'd grown even closer when Mom died a couple of years ago. I could always tell Amy everything. She was a great source of advice because she'd often experienced the current problem I was facing. But discussing my feelings toward Luke wasn't the same as the times I talked to her about my first day of high school, having a baby, or hot flashes.

Amy's marriage to Mitch was as solid as a rock, and she'd never understand how I could be interested in anyone other than Jerome— especially my son-in-law. Yet, I ached to tell her about my feelings to see if she had any ideas to help me. I knew sharing my ugly feelings was impossible, so I concentrated on Amy as she talked about some of the things going on in her office. When she started talking about a coworker who was having an affair, I had a perfect opening to at least touch on my guilty feelings, and perhaps get some insight from her.

"I can understand how affairs happen," I began.

"But this woman is married to a wonderful man," she argued.

"I am, too, but I've become interested in someone," I said softly.

Amy's eyes widened, and her mouth opened slightly.

"Nothing has happened between us," I added quickly. "I don't think that he's even aware that I'm interested in him."

Amy slowly set down the sack of frozen vegetables she was opening, and her gaze met mine. "Is he married, too?"

I nodded. My stomach grew tight as I realized how twisted the situation was.

She glanced into the living room at our husbands watching television, making sure we couldn't be overheard. "You've got to get your feelings under control before someone gets hurt and you ruin your marriage." Although she was whispering, I felt like I was being whipped. She assumed that the man was someone I worked with, and she lectured me about the problems with office affairs. Every so often she looked over her shoulder into the living room as though Jerome was going to walk in on us at any moment. "How could this happen?" she finally asked.

"It's like Jerome and I are two roommates sharing a house," I said. "Sometimes I don't think he knows I'm alive."

"Then you need to make him aware you're alive." Her blue eyes were like ice. "For all you know he's thinking the same thing about you."

"No."

"He could be," she argued. "What are you doing to make him feel appreciated or noticed?"

Her question was a blow to my stomach. I couldn't think of an answer.

"You see what I'm talking about?" my sister asked.

"I listen to him about his problems at work. I fix his favorite meals."

"How about a candlelight dinner? Or a sexy nightgown?"

I immediately pictured our dinners that we usually ate on our everyday china at the kitchen table. As for nightgowns, Amy probably wouldn't consider my faded T-shirts sexy.

"You need to get his attention. Once you get his attention and show him you're aware of him, he'll start paying more attention to you. It's like a cycle."

I nodded. As usual, Amy had good advice.

"And above all, you've got to avoid that other guy," she said in a stern voice.

"I will," I said, wishing it were that easy. Tomorrow was my lunch with Luke to discuss the surprise birthday party. An image of Luke flashed through my mind with his ready smile and deep eyes, and my heart skipped a beat.

I was pulled from my reverie when Jerome and Mitch walked into the kitchen with empty beer bottles. Remembering Amy's advice, I went over to Jerome and slipped my arm around him. He reached around and gave me a hug. Amy was right, I just needed to let Jerome know he was special to me and my marriage would get back on track.

The next day Luke was waiting for me in the restaurant when I arrived. We'd agreed to meet at a burger place at a convenient location between his school and the insurance office where I worked. The waitress showed us to a small curved booth made for two. I slipped into the booth beside him and tried not to sit too close, but the booth was small and it was impossible not to bump his thigh.

We quickly perused the menu and then both ordered teriyaki burgers. I kept telling myself I was with my son-in-law, but my heart wouldn't keep still and I kept having giddy feelings like I was on a date. I was glad when Luke pulled out a list of things we needed to work on. I returned to the role of Holly's mother as we talked about her favorite foods and colors. Luke had big plans, and a quick look told me he didn't have the money to do everything he wanted.

"I think you can save money if Amy and I prepare some of the food rather than buying it from the deli. She and I have done weddings and other special occasions together, so I think we can fix most of the food for you."

"That's great. Besides, what you prepare will be tastier than anything I can get from the deli." He smiled and covered my hand with his. I knew his gesture was meant to show his appreciation, but that didn't stop the heat from flooding through my veins.

Our hamburgers arrived, so we stopped talking about the party and dug into our lunches. The hamburgers were dripping with teriyaki sauce. They were delicious but messy to eat. I looked up at Luke once and found his gaze on me. He held up a sticky hand and we both laughed. We had a fun fight over the small pile of napkins on the table, and we giggled when the waitress brought us a huge stack. I couldn't recall when Jerome and I had laughed our way through a meal. I knew there had to be a time, but I couldn't remember when.

Luke and I only had a few minutes until we had to go back to work, so we quickly reviewed the party tasks. He'd already invited their friends, and he wanted me to invite Amy and some of our other relatives. "I'd like you to help me order the cake and pick out the party supplies," he said. "That's if you have the time."

"Sure," I said. I didn't mind helping him; I just minded his presence.

While we walked to our cars, Luke talked about the family reunion we were having in a couple of months and how his parents wanted all of us to have dinner soon. As I drove back to work I realized that avoiding Luke was going to be impossible. I'd thought things would be easier after the birthday party, but we were a close family and he and I would always be thrown together for projects and events. Working on getting Jerome's attention was my only course of action.

The next day I stopped at the mall after work and headed straight to a lingerie store Amy had told me about. I'd been by it a hundred times but had never gone in. Immediately I was in a different world, with the store's mauve wallpaper, thick carpets, and sweetly fragranced air. I walked around the displays of lingerie, letting my fingers brush the silky textures. I kept dismissing nightgowns, thinking they didn't look like me, but then I reminded myself I wanted to change my look. I wanted to get Jerome's attention. Gone were the cotton T-shirts, and in their place would be silk and satin.

Sometime later, I left the store, carrying a mauve bag filled with satin nightwear and silk panties and bras. All the while I had been shopping, Amy's suggestion that Jerome may feel unappreciated or ignored kept running through my mind. I didn't want to believe he could feel that way, but I had to admit that lately I hadn't gone out of my way to let him know that I loved or appreciated him. If anything, I'd withdrawn because I felt like he didn't notice me. The more I thought about it, the more I could see how a circle of behavior could develop. I felt unimportant so I withdrew. My withdrawal made Jerome feel unimportant, so he withdrew.

I knew a sexy nightgown and underwear weren't the answer, but they could be a catalyst to making things better between Jerome and me. Saturday night I was going to fix a romantic dinner for the two of us. I could only hope that showing Jerome that he was important to me would wake him up so that he was more aware of me. It would also help me to keep my thoughts off of Luke. And keeping my mind off of Luke wasn't easy.

Earlier that day Luke had thrown my emotions into turmoil when he had called me at work to see if I could meet him Sunday afternoon to order the birthday cake and get party supplies. Holly was going to a baby shower that afternoon so he had a perfect opportunity to shop for her birthday things. Luke had never called me before; Holly always called. The deep sound of his voice took me by surprise, sending my heart leaping as I instantly pictured his eyes and sexy smile. As we made plans for Sunday my mind drifted back to our lunch. I'd had so much fun. I blushed when I remembered how my body had tingled being so close to his in the booth.

I had to forget those thoughts and do everything I could to revive my marriage.

"Who's coming to dinner?" Jerome asked as he looked at the dining room table Saturday night. I'd set the table with my best tablecloth, formal dishes, and candles. I'd even put napkin rings on the napkins and placed them in the center of each plate.

"We are." I smiled at him and met his gaze. "I thought it would be fun to have a special dinner just for the two of us."

"It sure smells good." He followed me into the kitchen where I was making sauce for steak. Twice-baked potatoes were in the oven, and a Caesar salad was chilling in the refrigerator.

Jerome walked over to the counter and picked up the bottle of red wine I'd bought. It was one of his favorites and was more expensive than the bottles we usually had for dinner. His eyes widened and he turned to face me. "You really are going all out."

"I thought you'd like a special dinner."

"Your steak is always a treat," he said, "and with this wine, it'll be wonderful." He reached for the corkscrew and began opening the bottle.

We were at the table only ten minutes when my hopes for a dinner with lively conversation died. When we first sat down, we talked about his brother's new house, Holly's birthday party, and other things. Then, the conversation lagged and we finished our meal quietly. As we cleared the dishes I tried to reassure myself that I'd made progress. I'd fixed Jerome a special dinner, and he'd noticed. He also appreciated my efforts, because he remarked several times that he liked the steak. I just had to be patient.

That night as we got ready for bed I started to put on one of my new nightgowns and then thought better of it. Dinner hadn't worked out as well as I'd hoped, and I didn't want to be disappointed again. I knew my instincts had been right when Jerome fell asleep as soon as his head hit the pillow. It would take more than a silk nightgown to ignite his fire. I began to wonder if my marriage would ever be alive again. What if this was the way it would always be? Sleep wouldn't come as I imagined a lonely life with Jerome, while my feelings for Luke still burned strong.

The next afternoon as I drove to the shopping center to meet Luke, I told myself to put a lid on my emotions. I kept reminding myself how wrong my feelings were, and how much would be destroyed if I ever inadvertently let Luke know how I felt toward him. All my resolve to hold my emotions in check melted when I spotted Luke waiting for me near the shopping center entrance. He was wearing a navy blue T-shirt from the high school where he taught and a faded pair of jeans. The T-shirt stretched over his lean body, outlining a firm chest and strong arms, and the jeans fit snugly, making my imagination run wild.

Luke spotted me as I approached and walked up to greet me. He gently squeezed my arm, sending currents of warmth rushing through my veins. I smiled up at him and tried to think like a mother-in-law instead of a woman eager for his attention.

I told him we should select the colors of the party before we ordered the cake, so we went to the party store first. Most men could care less about the color of paper plates and napkins, but Luke took a deep interest in the colors we chose.

"Holly hates orange," he said matter-of-factly as he marched past the orange and yellow plates. "These look like her." He held up a package of turquoise plates with a flowered trim.

I nodded. I thought we were well on our way to leaving the store, but Luke had other ideas. "I had no idea there was so much party stuff here." We wound up going through most of the store looking at holiday displays, balloons, and other party items.

"This is fun," he said as we looked at a Halloween skeleton that glowed in the dark. In the next aisle Luke held up a bushy mustache next to his nose, and we both laughed.

I was having fun, too. Too much fun. I couldn't imagine Jerome even coming to a party store, let alone wanting to stay and look at things.

Eventually, we left the party store and walked through the shopping mall to the bakery. Again, I was amazed at Luke's depth of interest. He wanted Holly's party to be perfect, so he asked the bakery clerk detailed questions about the various cake fillings and frostings so that he would select just what she liked. Twinges of jealousy and envy crept into my heart, making me hate myself for having such feelings.

"Let me buy you a cappuccino," Luke said as we left the bakery. As usual, I was filled with mixed emotions. I wanted to be with him, yet I knew I should cut our time together short. When he said we needed to go over the menu one more time, I agreed to the coffee. He was right; we needed to finalize things. The party was next Saturday.

"It's a great party," Amy said. Holly's birthday party was in full swing, and Amy and I were taking a breather in the kitchen. I poured Amy a glass of wine, and then filled a glass for myself.

"Holly was genuinely surprised," I said as I recalled her scream of surprise and wide eyes as she walked into the living room and saw her friends and family.

"How are things going with you and Jerome?" Amy asked. All of the guests were in the backyard so no one could overhear us.

"I've followed some of your ideas, but no major changes," I said. I told her about the special dinner I'd prepared, and how I'd gone out of my way to show my appreciation toward Jerome and to let him know that I cared.

"It takes time." Amy took a sip of her wine. "What about that guy you were interested in?"

"I'm avoiding him as much as I can," I said. I gazed out of the sliding glass door to the patio and saw Luke give Holly a hug. I tried to stop the painful twinges of envy and jealousy, but they were too powerful to control.

"Things sure worked out for Holly and Luke," Amy remarked as she watched them laughing and teasing in the backyard. "They look so happy together."

"That's what I want," I said softly.

"What?" Amy asked.

"I want a marriage like they have—a marriage that is alive and exciting. Like mine used to be." Watching them was too painful, so I turned away from the door.

Amy followed me over to the kitchen counter. Her brow was knitted into a thoughtful expression, and her eyes were serious.

"I'm not sure candlelight dinners and sexy nightgowns are going to help me," I said.

"I don't think so, either." Amy's tone reflected the seriousness in her eyes. "I thought you were just feeling a little neglected at home, so you were attracted to someone at work. It sounds like you've got more serious issues."

"I feel like my marriage is dead. There's no excitement, no feeling."

"It may be a phase of life you're at." She leaned against the counter and looked thoughtful as she talked. "When we first get married, we're busy setting up our homes and starting families. Then comes the years of doing things with the kids and planning for their future. Then the kids leave home and there is suddenly a quiet period with just two people."

"Things did seem to change when Holly moved out and got married," I admitted. "It was like the pace of life slowed down."

"You and Jerome are alone for the first time in years with nothing to really focus on."

The more she talked, the more I thought her concepts had merit. Jerome and I had always worked together on projects and the future. Now, the projects were done, and our lives were on a more even keel. There was nothing for us to work toward.

"You came close to having an affair that could've destroyed your marriage," Amy was saying. "You need to tell Jerome what you're feeling, for both your sakes."

I cringed as I thought how right she was about the danger of my feelings toward Luke. My feelings were wrong and destructive.

Our conversation was interrupted when Luke stepped into the kitchen and said it was time to serve the cake. The rest of the afternoon I was busy with the party, but Amy's advice stuck in my mind and heart. Talking to Jerome about my feelings was the right thing to do. I just wasn't sure how to do it. Jerome and I had never talked about problems in our marriage.

A couple of days later I'd just gotten home from work when the doorbell rang. It was Luke. He was wearing his clothes from work—

10

dark wool slacks, a white shirt open at the neck, and a sports coat. In his hand was a pink mum in a pot wrapped in silver foil.

"A little thank you for helping with the party," he said as I showed him into the house.

Just seeing him made my pulses race, and I was speechless that he'd buy me a plant to show his appreciation. I hadn't done that much to help, no more than any other mother would've done for their daughter's birthday party.

I set the plant in the center of the dining room table and offered Luke a soda.

"After the day I've had, I feel like something much stronger, but I'll settle for a ginger ale."

"Bad day, huh?" I asked as he followed me into the kitchen and sat down on one of the bar stools.

"Just a personnel problem I've been working on," he said as he ran his hands through his hair.

I set a glass of ginger ale in front of him and stood across the counter from him—near, but not close. His sexiness filled the room, warming my body with sensations that I knew were wrong. I knew I should be as far away from him as possible.

"I'm not a mind reader," he began, his voice filled with frustration. "I've wasted a lot of time and created an unnecessary problem because the principal wouldn't tell me what was really wrong."

It was obvious Luke needed to unload about this problem and was happy to have a listening ear. While he talked, I couldn't help thinking about my situation with Jerome. My husband wasn't a mind reader, either, and in my own way I was creating a problem by not talking to him.

"The direct approach is best," Luke was saying. "That way issues can be dealt with before they become major problems."

I nodded in agreement, encouraging him to talk. The school principal had handled his problem much like I'd been dealing with Jerome. The direct approach may not be easy, but it is more effective. And Amy had said to talk to Jerome.

Luke slid off the stool. "I've got to get home, and it looks like you've got dinner to fix." He glanced at the box of pasta and jar of sauce sitting on the counter.

I nodded. "One of Jerome's favorites."

"Sorry to have dumped on you with my work problems. I'd just got done talking to the principal and I hadn't calmed down yet."

"No problem. It was interesting." And a good lesson for me, I thought as I walked him to the door.

I didn't plan to talk to Jerome right away, but that night I had a good opportunity when he joked about becoming a grandfather.

We'd just finished dinner and Jerome had been remarking how nice it was that Luke had given me the mum. "I expect Holly to make an announcement any day," he said as he sank into his recliner.

I plopped down on the sofa, kicked off my shoes, and tucked my feet under me. "Being grandparents will be something new for us."

He nodded in agreement.

I told him about the conversation I'd had with Amy about how marriages focus on different things through the years. "Right now I feel like we aren't at a phase."

Jerome's gaze met mine. "It's funny that you'd mention it, because I've been feeling out of sorts lately. It seemed like we were so busy and then Holly moved out."

"Sometimes I've worried that you're not interested in me," I said.

"What? Lynn, you're my life. How could you think that?"

"We don't talk as much as we used to over dinner, or sit on the patio together," I said.

Jerome was quiet, like he was thinking. I wondered if I'd offended him and started to say something, but then he spoke. "When I think about it, most of our conversations used to be about Holly or your job. We were planning for her college, or gearing up to meet the next boyfriend she brought to our door. Then you went through all that red tape to get your promotion."

"That's true," I said as I thought back to some of our conversations. My promotion had been a tough fight and every night I had given Jerome the latest blow-by-blow on what had happened that day at work.

"I know we haven't run out of things to talk about," he said. "I think we need something to focus on and build toward. Maybe our retirement plans."

"We really haven't talked about retirement," I said. "I know we've been saving money toward it."

"There's a lot to think about," he said as he straightened in his chair. "Do we keep living in this house? Do we move to Arizona where your friends moved? Will we want to work part-time or volunteer somewhere?"

"I don't know." He'd laid out some big questions that had no quick answers.

Jerome got up from his recliner and sat down next to me. "I do know that whatever we do, I want to do it together." He put his arm around me and pulled me against his chest. "And I want us to get back into our old groove again. I don't like feeling this way."

"I even bought a fancy nightgown to get your interest, but I thought we should talk instead." I giggled thinking about the nightgown stashed in my dresser drawer.

12

"Can't you wear your nightgown and talk, too?"

We laughed together and it began to feel like old times again. I wrapped my arms around Jerome as his lips came crushing down on mine, sending sensations through my bones until I was breathless. I never did get my new nightgown on that night, and we didn't talk any more, but we made love like we hadn't in years.

That night was the start of reviving my marriage. Change didn't happen overnight, but Jerome and I cared enough about our marriage to take steps to make it better. We are busy remodeling our house because we want to live there after we've retired. No way are we going to move out of town—according to Holly we're going to be grandparents soon and we want to be close to our grandchild.

Jerome and I have started doing more little things together, like taking walks around the neighborhood and talking with neighbors we've never gotten to know. In a month we're going on a vacation that we postponed because we were previously paying Holly's college expenses.

Like many problems in life, I found it was better to take the direct approach and talk about what was bothering me. Being direct can be scary at times, but the consequences of not speaking the truth can be devastating. My feelings for Luke have returned to the place that they belong—those of a mother-in-law. As for being envious of Holly's marriage, I'm too busy enjoying my own marriage.

THE END

MRS. PITT VS. MRS. PITT, THE SECOND:
He eats dinner with me—then spends the night catering to her needs!

I thought I could trust my new husband, but my patience was wearing thin. He sweared he loved me—

So why was he spending so much time at his ex-wife's house?

Garrett and I had just settled on the couch to watch Stargate SG1 when the phone rang. Somehow, I just knew it was my husband's ex-wife. Indeed, this was the second time that week that she called, and Garrett always responded to her pleas for help like a search-and-rescue dog called to service to locate the survivors of an avalanche.

"What does Izumi want now?" I asked after he got off the phone with her.

He sighed. "The water heater's not working."

"So what? Can't she call a repairman?"

"At eight o'clock on a Sunday night?"

"Then let them use cold water and she can call in the morning."

"Oh, come on, Mindy," Garrett scoffed. He stood behind me and massaged my shoulders, gently kneading them, just the way I like it. "You can't expect my boy to shower in ice-cold water. Sam has school tomorrow; if I can't fix it, I guess they'll have to manage, but I'd at least like to try."

Having witnessed, during Sam's visits, how dirty an eight-year-old can get, I reluctantly agreed. "Okay," I said, reaching up to stroke Garrett's face. "Do your best and hurry back."

He kissed me, picked up his car keys, and headed out the door. As his car drove off, I paced the living room, muttering nasty things about Izumi under my breath.

So, okay—she was Garrett's wife for ten years and she's the mother of his son. But she for damn sure isn't his wife any longer! Garrett really has no excuses for running over there whenever she calls.

As it was, each time he left me to go over to Izumi's house, I got the distinct feeling that she was using that time to try to get him back. I know it probably sounds silly and insecure of me to you, but honestly—I couldn't help myself. At the time, Garrett and I had only been married for nine weeks and already, I very clearly heard, saw, and felt myself acting every inch the overly possessive wife. But the way I looked at it back then, there I was—in a strange town, alone in the house, and my husband was over at his ex-wife's!

Isn't there something very wrong with this picture? I often wondered.

Garrett and I met two years ago in St. Louis, Missouri. Back then, he traveled to the city every couple of weeks on business, staying in the small hotel where I worked as a night front desk clerk. Whenever he was in town, staying in the hotel, after dinner and a couple of drinks in the bar, he'd come by the reception desk and talk to me. Like many businessmen away from home, I guess he was lonely.

At first, I was attracted to his gray-green eyes and his crooked smile. But then I started noticing: Gee. He's really very thoughtful, too; he always makes a point of saying hello to me and stopping to ask how I'm doing. Sometimes, if he arrived back late from a job and it was time for my break, we'd share Chinese takeout in the lobby; we both love Chinese food. And on one trip, he brought me a gift of a Justin Timberlake CD. Justin's my favorite singer, and I was very flattered that Garrett remembered that.

Garrett's more mature than the guys I usually dated, and he had a lot more to talk about than just the Cardinals' latest win, so I was thrilled when he asked me out on a date, and after that first date, we just got right into the habit of spending all of our free time together whenever he was in town. Truth be told—I looked forward to Garrett's visits with all of the breathless anticipation of a schoolgirl waiting for some rock star's upcoming concert. Pretty soon, things were serious between us, and when he asked me to marry him, I immediately said yes.

Garrett told me right from the very start that he was divorced; in fact, he often spoke about how much he missed being with his son. Sam was six then, and Garrett often showed me his pictures. He explained to me that he and his ex-wife, Izumi, married too young and for all of the wrong reasons, and finally they just grew apart, but that they remained on friendly terms and shared joint custody of Sam.

Garrett's ex kept the house as part of the divorce settlement, since Garrett didn't want any added upheavals in Sam's life. Nonetheless, living in St. Louis after we got married was out of the question (that would mean Garrett lived too far away from his son to see him regularly), so I agreed to relocate. My mom and her new husband are the only family I left behind and as it is, whenever they aren't working, Mom and Red spend practically all of their free time driving around the country in their R.V.

When Garrett and I moved into our own place in his hometown, I knew that his son would stay with us every other weekend, but right off the bat I insisted that Garrett fetch and return Sam alone so that I wouldn't have to meet "The Ex." Honestly—right from the get-go, I

15

had absolutely no interest whatsoever in talking to her or finding out what she's like. All of Garrett's old photos of Izumi were packed away in a box up in the attic and I never looked inside. I guess you could say that with all of the innocence of a new bride, I didn't see—or maybe just didn't want to see—any complications that might be looming up ahead.

How stupid I was, huh?

Believe me—I tell myself just that about a million times a day!

I pretended to be asleep when Garrett finally returned, even leaving a note on his dresser reminding him that I was on the early shift at the motel where I'd found work. But, as if he could tell just from my breathing that I was still awake, he undressed in the dark, got into bed, and snuggled up tight against me.

"I fixed it," he whispered.

To show him that I forgave him for leaving me alone, I murmured, "Good," and pulled his hand up to cup my breast. As it was, my nipples hardened the moment Garrett entered our bedroom and I found myself thinking, I'll remind him of what fun we have together and maybe next time, he won't be quite so keen to run off to her aid at Izumi's beck and call!

But during the drive to work the next morning, I became hurt and angry all over again with Izumi, and I decided then that I wouldn't stand for the situation any longer. As it was, my courtship with Garrett had been long distance and intermittent. Now that we were married, I dearly wanted to spend real quality time with him without him running off to his ex-wife's every five minutes. We planned to have a family of our own, naturally, and when that happened, I knew I'd need Garrett at our house, with our baby and me! And so as I drove along to work, I started thinking: I have to do something to cut his ties to Izumi before they really become a problem.

I suppose I was grateful that she wasn't greedy during the divorce; still, money was definitely tight those days. Garrett earns a decent salary working as a mechanical engineer, installing equipment in breweries and bottling plants, but he also pays a generous amount of child support, and we had our own mortgage and bills to consider. So if and when I did have a child, I always knew I'd have to continue working.

I'm prepared to make sacrifices, but is Garrett? I often wondered. After all, making sacrifices for our family just might very well entail not giving in to Izumi's every whim and demand.

That day during a quiet period at the motel, I thought about my chances of getting pregnant. Realistically, I knew it would probably take some time, especially since Garrett traveled a great deal. So I decided it was necessary to break him of his habit of giving in to

Izumi's demands before we became new parents. Indeed, after chewing on my pencil for half an hour, I decided to proceed methodically, trying one thing at a time.

I carried out my first idea a few days later. I finished cleaning up the kitchen while Garrett was on the computer, and then I joined him and placed a piece of paper on the desk beside the keyboard.

"Look at that when you have a minute," I told him, "and tell me what you think."

"What is it?"

"It's a written account of the amount of time you've spent at your ex-wife's over the last month. Not including driving time."

"What?" Garrett peered at the list of dates and times. "Mindy, you have to be joking! You're keeping track? Are you serious?"

"You're damn straight. After all, you don't believe me and take me for my word when I tell you how often you're over at her place."

At the look of annoyance in my husband's eyes, my heart sank and instantly I worried that I'd truly angered him. But his frustration disappeared quickly, replaced by weary patience. "But it's an old house," he countered, running a hand around the back of his neck as if to loosen the stiffness after sitting so long. "Things need just fixing over there every now and then. And it has a big yard—"

"And you're the only person who can do all of that work?" I folded my arms across my chest and scowled at him in disbelief.

Garrett saw the look on my face and chuckled. "You silly bunny," he said, pulling me into his lap and nibbling on my left earlobe. "Surely you don't want me to neglect Izumi and Sam—do you? After all, I do stuff around here, too, don't I?"

Although I love the tickly feeling of Garrett's hot breath on my neck and his teeth gently, teasingly nipping at my ear, I refused to let myself be sidetracked and concentrated on forming my next words. Then I turned to look him squarely in the eyes.

"Garrett," I said, "you're a very caring person and I like that about you; in fact, I love that about you—I honestly do. But sometimes it seems like I have to ask you more than once before you do a single chore around here." He pulled back and stared at me as if I were a sulky child, but I went on regardless. "Izumi calls and you're out the door before I can even turn around to watch you leave. Or else, you're late getting home after taking Sam back, and then you always tell me that you and Izumi were 'just talking and didn't realize the time!' "

"Give me a break," Garrett groaned. "I'm doing my best, baby." Then a knowing smile spread across his face. "Hey, now—wait a minute . . . you're not jealous, are you? Because you know you don't ever have to be, Mindy. I've told you time and time again: Izumi's the mother of my son, but other than that, she's no more to me

17

than a friend. And anyway, we do have to talk about Sam together sometimes, you know."

I leaned into Garrett's chest and slipped my arms around his neck. "What am I supposed to think, though?" I asked, planting little kisses around his mouth. "After all, you were married to her. You loved her once."

"Yes, and now I'm married to you," Garrett replied. "And I love you with all my heart, and I will never leave you, I promise. I truly love you, Mindy. Izumi and I are just friends nowadays. If you met her, you'd realize—"

"I don't want to meet her." I dropped my arms and stood, my body tense and rigid as I wondered, Why can't he understand? "She's supposed to be part of your past. Instead, she's very much in the present. Our present."

I couldn't get my head around the fact that Garrett and Izumi could be more than just civil with each other. Personally, I never wanted to see any of my old boyfriends again, preferring to move on with my life and not let them drag me back. Already, though, quite the contrary, Izumi was very much the fifth wheel in our relationship. And I wasn't about to stand blithely by and watch her steer my marriage into a ditch!

My father left Mom and me just after I turned fifteen. For a couple of years even before that, though, I used to notice him checking his watch every evening, and then around nine o'clock he'd grab his car keys and head out the door. He always told us he was "going out for a beer," but he was really visiting his mistress across town. Mom never suspected a thing, she told me afterward. She always trusted him. But then a so-called friend finally spilled the beans.

When the fights started, I'd pull the blankets around me in bed and turn up the volume of my stereo to drown out their angry, vicious, bitter voices. Things escalated quickly; Dad simply went out one night and never came back. A week later he sent a buddy around to collect his clothes and stuff. Needless to say, it took years of therapy for Mom to get over him and find someone new, and she often told me that she wished she never found out about Dad's affair because he would never have left if she hadn't given him an ultimatum: the mistress or me.

I always did my best to support Mom, but I felt the sting of rejection, too. I decided I never wanted any of that awfulness to happen to me, and I thought I chose my husband wisely. But if my own father could deceive Mom for so many years, I certainly knew it was possible that Garrett was deceiving me about the real nature of his relationship with his ex.

"Mindy," Garrett said, his voice bringing me back to the present, "I know you're very precise, but this is going too far, understand?" He crumpled up the paper and tossed it into the wastebasket.

All at once, I felt as if I'd been caught red-handed going through his pants pockets for clues.

"Don't look so crestfallen." Garrett got up and put his fingers under my chin. Lifting my face to his, he said, "I'll ask Izumi not to call unless it's really urgent, okay?"

I moved into his arms, fighting back tears, thinking, I mustn't let him think I'm comparing him to Dad, because he certainly knows all about what happened with my folks after all I've told him about my life before we met. "Thank you, Garrett. I'd really like you to do that for me."

But then, just as if Garrett knew exactly what was going through my mind, he said, "Don't ever forget, Mindy: I'm not like your father."

Things settled down for a while after that, and Izumi's calls more or less stopped. Good, I thought. I've achieved my objective at my first attempt. And so I relaxed and let myself enjoy life again.

And then Sam took up soccer.

Garrett, of course, had to go watch him play. And watch him practice. And drive Sam back and forth to games when he stayed with us. And Izumi was present at all of those soccer games and practices, of course, and so my insecurity returned.

One morning, Sam ran into the bedroom, where I was propped up against the pillows, reading True Story. It was a Saturday, and one of my rare weekends off. "Aren't you coming, Mindy?" he asked. Underneath his silky mop of straight, jet-black hair, his blue eyes were bright with excitement.

"No, Sam," I told him. "I'm busy today." Okay—I know it was a weak excuse, but I didn't want to hurt Sam's feelings. After all, Garrett and Izumi are the ones I had issues with.

Immediately, he clambered up onto the bed and snuggled up beside me. "I scored two goals last week, you know."

"Good for you, Sam." I reached over and ruffled his hair. "See if you can get three goals today, okay?"

"Okay." He jumped down and ran out of the room, leaving me with a smile on my face.

Sam's a sweet kid and full of energy. When Garrett and I married, I told Sam right away that I wasn't going to be a "substitute" mom, but rather, that I really, really wanted to be his good friend. Secure in the love of both of his parents, even though they live apart, Sam readily accepted my proposition. Not having had any previous real, hands-on experience with kids, I was pleased—and, I admit, quite relieved—to discover that Sam really doesn't need much in the way of hands-on mothering from me most of the time. Basically, he's pretty independent for an eight-year-old little guy.

Just then, Garrett popped his head in around the door. "Do you need anything before we go?" he asked me sweetly.

I smiled contentedly. "No, I'm fine."

"You won't come, then."

It was more of a statement than a question, seeing as he already knew my answer.

"Will Izumi be there?" I asked.

"Yes."

I sighed dramatically. "Can't you just ask her to miss a couple of games so I can go to a few?"

Garrett stared at me. "Would you like to be asked not to attend your kid's soccer games?"

"I suppose not," I replied, but I was thinking: Why can't Izumi get sick one weekend—food poisoning, maybe—and then I can go in her place?

"So you'll get dressed and join us?" Garrett asked, obviously thinking I'd softened my stance.

"No, Garrett; I'm not coming. But you could drop Sam off at the match and come right back. He probably won't even notice that you're not there. After all, he's only eight. And this is my weekend off; we should be doing 'stuff' together," I insinuated, wriggling on the bed suggestively as I licked my lips and gave him a devilish, desirous grin.

There was a slight pause before Garrett said, "It's precisely because he's 'only eight' that he still needs me, Mindy. Can't you just get it through your head, once and for all? I want to be actively involved in every aspect of Sam's life!"

His lips were tightly compressed and I realized immediately, just looking at him, that I'd crossed the line. "I'm sorry," I said quickly. "That was really selfish of me. Forgive me?"

"Sure." Garrett's features softened as if he suddenly remembered that I'm a lot younger than he is—not to mention, new to the parenting game. He came over and gave me a long, deep kiss. "I'll make it up to you later, huh, baby? How does that sound?"

"You'd better," I teased, running my fingers over his ribs, "because it sounds absolutely erotic!"

When the door closed behind him, I tossed the magazine aside. Although I felt bad about my remark, I still thought, Surely my feelings are understandable . . . aren't they? As it was, soccer had become the bane of my life. It seemed to me that Sam played the game seven days a week, and Garrett was absent ten times more often suddenly than he'd been even when he was always doing things around Izumi's house!

Once again, I thought angrily, gritting my teeth, SHE'S spending more time with my husband than I am! I frequently imagined her standing shoulder to shoulder with Garrett in the stands, cheering when Sam headed the ball or scored a goal. And in my mind's eye, I saw them smiling at each other, if not actually hugging, whenever Sam's team scored. I feared it was just a matter of time before Garrett started staying away longer and longer. Then I knew I'd just start to nag him about it all over again, and one day, ultimately, he just wouldn't come back ever again.

I couldn't bear that, I thought, feeling a dreadful ache begin to pulse in my gut.

No, I decided with a grim sense of fatalism, it's time to put another plan into action. I thought I'd give Garrett "a taste of his own medicine" by spending time away from him. I figured maybe he'd miss having me around, forever at his disposal and on his terms, and then he'd modify his behavior of his own accord.

I didn't know too many people in town at this point, but I had become very friendly with one of the other motel clerks. Her name's Chrissy, and she's a total movie buff. Garrett prefers to watch movies on DVD that we get from Netflix at times when it's convenient for him, so I asked Chrissy if she wanted to go to the movies, she said that would be great, and so our first "outing" was arranged.

"That's nice," Garrett said when I told him. "I'm glad you're finally making some friends here."

"You're sure you don't mind me going out without you?" I asked, hoping he'd drop to his knees, fling his arms open, and cry out, "I hate being apart from you, Mindy-my-darling! Please don't leave me! Promise me that you'll always be by my side—with me until my dying day!"

Instead, he looked up from the newspaper and replied, "No, I'm fine with it, actually. In fact, it'll give me a chance to clean up the garage later on. Oh, and by the way—you look smoking-hot in those new jeans."

"Thanks."

My throat felt tight with frustration as I kissed him good-bye.

Chrissy and I went to Chili's after the movie for margaritas and nachos, and it was past midnight by the time I got home. I imagined Garrett would be standing at the front window, watching out for me, or at least waiting up for me, reading a book in bed. But when I crept into the bedroom he was fast asleep. A note on my pillow told me that he hoped I had "a good time."

Once again, my idea didn't go as planned, but as I looked over at his sleeping face, I told myself: I must be patient. All in due time; all in due time. . . .

Chrissy and I went out several times over the next few weeks. We had fun, too—that is, whenever I could forget about Garrett. You see, instead of missing me, he was actually MORE THAN HAPPY to see me doing things outside the house with other people! He never once complained, as I expected—

As I dearly wished he would.

During my absences, Garrett worked on the car, read books, or did odd jobs around the house. If he was ever over at Izumi's, other than to pick up or return Sam, he didn't say, and needless to say—not knowing for sure that he really was just "home alone" started to drive me crazy. One night I told Chrissy I was too tired to discuss the film we'd just seen and instead, went right home. There, my suspicions were proved correct: The house was empty. Panic surged through me as I called Garrett's cell phone.

As soon as he answered, I yelled, "Where are you? Why aren't you home?"

"Oh, hi, Mindy. You got back early, huh? I'm, um—I'm at Izumi's, actually."

"Oh?" My insides did a flip, and then a flop. Garrett didn't deny being there, but all the same he sounded distant, like his mind was on something else.

"Why are you there, Garrett?" I demanded tersely.

"She—" He hesitated. "She needed me. It was an emergency."

"What kind of emergency?" I practically snarled.

"Can I explain later? I have to go. Izumi's waiting for me."

"Oh, well—then I'd hate for you to keep her waiting any longer!" I spat sarcastically—and immediately hung up on him.

When he came home an hour later, I was sitting up in bed—

Lying in wait.

"Hey, honey," Garrett said, peeling off his jacket. "Sorry about that, but I—"

I held up a hand. "I don't even want to hear it."

"But—"

"I said, I don't want to hear about why you were at Izumi's. I don't care about whatever excuse she made this time to get you there. The fact of the matter is—you're still running to your ex every time she calls. She has you wrapped around her little finger, Garrett! Can't you see that?"

Garrett pulled his T-shirt over his head, tossed it aside, and sat down heavily on the bed. His cheeks were hollow and his eyes drooped with fatigue. "Mindy, I don't want to keep any secrets from you. Please—just let me explain about—"

I lurched forward on the bed and wrapped my arms around his neck and pulled him to me. "It's okay, Garrett," I whispered. "You don't have to tell me what you were doing. I . . . I trust you."

I decided then and there that if I kept repeating that over and over

22

again, it would come true. I knew I had to have faith in my husband. But even if I truly believed that he would never willingly stray, could I trust Izumi not to keep after Garrett?

As I pressed my trembling body against his, I had the awful feeling that Izumi was waiting for him, all right—in her bedroom—

Previously known as their former marriage bedroom.

A few days later I had another idea, and I felt sure that this one would work. I decided I'd find out just exactly what Izumi was really like . . . and then copy the things she did. I know I sound like a total moron, but I guess I got to figuring that if Garrett was so happy to spend so much time with her, even though he was married to me, then he had to like the way she lived her life.

Maybe if Mom were more like his mistress, Dad never would've strayed in the first place, I thought. But I'm more than willing to try this trick; I'll do anything it takes to stop Garrett from leaving me—to stop Izumi from luring him away from me.

"What's Izumi like?" I asked "casually" one night as I handed Garrett the last of the dinner plates to put away.

He looked at me like I'd just grown a pair of horns on top of my head. "Izumi? But I thought you don't want to know anything about her."

"Well, I mean, I don't necessarily want to know what she looks like," I hedged, rinsing my hands. "What I really mean is—what was she like to live with?"

"Well. . . ." Garrett's lips lifted at their corners; clearly, he found my question amusing. "She's definitely very different from you."

"How so? Come on, Garrett; give me some details."

"Why the sudden interest?" he asked, suddenly looking suspicious of my newfound "Izumi studies."

I massaged hand cream into my fingers, taking my time formulating my response. "Well . . . I guess I just suppose it's time I finally found out more about her. That's what you've always wanted, anyway, isn't it?"

"In a way," Garrett said carefully. "I mean, I've always thought it would be great if you two could meet and get along decently with each other—you know—if not for my sake, then certainly for Sam's. You know, she still asks me to bring you over to the house. I think she'd really like to meet you."

I told him what I thought he wanted to hear: "Maybe I'll go over there, then, someday."

Garrett's eyes brightened instantly. "Okay, then," he began, grinning. "Let's see . . . well, for starters . . . she hates science fiction, spiders, and cheese. She's not in the least bit organized; I used to spend hours looking for things she'd put away and couldn't remember

23

where." He chuckled a little, remembering. "Once, I found my car keys in the dishwasher! And the house is always a mess. Not like this place, funny bunny." He raised a hand to tenderly stroke my cheek and then gave me a loving kiss.

"Thanks." Anyone could keep this little house in order, I thought. It hardly takes a minute. "Is that all?"

"Isn't that enough? All right, then; one more thing: It used to drive me crazy that she wouldn't make the bed."

"What?"

"Yeah." He grimaced. "She used to say, 'What's the point of making the thing when you only get in it again the same night?'"

"That's gross!"

He laughed. "I know. I tried doing it myself, but I soon got fed up with the job. So, my sweet, I do like the way you keep things neat and tidy. And everything's in the right place so I can always find it."

That's it, I thought as I followed Garrett into the living room. That's the problem in a nutshell: I'm a neat freak and Garrett's too nice to say what he really thinks. He obviously can't relax here, and that's why he stays so long at Izumi's.

I was excited to have the information I needed.

The following week Garrett went to St. Louis and I began putting my latest—and hopefully final—plan into action. I left my clothes laying around, stopped making the bed, and I let the dirty dishes pile up in the sink. I cringed every time I saw them, but I resolved not to do anything about a thing. I decided I had to let things slide—that I had to be more easygoing for Garrett's sake and mine.

Then one morning at work I was taking a booking over the phone. Looking at the dates on the calendar, I suddenly realized that my period was late. During lunch, I checked my diary—which only confirmed that I was six days late. On the way home from work that night I picked up a pregnancy test kit and followed the instructions.

I was pregnant.

Feeling lightheaded with excitement, I immediately started cleaning the house from top to bottom. I didn't care anymore about trying to be like Izumi; I just wanted my home to be perfect.

Garrett was thrilled, too, when I gave him the wonderful news. We spent the next few evenings cuddled up on the sofa together, talking about baby names, and how we would decorate the nursery, and whether or not we should find out the baby's sex before it was born. I was so happy; I didn't think anything could ever again possibly spoil my life.

But six weeks into the pregnancy, I started suffering from morning sickness—and evening sickness. In fact, I seemed to feel nauseated most of the time. My skin got spotty and my hair was always lank and greasy, seemingly no matter how much I washed it! I hoped it was all only temporary, since I figured if I couldn't stand to look at myself in the mirror, surely Garrett must hate the way I looked.

Then one Sunday night Garrett took Sam back to Izumi's. He left me sitting on the sofa with my feet up on the ottoman. I tried to concentrate on the movie I was watching, but instead, my eyes kept checking the time. He was gone an unusually long time and soon, I began to get jittery. The minutes ticked by as I started to fret, Has Garrett been carjacked? Has he been in an accident? Is he lying, bleeding, on the side of the road? Maybe even stone-cold dead already?

I called his cell; there was no answer. I knew he wouldn't pick up if he were driving; we both agreed that talking on cell phones while driving is dangerously distracting, and we always wait until we can pull over. But then I realized that he might not have even set off back home yet. And worse than a traffic accident, in my mind, was the thought that Garrett might be lying in Izumi's arms!

Panicking, I replayed in my head all of the previous occasions when Garrett was at his ex-wife's. I brooded on the thoughts I had about her trying to win him back. How she was always at Sam's soccer games. How she called Garrett with excuses about the house needing some repair or another when she probably really only wanted him to return to her. And then I had to wonder: Now that I'm tired all the time, ugly, and constantly throwing up, has Garrett finally succumbed to Izumi's mysterious charms?

I worked myself up into such a state that when Garrett's key sounded in the lock, I ran to the door and immediately let him have it.

"What the hell took you so long?" I screamed.

"What?" He took a step back, surprised by my reaction. His eyes swept the room as if he were sure the ceiling must've fallen in while he was out. "What's wrong?"

"What's wrong? I'm pregnant, and you leave me alone for hours—that's what's wrong!"

"But you knew exactly where I was. I was at Izumi's." Garrett looked at me like I was a madwoman.

"You're always at Izumi's! You're never here! You'd much rather be with her than with me! Don't you deny it!"

"Mindy, you're being absurd." Garrett reached out to me. "You need to calm down, honey. . . ."

"Don't you touch me!" I shrieked. "I hate you, and I hate Izumi, and I hate my life!"

Garrett's face drained of all color. A worried crease formed between his brows. "I think you should see your doctor tomorrow," he said carefully. "You might need something to help you feel better."

"Whatever!" I raced upstairs to our bedroom and slammed the

25

door shut. I felt like my head was going to explode.

Stupid, stupid, stupid! I told myself. I'm acting like a spoiled-rotten, maniacal brat again! I should apologize, right now.

But then a wave of nausea welled up in my throat, and I ran to the bathroom and threw up.

When Garrett finally ventured upstairs he found me in bed. "Can I get you anything?" he asked calmly.

I shook my head. "No. But I'm so sorry for acting the way I did tonight. I—I guess it's my hormones playing havoc with my emotions. I'll see my doctor, but I won't take any drugs. I'd rather put up with the sickness."

"But, Mindy," Garrett said, coming to sit by my side, "a prescription might ease your symptoms. I do hate to see you like this." Gently, he pushed my lank hair behind my ears.

I leaned against his chest and hugged him. "If you'll put up with my stupid outbursts, I'd prefer not to take anything. You don't want our baby harmed, do you?"

"Of course not. Only, Izumi took—"

I pushed him away. "Stop it! Stop it! Stop it!" I massaged my throbbing temples and breathed deeply for a few moments. "I know you've been through all this before—with her—but I don't care how she managed, or what she took, do you understand? I'm not her!"

"Whatever you say, honey," Garrett replied, tightlipped. He straightened the bedcovers around me and then headed for the bathroom.

Very early the next morning I heard the phone ring. Garrett's voice came faintly up to my ears from the floor below. A few minutes later he entered the bedroom and put my usual cup of coffee on the bedside table. But just the aroma of the java made me want to puke. Covering my nose with my hand, I said, "Please—take that away!"

He picked up the cup and turned to leave.

"Wait," I said. "Who was that on the phone just now?"

"My boss. I have to go to St. Louis today. Do you think you'll be all right without me?" He sounded like he was torn between wanting to do his job and being here for me.

Garrett's such a nice guy. He's constantly trying to please everyone, and I'm making life miserable for the both of us. Why do I do it? I pushed myself up slowly and leaned back against the headboard. I felt washed out; instead of putting on weight, I'd actually lost a few pounds.

"I'll be fine," I told him, managing a weak smile. "And after all, you can't risk losing your job. And I'll just take it easy at the motel and put my feet up whenever I can. Chrissy's on the desk with me; she'll help."

Garrett nodded and left the coffee outside the door. He returned a moment later to sit on the bed and I snuggled up against him. "I should only be away for a couple of days."

26

"Is it some sort of emergency?" I asked, inhaling his fresh-from-the-shower smell and feeling his chest rise and fall in rhythm with mine. It made me feel safe and instantly, I wondered, Why can't I always feel this safe? Will I only be happy if I keep Garrett in my sight twenty-four hours a day? Even I know that's not possible.

Garrett eased himself out of my embrace and kissed my forehead. "It's always an emergency. They're like a bunch of old women in that brewery."

I watched him pack his bag and then he kissed me good-bye.

"I'll call you as soon as I can," he said. "I love you, Mindy."

"I love you, too."

I got out of bed feeling as weak as a newborn kitten. I wasn't looking forward to the next eight hours, but with Chrissy's help, I got through my shift and then drove home. I only threw up three times that day, but no sooner had I turned the corner onto our street than I felt my stomach begin to constrict again. I entered the house and ran upstairs to the bathroom.

The dry heaves left me exhausted. There was nothing left in my stomach to bring up, though, and I didn't feel like eating anything. In fact, the very thought of food made me queasy. So I filled a glass with water and sipped it slowly as I sat on the sofa. The telephone rang and I snatched it up, certain that it was Garrett. I didn't bother to glance at the caller ID.

It was a woman's voice.

"Oh, hello," she said. "We speak at last. This is—it's Izumi."

I was totally unprepared to hear the voice of Garrett's ex—as well as disappointed that it wasn't my husband calling. "Garrett's out of town," I said, more abruptly than I intended.

"I see. Then I guess he won't be able to help me out. . . ."

"No." I wanted to tell her then that after our baby was born, Garrett wouldn't be "helping her out" as often as he had in the past, but suddenly, another wave of nausea washed over me, causing me to gasp, "Listen—I . . . I—I can't talk right—" I slammed the phone down and fled to the bathroom.

Half an hour later, feeling like I'd been flattened by an eighteen-wheeler, I dragged myself downstairs and stood by the phone, debating whether or not to call Izumi back. As it was, it'd certainly been a strange experience, talking to her. I had to admit—she sounded warm and friendly, and my long-held images of her as a vengeful ex-wife plotting to steal back my husband hardly fit the voice I heard.

But having avoided Izumi since I married Garrett, do I really have the courage—especially now—to reach out to her, after all this time? Maybe I'll wait until I feel better, and then Garrett and I can talk this through first. . . .

But I knew then that I couldn't go on as I had been. I didn't want to end up like my mother—angry and bitter for so many years. I could just picture myself standing at the door, holding a crying baby in my arms, pleading with Garrett not to go over to his ex-wife's again. . . .

Tenderly, I placed my hand on my abdomen. "That's not going to happen," I told my unborn child. "This has to stop, now."

Picking up the phone, I hit speed dial for Izumi's number, but there was no answer. I tried a couple more times, but hung up rather than leaving a message on her answering machine because I simply felt I had to talk to her in person. Honestly—I felt I owed her an apology, and I didn't want her to hear it "secondhand."

Wandering into the kitchen, I stared at the pantry shelves, wishing Garrett would call. I wanted to tell him that I loved him, and that I was truly sorry for my actions. Instead of trusting my instincts, I'd let my childhood insecurities about men grow out of all proportion, and made an utter fool of myself in the process. But it wouldn't happen again.

I found a box of crackers and took them through to the living room. Sitting on the sofa, I reminded myself that my husband is nothing like my father, and that Garrett should not be made to pay for Dad's deficiencies of character.

The doorbell rang.

When I opened the door I found Sam's face beaming up at me. Behind him stood a tall, slender Asian woman with Sam's thick, straight, jet-black hair, Sam's solemn features . . . and Sam's lovely smile. Her hands rested gently on Sam's shoulders.

My heart hammered in my chest.

Izumi?

"Oh, boy—you look as awful as you sounded on the phone!" were her first face-to-face words to me. "Pregnancy's not all it's cracked up to be, is it? Can we come in?"

I held open the door with trembling fingers. My earlier courage suddenly failed me and my knees felt wobbly, but then Sam gave me a quick hug and ran over to the cupboard where we keep his toys. He pulled out the rug covered with road signs and streets, and a bunch of little cars.

I watched Izumi remove her jacket and drape it across a chair. She carried an overstuffed leather purse in her hand as her eyes swept the room and came around to rest on my face.

"You're very pale," she remarked, her face showing genuine concern. "Maybe you should sit down before you fall down."

Silently, I did as I was told. She seemed so . . . self-assured, as if she knew everything about me already—even my secrets.

Izumi removed a magazine from a chair and sat down facing me. She smiled. "I hoped we'd meet well before this," she began pleasantly.

Well before what? I thought. Before I got pregnant? Or before I almost drove Garrett back into your arms with my stupid efforts to stop him from being with you?

I looked down at my hands. My wedding ring glinted harshly in the light, mocking me; after all, I realized then that I was hardly the perfect wife.

But maybe, I considered, just maybe . . . it isn't too late to make amends. . . .

"Garrett sure picked a stubborn one this time," Izumi went on as if reading my thoughts. "Why wouldn't you ever meet me? Has he blackened my name that much?"

"Garrett?" Instantly, I was confused. "Garrett's never said anything bad about you."

"Then, didn't he ever bother to explain to you that we aren't in love anymore? That we got divorced so we'd each be free to find a soul mate this time around?"

"Well. . . ." My spirits lifted instantly as I wondered, Does that mean Garrett thinks of me as his soul mate?

"It's perfectly straightforward, Mindy. Our marriage lost its spark after the first five years. We tried counseling and relationship clinics, but nothing brought it back. In the end, we were more like brother and sister than man and wife. Surely, though, Garrett's already told you all of this?"

I shook my head. "I . . . I—wouldn't let him say anything," I confessed, blushing. "I—I didn't want to know the details."

"I see." She sat back and looked around the room.

Meanwhile, I chewed my lip. My explanation sounded childish—even to my own ears. After all, surely if I'd been adult about it, I would've found out the reasons why Garrett was divorced so that we could avoid the same pitfalls.

But I guess once the spark's lost, there's often little you can do to relight it, and at least they tried. . . .

Before I could say anything, Izumi added, "I like this house; it's great. Garrett's always going on and on to me about how neat, tidy, and organized you are. Has he told you that my place is a total disaster area?" She grinned and chuckled easily.

"Well," I admitted, blushing again, "as a matter of fact, he did say something the other day."

She laughed. "Really? Well! I have to say—I'm both surprised and delighted. Garrett usually manages to find the good in people, so I guess he has an explanation for me being a slob. Truth be told, though? I drove him up the wall. But he was always too kind to keep on ragging at me, and eventually I guess he just learned to accept it . . . or maybe not, huh?" She grinned. "He was always the one to clean the house on the weekends, and he taught Sam to make his bed as soon as he was old enough to sleep in one! But I just feel that life's too short to worry about a few cobwebs and stuff—you know what I mean?"

So Garrett's been telling me the truth all along. And he's probably too proud to tell me that I'm ruining our marriage with my warped view of relationships.

"Anyway—" Izumi lifted the purse into her lap. "I've brought you a few things—for your nausea."

"Oh? Thank you," I croaked.

She started placing things on the coffee table. "This is a can of ginger ale—it's good for pregnant women. And here's a packet of ginger tea, though I never tried this myself. I preferred to nibble on ginger cookies, so I've brought you a box of those, too."

I looked at the items in front of me, overwhelmed by Izumi's kindness. I'd been spending all of my time thinking bad things about her—and I hadn't once considered her reaction to Garrett marrying me!

Shame washed over me as I deeply realized: All this time, I've only been thinking of myself.

As if she were aware of my feelings of guilt, but didn't want me to wallow in them, Izumi thrust two sheets of paper into my hands. "And here are some more suggestions that might help; you know—things like, 'Eat a little something every two hours to keep your stomach from feeling empty.' I got them off the Internet. And try eating a couple of soda crackers before you even get out of bed in the mornings; that worked for me for a while, but I still needed help from my doctor." She stood. "Shall I pour some of this ginger ale into a glass for you?"

When I nodded, she walked into the kitchen. After she returned, I accepted the glass from her and took a few bubbly, tingly sips of the fizzy liquid.

"Why did you call the house earlier?" I finally asked her.

She sat down again, glanced quickly over at Sam, and then leaned in toward me. "I had a date this evening, and my babysitter couldn't make it. Garrett was kind enough once before to step in at the last minute; that time, Rachel had to leave at ten since it was a school night, but my car had a flat on the way back from dinner with Jason, and I had to call Garrett for help."

"What happened?" I asked.

"Garrett went to my house and after Rachel left, he bundled Sam into some blankets, drove to where I was stranded, and put on the spare." Her eyes caught the shock revealed on my face. "He did explain everything when he got back, didn't he?"

"I, um—wouldn't let him," I confessed, blushing again.

She sat back, a look of confusion on her face. "Then what on earth did you think he was doing at that hour?"

I swallowed hard, realizing it was time to tell the truth. "Every time you called, I thought you wanted to see Garrett . . . alone. I refused to hear his explanations in case they were lies. . . . Instead, I asked him not to say anything about you to me at all. Ever."

"You poor thing! All that worrying over nothing," she said, and clasped her hands together. "It's my fault, you know. I shouldn't have depended on Garrett being my handyman 24/7—especially after he became a newlywed again. It's just that, well—I've gotten so used to calling him. However, in my defense, I did expect him to bring you with him sometimes—especially when he collected Sam. I've been wondering why you never came."

I shook my head. "It's nice of you to take the blame, but it's my horribly overactive and self-destructive imagination that's at fault. Anyway, what happened to your date tonight?"

"I cancelled. Jason says he understands, though, and if he doesn't—then he's not the guy for me." Izumi shrugged. "I may have to break many more dates with him, after all; you never know what's going to happen when you have kids, do you? I didn't invite him over to my place since I don't want Sam getting attached to Jason in case things don't work out—know what I mean?"

That sounded to me like a very sensible idea. Garrett did the same thing with me, I remembered then. I didn't meet Sam until after we were engaged.

"Now, why don't you put your feet up on that ottoman?" Izumi kindly suggested. "I'll make you something to eat. What do you want?"

"Well, there's some leftover roasted chicken in the fridge," I told her. By this time my queasiness had passed, and I decided I'd feel even better if I ate something. "And you might want to check the salad bin; I'm sure there's something in there. But—will you and Sam stay and eat with me, please?"

Izumi smiled. "Yes. That'll be really nice, actually."

My husband called later that night.

"Mindy, honey, are you okay?" His voice was husky with concern.

"Hi, darling," I said warmly. "Yes; in fact, I'm feeling much better, thanks."

I heard his long sigh of relief. "That's great. I really miss you, you know," he said wistfully. "What are you doing?"

"I have a visitor, actually, and I'm having a lovely time getting to know her."

"Who is it? One of the neighbors?"

"Why don't you speak to her?" I said—

And handed the phone to Izumi.

THE END

31

3 SISTERS, 1 MAN
Who will he choose?

Having two sisters has always been, at the very least, interesting. Sharing an apartment with them? That defies logic. They've never been very good at sharing.

My older sister, Megan, is a junior accountant working on her master's degree at night school. Mandy, the baby of the family, is a sales manager at an upscale women's clothing store. She is pursuing her "Mrs." degree. As for me, I have my path neatly laid out, too. I'm a nurse working the graveyard shift, trying to save enough money to move out on my own.

Since we're never home at the same time, the three of us have been getting along pretty well.

That is, until Tyler Ashford came along.

I knew the man was trouble the first time I saw those eyes and that killer smile. To be fair, it wasn't his fault.

Megan brought Tyler home to review his taxes. The poor guy was being audited. When Mandy got one peek at his estimated earned income, it was all over.

Megan and Mandy were in the kitchen arguing, yet again. All I wanted was a little peace and quiet before I went to work.

"Would you two stop yelling?" I said to them.

"Melissa, please tell Mandy that Tyler is my friend. I will not have him exploited because he earns enough to keep her in the style she would like to become accustomed to," Megan said.

"You're jealous because he's attracted to me instead of you," Mandy shot back, admiring her perfectly manicured nails.

"You had no business looking at his tax forms," Megan said.

"Stop," I demanded.

As though ending round one, the doorbell chimed. Neither of my sisters moved from their corners to answer it. I stomped through the living room and yanked open the door.

He smiled, and in that moment I realized how one man had turned our household into a battleground.

"Tyler." I was talking to myself, but he thought I was greeting him.

"You must be Melissa," he said. "Nice to meet you. Is your sister here?"

"Oh, they're both here," I said. And as if on cue, they appeared.

"Tyler!" my sisters cooed, pushing past me.

"Take your pick," I muttered, grabbing my coat to leave.

When the elevator door opened, I was more than a little surprised to see Tyler right behind me.

"That was quick."

"Just had to drop off some deductions. Besides, it was kind of tense in there."

We stood in awkward silence for a moment as the elevator descended. Then he spoke. "I've always wanted to wear pajamas to work."

I looked down at my pink scrubs and laughed. "I like it."

"Which hospital do you work at?" he asked.

"St. Paul's. I work in the geriatric unit."

"No kidding? My grandmother's there right now, in rehab. She broke her hip. Abby Ashford."

"Miss Abby is your grandmother?"

"None other than."

"I adore her. She's such a great lady."

"I think so, too. In fact, that's where I'm headed."

We were out to the street. "Well, I'll see you there. There's my bus," I said.

"Let me give you a ride," he offered.

I'm not stupid. Of course I took the ride. Saving money on the bus meant it was that much sooner that I could move out of that apartment. And Tyler was great company, too.

"So how come I never see you on my grandmother's floor?" he asked as we drove.

"I normally work nights. Today I'm working a double, covering a swing shift for a friend."

"Nights? You aren't the one who plays cards with Grandma, are you?"

"I've played a few hands of poker with Abby when she's had insomnia. She refuses a sleeping pill, you know."

"I think the word she used to describe you was card-shark."

"Hey, I won those cookies fair and square."

Tyler laughed. "Oh, sure. That's what they all say."

I pretended to be outraged. "I'll prove it to you during my dinner break. Stop at the bakery across from the hospital and I'll run in. We're going to need more cookies."

Bending the rules a tiny bit, I allowed Tyler to stay a little longer than the posted visiting hours. His grandmother enjoyed it. I was sorry to see him leave.

I only wish all my shifts went as fast as that one did. The night shift crept by, and I was only too glad to walk out of the hospital into the fresh air in the morning. In my usual zombie-like morning trance, I walked along the route home until a car's persistent horn got my attention.

"Hey, Melissa."

It was Tyler.

"Hi there, Tyler. What're you doing here?"

"I wanted to see you again."

"I'm too tired to play cards," I said. "Beside, you won most of the cookies."

"Hop in, I'll take you home."

"No, I'll fall asleep and then you'll have to carry me in the house." I shook my head. "And frankly, I'm no lightweight."

I heard him laugh. A second later he was striding next to me.

"Got any plans for your time off?" he asked.

"You bet. Today, I'm sleeping until noon. And then I'm going to roll over and look at the clock and go back to sleep." I sighed with anticipated pleasure.

"How about a movie tomorrow night?"

"That's a wonderful idea," I said. "You rent the movie, and I'll borrow the VCR from administration. We can make popcorn in the nurse's lounge. Abby will love it."

"That wasn't exactly what I had in mind." He paused. "But sure. Okay."

"What time?" I asked.

"I'll pick you up at six."

"Great!" I dashed into my building, waving good-bye.

That evening I sat on the stairs outside my building, bleary eyed. My sleep was interrupted at eleven by the vacuum cleaner. Megan came home early to clean the house.

She'd invited Tyler over for dinner to celebrate his successful tax audit. I was the first to point out that she didn't make me dinner when she did my taxes. But she didn't hear me over the noise. My sisters were at it again. They were arguing over Tyler.

"Why so glum?"

It was him, standing over me, hands in pockets. He looked wonderful as usual.

"Men," I said.

"Men?"

"Never mind." I stood and linked my arm in his. "I hope you're hungry. Megan has been cooking all day. Be sure to mention the pasta sauce. Oh, and Mandy got her hair done. You'd probably better notice that, too."

"Okay," Tyler said, giving me a quizzical look.

Thanks to Tyler's lavish compliments, dinner went very well. In fact, my sisters called a temporary truce. They decided Tyler liked them each equally, and they were subdued. I knew he was going to have to make up his mind soon.

The next evening I waited for him outside the building. My sisters didn't know Tyler and I had plans. Since their temporary peace was

34

so tenuous, I figured what my sisters didn't know wouldn't hurt me.

We had a lovely time with Abby. When she fell asleep at the end of the movie, Tyler and I quietly slipped out. The night was warm, so we walked.

After ice cream cones, we walked some more. We found an all-night coffee shop and talked for hours. When we realized it was morning, we reluctantly headed back to my apartment.

"Melissa, do you believe in love at first sight?"

"No," I said. "But don't let that stop you. Is it Megan or Mandy?"

"Neither."

I shook my head. "That's not good," I mumbled. My sisters were going to be extremely unhappy.

"What about you and that man you were talking about?" he asked.

"Man? What man?"

"The other night. You were muttering something about men."

"Oh, that was a generic muttering. Why?"

"Melissa." He took my hand. "You are the only sister I'm crazy about."

I didn't know whether to throw my arms around the man or slug him. Did he realize how much trouble I was going to be in?

"Me? Are you sure?"

He laughed. "Of course I'm sure."

"But Megan thinks you're an accountant's dream. You keep alphabetized receipts. And Mandy is in love with your tax bracket."

"And you?"

"Well, of course I like you."

He frowned.

"I more than like you, Tyler. I'm crazy about your grandmother. And I adore playing cards with you. And I could talk to you forever."

"Forever is good," he said, no longer frowning.

We reached my building.

"We should take it slow," I said. "Forever is a long time, you know."

He smiled. "Do you think a kiss would be okay?"

"Have you kissed my sisters?"

"Of course not. I mean, they're nice, but I was waiting to kiss the right sister."

"Good answer," I said, leaning toward him.

It was a good kiss. A forever kind of kiss.

From behind us a terse cough and an astonished gasp ended it all much too quickly.

"Good morning, Megan. Good morning, Mandy. Have a great day," I said, never taking my eyes off Tyler.

And the right sister finished her forever kiss.

THE END

WHO'S THAT GIRL?
And what's she doing with my dream man?

I was upset with myself as I drove the fifteen miles to work. A good job, and here I was going to be late my very first day. Well, at least I'd be working for my uncle, if that were any consolation. Still, not a very good impression for a new employee to make her first day on the job.

I banged my fist against the steering wheel and muttered to myself. I'd really wanted this job and had finally earned my credentials as an accountant with my new college degree. When Uncle Alden offered me this opportunity, I'd given my two weeks notice at the bank the next day.

As I rounded a curve in the road I suddenly noticed a guy on the side of the road, standing beside the bed of his truck. The road was wet and muddy from a heavy rain the night before, but I didn't want to slow down or I'd really be late for work.

When I got closer I saw him lift a tire from the bed of his truck and start to carry it over to what was obviously a blown left front tire. Puddles of water and mud lined the street and he was on the narrow shoulder, his back to me. As I zipped past him, water and mud shot out from under my car tire and splashed him. He quickly turned and looked at me, a look of surprise and anger on his face.

Our eyes locked for a minute as I drove past. I felt bad about getting him soaked with mud, but figured I'd never see him again. I glanced in the rearview mirror and noticed him shaking his head. I admitted he had a right to be angry. I knew I would be. Still, I kept driving.

First things first, I told myself. I have to get to my uncle's store.

As I walked into Uncle Alden's building supply store one of the clerks looked at me, and then turned and shook her head. She apparently thought I was taking advantage of being the owner's niece, as if I thought I could come in when I pleased. Seemed like I was making lots of people upset that day.

At least Uncle Alden was happy to see me. He gave me a big hug, and then introduced me to his secretary and office staff. They may have been wondering why I was almost half an hour late my first day, but no one said anything. I knew Uncle Alden was well liked and treated his employees well. I also knew I planned on being an excellent employee, in spite of my initial tardiness. And I also knew I'd be judged more harshly than most because I was related to the owner of the business.

Uncle Alden wanted me to learn every aspect of the business before I worked as an accountant, and had me start on the floor. I helped stock the shelves with everything from faucets to nails, ran the cash register for a while, and even answered the phones.

The rest of the day went pretty smoothly, and I was beginning to think my troubles were over when I happened to glance up from the computer screen where I was searching for a product, and looked straight into the eyes of someone I'd hoped to never see again—the guy at the side of the road who'd been fixing his tire.

He stared at me and I stared at him, a big lump settling in my throat like a piece of bubble gum that got stuck. Then he grinned and winked. I knew I blushed because my face felt as hot as a bad sunburn.

I thought it couldn't get any worse, but it did. Uncle Alden walked over and shook the guy's hand.

"Hi, Sean," Uncle Alden said. "Have you met my niece, Michelle?"

Sean furrowed his brows like someone deep in thought and said, "You know, Alden, Michelle does look familiar. Now where have I seen her before?" Then he grinned at me again.

I wanted to be anywhere but in that spot at the moment, but I was stuck. I didn't say a word, and probably couldn't have if I'd tried.

Fortunately, the other customer I was helping asked more questions and I turned my attention to him, while Alden and Sean talked about an order as they walked away. About twenty minutes later, as Sean was leaving, he walked over and said, "Much better meeting you this way, Michelle."

I bit my lip, and then noticed his shirt was clean and pressed. Obviously he'd changed clothes since I'd sprayed him with mud. I simply nodded. He smiled that big smile of his and left.

I watched him as he walked out. It seemed everyone in the store knew the guy. Many clerks and customers said hello to him or stopped him for a minute to talk.

He sure is tall, I thought to myself. Good looking, too.

The phone rang at the desk I was assigned to and I picked it up while still staring at Sean, trying to figure out how to apologize.

"Dana? It's Phil," the voice on the phone said.

That caught my attention. "Phil, don't call me here. How did you get this number, anyway?" All I needed for the day to end out even worse than I possibly thought was for Phil to call me.

"It didn't take long to find the number," he said. "You should've given it to me."

I briefly closed my eyes. "Phil, don't call here again. I'll talk to you soon." I put down the phone.

I'd dated Phil for my last three years of college. At first I'd thought he might be the one for me. But the spark wasn't there, probably never had been. We really hadn't broken up, but I'd been gradually trying to get him to understand it was over. Trouble was, Phil wasn't getting the message. I didn't want to hurt Phil. He was a good guy, and would make some girl a wonderful husband, but I knew that girl wasn't me.

After we'd closed the store for the day and were getting ready to leave, Uncle Alden asked me how it'd gone.

"Fine," I said. "But just who is Sean?"

Uncle Alden smiled. "Sean Zander is my best customer. He's one of the biggest contractors in town. Great guy, too. Pays his bills on time, easy to work with. I'm lucky to have him be so loyal to my company."

I took a big swallow and attempted to smile. "I'm glad he does his business here," I said. I silently wondered if he'd continue to do business with my uncle, now that Sean knew I was Alden's niece.

I drove home with a lump in my throat. Should I tell my uncle about splashing Sean with mud? But what good would that do? I decided to wait a few days and see what, if anything, happened.

I couldn't get Sean out of my mind that night, or out of my dreams. I kept driving by him, splashing him with mud, and then he'd hop in his truck and race after me. The dream stopped there, leaving me wondering how I really wanted it to end.

The next few days went by in blissful normality. Sean didn't show up, I wasn't fired, and Phil didn't call. Well, he didn't call at work. He called me every night at home, but I didn't return his calls.

The less I saw of Phil the more I knew we didn't belong together. I felt guilty, though. My friends couldn't understand me, and I guess I couldn't, either. Phil had a good job and promising future, was a nice-looking guy, treated me with love and tenderness, and he wanted to marry me. But I just couldn't help it. I loved Phil, but I wasn't in love with the guy. We'd have to have another serious talk soon.

Then on Friday, as I sat at a computer terminal checking account balances in a back office, I saw someone standing in the doorway out of the corner of my eye. I slowly turned and looked into the eyes of a handsome man with a smile on his face. He slowly walked into the office and sat down.

"Hello, Michelle," Sean said. "Now it seems to me that our brief conversations have been one-sided, me talking, you listening. So I thought I'd just drop in and say hello and find out if you do talk. I mean, a pretty girl like you, I bet you have the sweetest voice."

My face heated up and I just knew I was blushing again. Before I could say anything, one of the clerks, Megan, walked in with some accounts. She never took her eyes off Sean, though, and it was obvious she'd had her mind on him for some time.

"Why, Sean, where have you been?" Without looking at me, Megan tried to set the papers on my desk, and would've missed the desk completely except that I leaned over and grabbed them out of her hand.

"I thought you'd have called by now," Megan said, her back still to me as she focused on Sean. "Did you forget the concert next Saturday? I have two tickets." She set one hip on the corner of my desk.

I'd seen women flirt before, who hasn't, but this was an out and out assault. Megan was clearly after Sean, and it was as if I didn't even exist. This woman meant business.

To my surprise I noticed Sean was obviously uncomfortable. He moved slightly in his chair, as if trying to back away as much as possible from this woman who was on the attack, big time. His smile didn't reach his eyes any longer and he gripped the edge of his chair with one hand.

"Uh, Megan, I explained that I was busy that night," Sean said.

"Now how could you be busy?" Megan somehow managed to wiggle her hips while still halfway sitting on the corner of my desk. I was amazed at her agility, and knew I could never compete in her league. Then I realized I didn't want to.

"I just am," Sean answered, "and I can't attend the concert with you."

That didn't seem to phase Megan, who giggled and, like a magician's slight-of-hand trick, produced the two concert tickets out of a shirt pocket and held them up. "See, Sean, told you I had the tickets. I know you love blues music, and I bought these tickets especially for you."

Sean just stared at her and I was really getting annoyed. Megan seemed oblivious to me and the fact that her rear-end was planted on my desk, performing gyrations I'd never witnessed before.

"Thank you for these documents, Megan," I said, rather loudly. "If you'll excuse us, Sean and I were discussing business and our time is limited."

As if she'd suddenly become aware I was even present, she whipped around and stared at me. My sweet smile did nothing to shake the angry look on her face, but she swallowed and nodded, and then looked once more at Sean.

"Megan? If you'll leave now, please," I said.

She lifted her chin, straightened her back, stood up, and stormed out.

"Whew!" Sean wiped his brow. "I don't know what I'm going to do with that woman. She just doesn't get the hint." Then he smiled at me. "You were awesome, Michelle. I think I owe you my life."

Before I could respond, Uncle Alden walked in and told Sean he had some specs he wanted checked. Sean gave me one last smile and left with my uncle.

Well, I sure hadn't made a friend of Megan, but I had to admit I could understand what she saw in Sean. Those big shoulders and arms that bulged under his shirtsleeves were enough to make my

39

imagination soar. I told myself to stop it. Sean probably had a steady girl and I didn't want to get involved with a customer, anyway.

But I had to smile once in a while as I worked on the accounts that day. I even chuckled to myself once as I thought about Megan's astonished look when I asked her to leave.

So when Uncle Alden walked in and asked if I'd drive over to a construction site that Sean was working on to check some figures for a shipment, I almost leaped out of my chair in a rush to be on my way. Thankfully, I stopped short of leaping and managed to tell Uncle Alden that I'd be happy to go.

I located the construction site, but there were so many men, trucks, and equipment working on the place that I couldn't see Sean. When a man in a hard hat scowled and asked if I hadn't read the warning signs about wearing a hard hat, I apologized. I explained what I was there for and he handed me a hat and pointed in the direction of a building.

I stepped over boards and nails and managed to get to the building without incident. But when I finally found Sean talking to several men as he pointed out something on a diagram, I forgot to watch where I was going. As I walked up to the men I tripped over a bucket of paint, which tipped over and dumped its contents out onto the ground, and onto the pant legs of you-know-who.

Sean looked down at his feet, then up at me, briefly closed his eyes, then burst out laughing. "Michelle," he managed to say between bouts of laughter, "are you some kind of walking disaster?"

The other men, who'd also received their share of splashed paint, grinned. "At least it's our old work clothes," one of them said.

I said a quick prayer of thanks for that one, but my brief consolation was interrupted when a girl about my age walked up and put her arm in Sean's. She wore a hard hat, too, but she didn't look like any of the other employees. In fact, I had to admit she was downright beautiful. She looked like a model on the cover of a fashion magazine.

Sean leaned down and kissed her cheek, with that grin still on his face. "Marsha, I'd like you to meet Michelle. She works at Alden's supply store."

Marsha put out her hand and welcomed me to the construction site. "What happened to you guys?" she asked the men. "You look like someone threw paint all over your pants."

"My fault," I said. "I'm sorry."

Marsha raised her eyebrows at me. "Construction sites can be hazardous, Michelle. You know, if you want, you can ask one of the workmen to get you what you want."

Then she ruffled her hand through Sean's hair and said, "See you later, boss."

A wave of jealousy swept through me, although I told myself that was ridiculous. Sean sure did attract the women. I could see why, but I wasn't exactly making a good impression on the man. I assumed that Marsha was his girlfriend as I watched her walk away. It looked like she worked in the construction area, not as a secretary or bookkeeper. Another guy handed her some drawings and she stopped and looked at them, then walked away with the guy in deep discussion.

I looked back at Sean, who'd taken a paper towel and was wiping what paint he could off his pants.

"I'm so sorry," I said. "I honestly don't mean to do these things." I handed him the papers Uncle Alden had given me.

Sean barely glanced at them, initialed his name in several places, and handed them back. "I trust Alden has done his research like he always does and found me the lowest prices."

His cell phone rang, Marsha returned with a question, and a guy called out that he needed to talk to Sean about something. Clearly, I wasn't needed. In fact, I was a definite liability, so I quietly left.

I glanced back at Sean before leaving the area. He stood there talking on his cell phone, Marsha by his side. I had to admit they were a good-looking couple. I didn't belong in the picture, as much as I'd have liked to know Sean better.

Megan stuck her chin up when she saw me walk in the door to the supply store. I smiled. At least Sean had no interest in her. But that was small consolation, because he had a real woman in Marsha.

Phil didn't call that night. He simply came over to my apartment.

"I'm tired, Phil," I said as I threw my briefcase on the table and shrugged out of my jacket. I kicked my shoes off and sat down on the couch and rubbed my temples. How could I get this man to realize it was over?

"Just give me a chance, Michelle," he said. "One more try. We've been together three years now. How can you throw that away?"

"I'm not throwing anything away, but if it doesn't feel right now, we need to stop here, rather than years down the road." I shook my head. "You're a nice guy, Phil. A wonderful guy in fact. It's just not there for me."

He looked off into the distance. "Can I at least take you to dinner tonight?"

I knew I should say no, but I was tired and to be honest, hungry. I didn't feel like cooking anything anyway, so I said yes.

We walked into my favorite Chinese restaurant and who should be standing at the counter, but Sean and Marsha. It seemed I was destined to keep running into this guy. My pulse picked up a notch just looking at him.

Sean smiled and walked over to us and said, "Why don't you two join us?"

41

I introduced Phil and we followed the waiter to a table. I felt awkward, but no one else seemed to. We ordered a drink then looked at the menus. I knew the menu by heart, having come here so many times before with Phil, but I needed to look at it. Anything, other than Sean.

He and Marsha seemed so comfortable with each other, and I realized they'd known each other for a long time, probably years. They seemed to know a lot about each other's families, too, and talked and laughed like old friends.

I even got my hopes up for a minute and thought that maybe they were just friends, until Marsha mentioned she'd finished doing the laundry, but next week it was his turn. So much for that thought.

Somehow I managed to keep up my end of the conversation and didn't have to contribute that much, because the guys got to talking about the latest baseball scores. The waiter brought our drinks and I carefully put my hand around mine. The last thing I wanted to do was spill wine on Sean.

Marsha asked me about my job and told me about hers. She was one of the foremen and had worked for Sean for over a year. I did ask if she'd known Sean before working for him and she laughed, but before she could answer my question the waiter came for our orders.

I had to admit that I liked her. She was easy to talk to and didn't hang all over Sean. Of course, I didn't hang all over Phil and really never had. What was I going to do about Phil?

We had a nice, leisurely dinner and walked out together. Sean said he'd like to do it again sometime and before I could say anything he and Phil agreed on dinner the next weekend. I watched Sean and Marsha walk to his car and drive off. They seemed so comfortable with each other, like wonderful friends. And they were also probably wonderful lovers, although they didn't make a show of holding hands or touching each other.

"Why did you do that, Phil?" I asked him as he drove me home. "Agree to next weekend?"

"Why not? They're a nice couple. And it gives me a chance to see you again."

"That's what I mean," I said. "Look, Phil, we're the best of friends, and I think that's what we were meant to be. Can't we leave it at that?"

He didn' t answer, but just kissed my cheek as he dropped me off. "See you next weekend, Michelle."

It was a restless sleep for me that night. My mind swirled with thoughts about what to do. I finally had my college degree and the job I'd wanted, but my life felt empty. And I couldn't put a certain guy out of my mind, even though I barely knew him.

My folks had known each other only a week before Dad proposed, and they'd been married over forty years. Maybe there was such a thing as love at first sight. I just knew I'd fallen for Sean, even if he thought I was a total klutz. At least I felt sure that's how he looked at me, and who could blame him? I acted like one whenever I was around him.

The following week was busy at work. I didn't see Sean and was disappointed. Megan continued to snub me but I learned she wasn't anyone's favorite, anyway. I wondered what she thought of Marsha, and why she pursued Sean when she must surely know he had a girlfriend.

The nights were lonely, though. Phil didn't call, something new for him, and I had to admit I missed him. I only wanted to talk with him, connect with someone. My best girlfriend had moved the year before, and I'd never been one to confide in a lot of friends. Come to think of it, I couldn't confide to Phil, anyway. He wouldn't want to hear I couldn't get Sean out of my mind.

Marsha did come in on Friday. "Hi, Michelle," she said when she saw me behind a counter. "How about Italian food this time? Sean and I are looking forward to seeing you guys again."

She was so friendly and warm that I couldn't help but smile. "Sounds fine to me, and I'm looking forward to it."

"I really enjoyed meeting Phil, too," she said. "He's such a nice guy."

"Yes, yes, he is that," I said.

I watched her walk out with another foreman from Sean's company. She was actually quite beautiful—tall, same colored hair as Sean, high cheekbones. I envied her. She had a good man and probably everything else going for her in life. Plus, everyone seemed to like her. I decided I'd like her, too, and would enjoy the evening that night. But I reminded myself that Phil and I needed to have a good, old-fashioned talk.

Phil was pleasant and polite when he picked me up and didn't say anything about our relationship, which was fine with me. When we walked into the restaurant I was surprised to hear music and see people dancing. Sean and Marsha were already seated and waved to us to come on over.

"We ordered a bottle of chardonnay," Sean said. "Hope you like it."

"I love it," I said. I couldn't help notice how handsome he looked in a shirt that exactly matched the color of his eyes. I knew Marsha had probably chosen it for him, and I had to admit she took good care of her man.

"I didn't get into the store this week," Sean said. "How are things going?"

"Well, I haven't spilled or dumped anything on anyone," I said. "So I guess that's an improvement."

Sean and Marsha both laughed, although Phil just looked at me. I

43

realized I'd not told him the story. We hadn't talked much lately.

The little orchestra played a romantic ballad and we all got up to dance. When the next piece started, Sean asked Phil and Marsha if they'd mind changing partners, and soon I was in Sean's arms, dancing to romantic Italian music.

To my delight he was a marvelous dancer, and even when I flubbed a few times until I learned his steps, he easily led us around the floor. The fragrance of his after shave lotion lingered on his neck and I almost nuzzled my face in it.

I hoped he didn't feel my heart pounding. He leaned his cheek on the top of my head and I thought I'd melt in his arms. He was so strong, a terrific leader on the floor, and yet so gentle.

I noticed Phil and Marsha as they moved by, and they both seemed engrossed in each other. Poor Phil, he deserved a better woman than me. I may not be able to have Sean, but I'd do the right thing by Phil and break it off.

We danced another dance, then another, when Sean whispered, "I could do this forever, but I guess we'd better go back to our salads."

I hoped he wasn't making a pass, because I'd never date a man who belonged to someone else. But then again, I hoped he was making a pass, because I'd really fallen for him. Fallen for a man who had no interest in me and never would.

We danced between courses, alternating partners, and stayed for several hours after finishing our dinner and another bottle of wine. By the end of the evening I felt like I could dance with Sean forever, he was that good.

"You're a terrific dancer," he whispered in my ear. "About the best partner I've ever had."

"You're just a terrific leader," I said.

He held me back a few inches and looked into my eyes. "No, that's not it. After all, I danced with Marsha, too, and she's not nearly as good as you."

I didn't know what to say. Naturally, I was flattered, but I didn't want to encourage him to say anything against Marsha.

"Phil's not crazy about dancing, I have to admit," I said. "He does it just for me."

"Well, looks like he's doing fine with Marsha," Sean said.

I glanced over at them. They did appear to be having a good time, although Phil would never make a great dancer, and never wanted to be, anyway.

Once again the four of us walked out together and headed toward our cars. We talked about doing it again next week, although Phil said he'd rather go someplace where he didn't have to dance. Surprisingly, Marsha agreed with him.

Phil was quiet as he drove me home, in fact he didn't say anything. I just couldn't find it in my heart to talk to him that night, but promised myself I'd do so within the week. He didn't seem like he wanted to talk, anyway.

Monday morning was a disaster with a shipment delayed in transit and several employees calling in sick. I couldn't get the accounts to balance and later that afternoon our computer system crashed.

We were all in a bad mood by the end of the day. So when Megan waltzed in and plopped some papers onto my desk, on top of other documents I was struggling with, I decided enough was enough.

"Look, Megan, I do have an in-basket and I'd appreciate it if you'd put anything new in there."

She finally met my eyes and I guess she was tired, too. "Just because you think Sean's interested in you, you don't have to lord it over me."

I stared back at her. "Sean? He's got a girlfriend."

"Since when?" she asked. "He broke up with her last year, and as far as I know he's not dated anyone since."

"You don't know about Marsha?" I asked. How could she not know? This gal seemed to know all the gossip in town.

"What about Marsha? What's she got to do with this?" Megan stood there with her hands on her hips.

"She's Sean's girl," I said.

To my surprise she burst out laughing. "Oh, no, she's not." And she walked out.

Now what did that mean? I thought that one of us was losing it and was afraid it might be me.

The phone rang and I picked it up as I continued to stare out the door that Megan had just walked through, as if she might come back and explain herself.

"Hi, Michelle," Phil said. "I think we need to talk. Is tonight okay?"

"Sure, Phil, sure. I agree. We need to talk." Well, we might as well get our conversation over with, and the way the day had gone this was as good a night as any.

Phil arrived shortly after seven. "I guess I've not really paid much attention and I should have," he said. "You're right, we've been best friends for so long I just assumed we were in love and would be married someday."

I waited. He was doing the talking and I wanted to see where this conversation would go before I said anything.

Phil ran his fingers through his hair. "Michelle, I'd kind of like to date Marsha. In fact, I asked her out for next weekend and she said yes. I mean, you're the one who said we should break up, just be good friends."

45

I stared at him. How could he ask out the girl who dated Sean? Then I remembered what Megan had said, that Marsha wasn't Sean's girlfriend. I came to the rapid conclusion that everyone else was mixed up and confused or else it was me, and quickly decided the odds were that it was me.

"Uh, Phil, I think that sounds really nice. But, what does Sean have to say about all this?"

Phil shrugged. "What does he have to do with this? It's her decision. Why should he care?"

I took a deep breath. "Well, I thought . . ."

"You thought what?"

"I thought Marsha and Sean were a couple," I said.

"Well, I suppose they are in a way, but it's just out of convenience. You know, so they'll have someone to do things with."

I nodded, although I didn't understand at all. "Phil, Sean won't be hurt if Marsha dates someone else?"

Phil stared at me. "Of course not. Why should he? They're really close to each other. Did Sean tell you that his mother raised Marsha after her mother died?"

I shook my head. "No, I didn't know that. It was sure nice of her. I guess Sean and Marsha must think they're like brother and sister."

"Yeah, I guess you could say that. Sean's mom was really close to Marsha's mom. Of course, they were twins and I hear that twins are really close."

I suddenly stood up. "Twins? Then Sean and Marsha are actually cousins?"

Phil stood up. "Sure. What did you think they were?"

I closed my eyes. I didn't want to answer that question.

"Oh, I see. You thought they were dating," Phil said. Then he burst out laughing.

"It's not funny," I said.

"Yes, it is," he said. "Sean wants to ask you out, but he thinks you and I are still a couple. Once I heard that from Marsha, the night we danced together, I told her we were best friends, and always would be."

I couldn't help it. I laughed. "Oh, Phil, and here I thought, well, never mind."

We stood there together and looked at each other. I think that for both of us the last three years came to our minds, a lot of good times, and in a way it was sad to let go. But it was time. We reached for each other and he held me in his arms, his cheek resting on mine.

When he left I sat alone, trying to figure out what to do. So Sean had wanted to ask me out. Well, what was there to lose? I picked up the phone and called him.

46

"Hey, mister," I said. "How about me picking you up and we'll go out to dinner."

"No, I don't think so," he said.

My heart sank.

Then he said, "I'll pick you up and take you to dinner. And we'll go alone this time, to our Italian place, where we can dance the night away."

He drove over in record time and stood there in my doorway, the man of my dreams. Then he slowly walked toward me, tilted my chin up, and softly kissed my lips.

"I've been wanting to do that ever since the second time I saw you," he said.

I felt the heat of my face and knew I was blushing again. "I guess the first time wasn't the best," I said. "But I'll make up for it."

"You already have, darling." He kissed me again, deeply and with passion. Then he took my hand and led me to his car. We drove to the Italian restaurant, and we did dance the night away, in each other's arms.

THE END

LOVE KILLED
OUR MARRIAGE

From the very beginning, Mom had known that my friendship with Jolene Everett was dangerous. "You're born to the place where God wants you to be in this world," Mom told me. "It's up to you to make the best of your lot. Don't waste your time and strength wanting to live someone else's life."

Mom's words had upset me, but they hadn't stayed in my mind. It was a long time later that they came back to haunt me. . . .

Mom never seemed to envy anyone else, despite all the hard times that our family had endured. It was different with me, though. Even though I'd liked Jolene very much and considered her the best friend I'd ever had, I'd also envied her.

Mom's words had upset me, but they hadn't stayed in my mind. It was a long time later in life that they had come back to haunt me. . . .

Mom never seemed to envy anyone else, despite all the hard times that our family had endured. It was different with me, though. Even though I'd liked Jolene very much and considered her the best friend I'd ever had, I'd also envied her.

I'd known Jolene about a month when I'd spent my first weekend with her and her family.

Late that Sunday night, she'd driven me home in her expensive foreign car. I hadn't invited her to come into the house because it was late, and we'd both had to study for a science test the next day.

After she'd gone, I'd stood by the front gate for a few minutes, remembering the big Everett ranch. Suddenly, I'd hated to turn and head up the path to the shabby, old-fashioned farmhouse where my own family lived.

I'd never seen anything like Jolene's house, except in the movies. The house was professionally decorated. The big chairs and sofas made you want to sink into them and stay forever. All the rooms on one side of the house had glass walls that could be opened onto the terrace and the swimming pool.

Jolene's own room was beautiful. Her closet was almost as big as a room, too. It was filled with racks of gorgeous cashmere sweaters and skirts, designer jeans, and luscious gowns.

I'd felt a sudden, sick longing, knowing that I'd never have things like those myself. I was ashamed of my envy, though. It had seemed so disloyal to my mother and father. I'd realized that they did all they could to give my sisters and brothers and me a happy life. It wasn't their fault that we'd always seemed to be getting hit by some new trouble, such as Mom's baby turkeys dying, or some new insect that was attacking the crops.

Deep down, I was really as proud as my folks were that our family still lived on the farm that my great-grandparents had passed down to us. A lot of other small farmers had sold out to the big ranchers like Mr. Everett, but we'd managed to hold on to our place. Those big ranchers had modern machinery and equipment and hundreds of men to work for them, though. The crops they were able to raise were better and brought in more money than crops from small, old-fashioned farms.

Since I'd met Jolene, my feelings had bewildered me. Our eighty acres had suddenly seemed pitifully small, and our house had seemed old and bare and ugly, compared to the way she lived.

And Tom Podlas—my feelings about him were all mixed-up, too. Tom's farm was right next to ours, and it had been in his family as long as we'd owned our land. Tom was only nineteen, but he had the full work and worry of the Podlas place, because his parents were dead. Lately, whenever I'd thought of Tom, love and discontent had sort of twisted together inside of me.

Tom had always been a part of my life. From the time when I was ten years old, I'd dreamed of marrying him. When I was fifteen, we'd started dating, and just that past Christmas, Mom and Dad had agreed that we could be engaged if we waited until June, when I graduated, to be married. At first, I didn't think that I could stand to wait. Just the sight of Tom, with his handsome face and tousled hair, could make me go weak. When he kissed me, I blacked out to everything but the sweetness of his touch.

Since I'd met Jolene and seen what it was like to have a lot of money, I'd kept thinking about Tom and myself. After we got married, we'd probably lead exactly the same kind of scrimping lives that our parents had lived.

There were so many things that I wished I could buy for Mom and Dad, and my brothers and sisters—and for Tom. I didn't want a lot of extravagant luxuries for us, though. I longed for a better house to live in, and new farm machinery for Dad and Tom. For Mom, I'd have liked a new kitchen, with modern appliances in place of the old, worn range and the washing machine that was always breaking down. Things like that.

I'd thought of Mom, especially. She was young and still pretty, but years of hard work and poverty had taken a toll on her health. And, she was pregnant again, and she hadn't seen a doctor. We just couldn't afford it.

If things were different, I'd have bought my sisters and brothers the clothes and shoes that they needed. They wouldn't have had to wear patched jeans and faded shirts and sweaters to school. Cassie was fourteen, and the twins, Annie and Meg, were eleven. They were old enough to long for pretty things. My brothers, Kevin and Corey, eight and nine, dreamed of having bicycles, but there wasn't a chance that they'd ever get them—not with the way that things were.

I was exhausted by my longings when I'd turned and headed up the path to our house. I'd braced myself for the let-down that I knew I was going to feel after I'd stepped into the bare, shabby rooms. I was glad the lights were turned off, because that meant everyone had gone to bed. I didn't feel like talking.

But as I'd crossed the front porch, the sagging old glider had squeaked, and my mother had moved out of the shadows.

"It was such a nice night," she told me. "I couldn't sleep."

I knew that wasn't true, though, because she was always tired lately. She'd just wanted to wait up for me. She and I had always been very close. Sometimes I could almost sense what she was thinking, and how she felt about things.

"Tom was here," she said. "He waited, hoping to see you, but, finally, he went home. He was awfully disappointed when you didn't remember that you'd promised to be here early."

Suddenly, all of the mixed-up anger and guilt and discontent that had been bubbling inside of me lately rose to the surface. "Mom, it isn't fair!" I burst out. "Jolene's life is so different from ours. It was so beautiful over at her house. It's hard to—" I broke off.

"To come home?" Mom finished the words I was ashamed to voice. "Katie, don't go to Jolene's house if you can't see what she has without jealousy."

"I'm not jealous of her. She's the best friend I've ever had!" I protested, half ashamed, half angry.

"But you hate to come back to your own home and family after you've been with her," Mom went on. "Don't let your father hear you say that, Katie—or Tom, either. Tom wants to offer you more than he can. A man longs to give nice things to the girl he loves. Sometimes, though, he can't do what he'd like for her. All that he can do is love her—and hope that love is enough."

"Mom, I know it may sound as if I'm jealous, but I'm not," I insisted. Still, deep in my mind, a nagging voice seemed to ask: If it isn't jealousy you feel, what is it?

It was then that Mom said how it was wrong for a person to want to live someone else's life.

Just as she'd finished, Tom drove his old truck up our lane. It was making a dozen different kinds of engine noises. I'd tensed. I loved

50

Tom, but I didn't want to be with him, or talk to him, just then. I wanted to get over the crazy mood I was in.

He got out of the truck and came over to the porch. "So you got home safely," he said.

Mom went inside and left us alone.

"Hi, honey," Tom murmured. "I missed you. A couple of times this weekend, I almost went over to the Everett ranch to bring you home."

In the moonlight, he looked more handsome than ever. His cotton shirt was old, and it was really too small. The muscular leanness of his shoulders strained against the fabric.

I yearned to have his arms around me. Yet, at the same time, I'd resented that longing. I'd even resented the strong attraction that had always existed between us.

"Do you want to go for a ride?" Tom asked.

"No. It's too late." As I'd said the words, I couldn't help remembering how it had felt to glide along the road in Jolene's sleek car.

"Maybe my truck isn't good enough for you, after what you've been riding in," he mumbled, seeming to sense my thoughts.

I started to snap back at him, but he reached for me. "Honey, I'm sorry I said that," he apologized.

The next second I was in his arms, melting against him, wishing that his kisses would never stop. Yet, I wanted to fight against them— against what they stood for.

"I know we promised your folks that we'd wait until you graduate to get married, but that's such a long time," Tom told me. "I want you in my house now. I want to look after you and care for you. You could be married and still go to school."

I'd pulled away from him, feeling a crazy kind of panic as I'd pictured what my life would be like with Tom. It would be what Mom's life had been like with Dad—and possibly worse.

I was sorry after I'd broken away from Tom, though, because he'd looked so hurt.

"You're different after you've been with that Everett girl," he said, his voice hard and cold. "I'm not good enough for you anymore. Is that it?"

"Don't be silly, Tom!" I protested. "I love you. You know that, but I guess I'm afraid. What is there for us to look forward to, if you go on farming? You're not doing any better than Dad. We'll never have anything if things go on the way that they have been."

He caught my wrists and held them so tightly I'd felt as if they'd snap. "You belong to me, Katie!" he insisted. "You always have, and you always will. I won't let Jolene Everett and her family change you."

"I haven't changed, Tom. It's just that I can't help—" But I found that I couldn't go on.

51

Tom left me there in the dark. I'd heard the rattle of his truck engine as he'd started home. It was a lonely sound. After he'd gone, I'd stood there, crying inside.

Oh, Tom, I didn't mean to hurt you, I thought. But I knew that I had hurt him—badly.

I went inside and upstairs to the bedroom that I shared with my sister, Cassie. She must have been waiting for me, because she'd turned on the light and stared at me as if she'd hated me.

"Tom was here all evening, waiting for you. You promised him that you'd get home early," she snapped. "Or isn't Tom important to you anymore, now that you're so busy with Jolene?"

"You're only fourteen. You don't know anything about it!" I responded angrily. "Maybe if you were nicer to Jolene, she'd ask you over to her house, too. You're so jealous ,you won't even act properly."

"I've got too much pride to play up to her," Cassie said heatedly. "And I'm sick of the way you hurt Tom."

I was sorry then that I'd accused her of jealousy. It wasn't like her to envy anyone. "Cassie, please try to understand," I begged. "I don't hurt Tom on purpose."

I'd wondered, though, how she could understand me, when I didn't understand myself. I'd undressed in the dark, wondering why my friendship with Jolene seemed to be changing everything for me.

I'd felt as if I'd known Jolene most of my life, but actually, we'd met only a month before. I'd always been aware that Jolene existed, of course. The kids in my high school used to talk about her often. Some of their fathers worked on the big Everett ranch, so they knew a lot about Jolene. They were always talking about how she had her own car, and all the money she wanted to spend.

Until that year, Jolene had gone to a private boarding school and was home only on vacations. But that fall, she had enrolled in our local high school to finish her senior year, because her mother had decided that she'd wanted her at home.

Frankly, I wasn't even curious about what she was like. I'd noticed that she had nice clothes and that she probably had her hair professionally styled often. But my dates with Tom and my schoolwork filled my life, and I had never cared whether I'd ever gotten a chance to know her or not.

The kids in my crowd thought that Jolene was a snob. Nobody ever forgot for a minute how rich she was. Then, one day when she was sitting alone in the school cafeteria and I was with some friends at another table, I'd glanced up and seen her watching us. She'd looked so lonely. The realization had dawned on me then that she might really be nice—not conceited or snobbish.

I'd gone over and asked if I could sit with her.

"Would you?" Jolene asked. "I thought I'd never get to know any of you. I'm too shy just to barge into a crowd."

She was serious, too. During those first few days when we were getting acquainted, I'd realized over and over again that Jolene really was nice. And, all that money she had didn't seem to mean much to her.

I'd introduced her to all of my friends, and they'd liked her, but the two of us became really close friends. I was amazed at all the things that we had in common, despite the differences in our backgrounds.

I was engaged to Tom, although I didn't have a ring, and Jolene was engaged to Richard Grey, one of her father's business partners. She was just crazy about him, and wore his diamond on a chain around her neck. She thought her ring was too big and ostentatious to wear at school.

Jolene wanted to talk about Richard all the time. When I'd first met her, he was away on business. Even so, I'd begun to feel as if I knew Richard, too.

He was only twenty-three, but was already very successful. He'd inherited his part ownership in the Everett ranch from his parents, who had died a few years earlier. In addition, he had his own big ranch.

Even though Richard had had a lot of money all his life, Jolene told me that he'd never been really happy. "When we're married, I'm going to make a real home for him," she said. "We'll have a big family, and we'll all have fun together. Richard has a sister and brother, but he hardly ever got to know them. His mother and father were divorced when he was just a little boy. Mrs. Grey took his sister and brother and moved away, and Richard stayed with his father. He always hoped that they'd all get back together, but his mother and father both died before that could ever happen. His mother died of cancer, and his father had a heart attack."

After I'd met Jolene, I still rode to school on the bus in the mornings, but every afternoon, she drove me home in her car. We took rides first, sometimes going all the way into Middletown. I usually got home even before the school bus had passed our gate, though, because it followed a long, roundabout route and didn't come down our road until after five.

It was a shock to me when I'd realized that my family resented my being with Jolene so much. The first time that anything was actually said about it, though, was one night at the dinner table. I'd been talking about Jolene going into a big store and buying a dozen pairs of shoes at one time.

"Can't you talk about anything else, Katie?" Mom cut in. "We're interested in other things besides Jolene's money, even if you aren't. Besides, I'm not so sure that she's a good influence on you."

I was hurt, but at the same time, I knew that I probably did talk about Jolene too often. I'd tried not to mention her so much after that, but I could still feel resentment from everyone at home—and from Tom, too.

Mom and Dad had always wanted us to bring home our friends. They'd always made them feel welcome. It had seemed to me that they were different with Jolene, though—sort of distant, and too polite.

The first time I'd brought Jolene home, Mom had been cool toward her. "We're always glad to meet Katie's friends," she said stiffly.

My father just nodded. Cassie and the younger kids stared.

After Jolene had gone home, I'd let them know how angry I was. "You all acted like snobs! You were so cold to her!" I exclaimed.

"You'd best make friends with your own kind," Dad advised.

"My own kind! What does that mean?" I asked. He'd never said anything like that to me before. We'd been raised to believe that God had created everyone—and that we were all equal. What he'd said just didn't make sense. "Jolene's the nicest person I've ever known. You act like it's a crime for her folks to live decently."

"We live decently, too," my mother reminded me. "You just remember that, Katie. Lately, you seem to forget it pretty often—the way you compare everything that you have with what Jolene has. If you can't be friends with the girl without envying her, then you'd better drop the friendship."

I was so furious that I was shaking. Yet, I was ashamed that I'd made that remark about Jolene's life being decent because I'd implied that ours wasn't. It wasn't true. It wasn't what I'd meant, really. Sometimes, I didn't know myself anymore.

I'd remained friends with Jolene, though I'd gone to her house more often than she'd come to mine. In sharp contrast with the way my family had acted with her, her parents had accepted me immediately as her best friend. They'd treated me as if they'd always known me. They adored Jolene, and they wanted to be a part of everything that she did.

Every time her father went into the city or took a business trip, he'd bring her a surprise gift, and often, he'd give me the same thing. Sometimes it was perfume, or a book, or a beautiful handbag.

Once, he gave us beautiful silk dresses that he'd brought back from Europe.

Tom happened to be at our house for dinner on the night when I'd brought mine home. "Don't they like the way you dress?" he asked, his face dark with anger. "Maybe this is none of my business, Katie, since we're not married yet, but I don't want you to keep these gifts."

"Yes, you'll have to return the dress," Mom agreed. "It's too expensive for you to accept."

"You don't have to take charity from the Everetts, or from anyone else," Dad put in. "I can support my own family."

Mom had taken me aside and apologized later. "Maybe it doesn't mean that Jolene and her parents feel sorry for you, if they give you expensive gifts. But it hurts your father's pride, and Tom's, too, when you make so much of the luxuries that your friend has, Katie."

"What about my pride?" I asked indignantly. "How can I explain things to Jolene without hurting her?"

I did give back the dress, of course, and Jolene was nice about it. Tom tried to be extra sweet with me after that, but it didn't help. I'd still felt hurt because he couldn't seem to realize that Jolene and I were like sisters, and that her money meant nothing to me.

One day when I'd gone home with Jolene after school, there was an expensive luxury car parked in the driveway.

When she saw it, Jolene gasped. "Richard's here! Richard's home!" she exclaimed. Ordinarily she was just pretty, but her face had looked really beautiful then.

She'd run through the big living room and dining room, calling Richard's name.

When he'd hurried in from the terrace, I'd felt like an intruder. They'd stood there locked in each other's arms, seeming to be completely unaware that I was in the room.

I'd started to slip away, but Jolene had stopped me. "Wait, Katie!" she called. "My two favorite people have to get to know each other."

"I feel as if I already know Katie," Richard said. "You've written so much about her in your letters."

I'd seen photographs of Richard, but they hadn't done him justice. He was an incredibly handsome man, but the special thing about him was his personality. He was so friendly and warm. And the way he looked at Jolene, as if he worshipped her, thrilled me.

That night, after Jolene and Richard had taken me home, I was glad that Tom hadn't come over to see me. I wanted to be alone. I went out onto the porch and sat in the dark. I'd kept thinking of how perfect Richard and Jolene were together, and I couldn't help comparing them to Tom and me. Somehow, their romance seemed different than Tom's and mine. They were so glamorous, and we were so ordinary.

A few months later, my mother gave birth to a little boy, Liam Michael. After that, it seemed as though I was always fighting for time to see Jolene. Even though I did my share of chores around the house, Mom and Dad seemed to resent even more every minute I'd spent at Jolene's house.

Tom had started trying to talk me into marrying him at Christmas, instead of waiting until spring, even though we seemed to argue every time we were together. My parents had agreed to give their consent, too.

"You can still finish school. I'll take you to school every day," Tom insisted. "There isn't a lot of work in the winter for a woman. You don't need to plant a garden, or raise chickens or turkeys, this year. You can spend your spare time fixing up the house the way you want it. We'll scrape up money for paint and some new curtains. I guess the old furniture will have to do, though, until I get more of a return from the farm."

At the thought of moving into Tom's house, I'd felt an increasing sense of panic and dread. I just wasn't ready to get married, and I was beginning to wonder if I would be at graduation time.

Once, I'd been thrilled when I'd dreamed of being Tom's wife. Suddenly, even though the attraction between us seemed stronger than ever, as soon as his kisses had ended, I'd always felt as if I were trapped.

Jolene and I were both taking home-economics courses at school. I couldn't understand why Jolene got such a kick out of learning to cook and sew. Richard had so much money—she'd never have to worry about doing housework.

Just before the Christmas vacation, the school chorus and the home-economics club planned a holiday party for the PTA. The chorus was going to sing Christmas carols, and the home-ec students would serve cookies and hot spiced cider.

Mom had promised me that I could have a new outfit to wear to the party, but in the end, she wasn't able to give me the money. I'd have to wear my same old worn sweater and faded jeans.

When Jolene showed me the outfit that she was going to wear, longing and envy had swept over me. It was the first time that I'd realized that you could actually want something so badly that it could make your head ache. Just once, I'd wanted to look as well dressed and pretty as Jolene.

The next day, Jolene had some shopping to do, so we drove into Middletown after school. While we were in the store where she often bought clothes, I fell in love with a cashmere sweater. It was a beautiful soft winter white, and I'd tried it on just for fun. I couldn't believe how that sweater had transformed me.

"Katie, you have to have it!" Jolene exclaimed. "Let me buy it for you, please. It can be a Christmas present."

Of course, I hadn't let her buy the sweater. I'd known right away that Mom and Dad would never approve. Instead, I'd tried to put all thought of that sweater out of my mind.

Then, after classes on the afternoon of the party, Jolene had told me that she had an errand to run in Middletown. It was late, but we drove into town, anyway.

At the clothing store, she picked up a package that was waiting for her. "I bought that cashmere sweater for myself," she explained. "I'm crazy about it. You can borrow it tonight, Katie. I'd feel terrible if you didn't."

I knew that she didn't really want the sweater. She had many similar cashmere sweaters in her closet at home. She'd just bought it so that she could lend it to me. I decided that I'd wear it, no matter what Tom and my parents said.

It was a cold, wet night and already dark when we'd started back home. Since it was so late, we'd taken a shortcut—a back road that was used mostly by farmers and truckers. Jolene drove pretty fast, even though the rain was coming down hard.

I never really knew what happened. One second, Jolene and I were listening to the radio and laughing, and the next, her car had skidded and plowed straight into a big truck.

I was thrown clear. Just before I'd hit the ground and my head had seemed to explode in pain, I'd heard Jolene's screams and the smash of metal and glass.

I was unconscious for several hours, but my injuries weren't really very serious. When I woke up, I knew that Jolene was dead. No one had to tell me. Mom held me in her arms while I cried.

My whole family, as well as Tom, did everything that they could to make it easier for me to get through that tragic Christmas. I didn't know how I'd have faced it without them.

When I went home from the hospital after five days, I saw that Dad had painted the room that Cassie and I shared. It was a beautiful shade of peach.

"You need a cheerful place," he said, almost shyly. Mom had made pretty white curtains.

Annie and Meg and Corey and Kevin put on what they called "a show" for me. They'd tried so hard. But while they were reciting poems and singing songs that they'd learned in school, I'd kept thinking of Jolene. I couldn't believe that she was gone forever.

Tom came over to the house every night during the Christmas holidays. He took me for long walks.

"That's what I always do when I can't think of any way to change what happens in life, Katie," he said. "It sort of quiets me inside."

He went with me, too, when I went to visit Mr. and Mrs. Everett.

I'd had no idea what I could possibly say to Jolene's parents. I only knew that I wanted to help them in any way that I could. I was haunted by the memory that we had gone into Middletown that last night because she'd wanted to do something nice for me.

Mr. Everett had grown old since I'd seen him last. His face was pale and his eyes swollen from crying, even though Jolene had been dead for nearly three weeks.

"Oh, Katie!" he cried when he saw me. "We've lost our girl forever."

Mrs. Everett, who was under the care of a nurse, seemed dazed and confused. Even so, my being there had seemed to help her. She'd clung to my hand. "Jolene is so fond of you, Katie," she murmured, as if Jolene were still living.

Another awful moment had been when Mr. Everett had explained that Richard Grey had been so crazed by grief that he'd gone to Europe. He'd said that he wanted to be as far as possible from everything that he and Jolene had known together.

On the way home, I'd cried so hard that Tom had stopped the truck and held me in his arms.

A few days after I'd visited the Everetts, Mr. Everett had called my mother and asked her if I could come to visit his wife again. Of course, Mom was glad to have me do all that I could to comfort Jolene's mother.

It was only later, after Mrs. Everett had begun to want me with her every day after school, that Mom and Dad, and even Tom, had begun to complain that I was going to the Everetts' house too often.

"We're sorry for Mrs. Everett," Mom said gently, "but it's wrong for anyone, even in grief, to take up another person's time completely, Katie. You have a life of your own to live."

Tom had objected even more than my parents. "You should be planning our wedding," he protested. "It's a tragedy that Jolene was killed, but she's gone. Her mother has to face that. She can't keep on clinging to you."

Dad had started grumbling that it was time that I got rid of any ideas of fancy living that I'd gotten from the Everetts.

What none of them understood, I'd kept telling them, was that Mrs. Everett needed me. Only when I was with her did she seem to take any interest in anything. I was the only one who could get her to eat.

"When you're here, Katie," she told me once, "I can pretend that nothing has changed. I always feel as though Jolene could be in the next room, and that she might come running in to me."

A few months later, Mr. Everett took Mrs. Everett on a vacation, thinking that the change might help her. After they had gone, and I'd had no need to go over to their ranch after school every day, a strange depression and sadness had settled over me. I just couldn't shake it off.

When I went home after school, our house looked shabby and drab. The rooms seemed to be crowded to bursting with noisy people. Everything seemed to smell of frying potatoes or dirty diapers. I couldn't find a place in the house to be alone. Cassie and the other girls were always in our room.

I'd remember the big, quiet rooms in the Everetts' house, and I'd think about how there was always privacy there, if you wanted to be alone. I was ashamed of thinking about it so much, but I couldn't seem to stop. Sometimes, I'd wake up in the middle of the night, crying.

I'd told myself that I just couldn't get over my grief about Jolene, and that was partly true. But, at the same time, I knew that I was depressed because the only glamorous part of my life had ended, and I'd never get it back again.

After just one week, Jolene's parents had come home unexpectedly. Mrs. Everett had collapsed while they were away. She was asking for me, and Mr. Everett had called and asked me to come and stay with them for a while—at least until my graduation.

Mom and Dad were against the idea, of course. But Mr. Everett was so worried and pathetic that they'd agreed to let me go, if I decided that it was something that I wanted to do.

Tom had really made things difficult for me. When he'd heard that I was going to live with the Everetts for a while, he'd said terrible things—things that I almost couldn't forgive.

"You're going to marry me after you graduate," he snapped. "Maybe if you get used to living the way those people do, you'll turn your nose up at what I can afford to give you."

"You don't know me very well, do you, Tom?" I asked. "Maybe you don't love me, either, or you'd have faith in me."

I'd have gone to help Jolene's mother if she'd been living in a shack. But, after I'd been staying with the Everetts for a few days, I'd often felt a secret stab of guilt because I did enjoy the luxurious way in which they lived.

Mrs. Everett improved, but very slowly. After I'd graduated, she'd begged me to stay on a little longer. I didn't give her a definite answer, but I didn't move back home, either.

I saw my family two or three times a week, but somehow, those visits with them had never turned out well. Mom and Dad and the kids seemed so quiet and reserved with me. They'd acted hurt, as though I'd deserted them. Only, I hadn't deserted them. I was just doing a favor for the Everetts. I was still going to marry Tom.

Tom and I still went out on dates, but suddenly, our times together had turned out to be torture for us. The main problem was Tom's attitude. He was moody and quiet. He could never say much to Mr. and Mrs. Everett when he came to pick me up. He owned a good suit, but he often came to take me out wearing torn jeans and work boots— almost as if he wanted to embarrass me.

The Everetts were against my marrying him. "He's a nice young man, I'm sure," Mrs. Everett commented, "but you could do so much better, Katie."

"You're like our own daughter, so we want the best for you. Otherwise, we wouldn't interfere," Jolene's father told me. "From what we've seen of Tom, he seems to have a bad temper, and he's quite sullen."

They were sincere in their criticism of Tom, but I had a nagging feeling that maybe it was my fault that they'd never seen him at his best.

A few weeks later, Richard Grey finally came home from Europe. Jolene had been gone for six months, but Richard looked as if he had lost her only a few days before. The afternoon I saw him, every detail of our first meeting had come back to me. I'd remembered Jolene running into his arms, and how they'd seemed so special—so perfect—together.

Neither of us could speak at first. "Jolene's mother and father have told me how good you've been to them, Katie," he said finally. "I appreciate it, and I know Jolene would, too. I should have stayed with them, but all I could think of to do was to run—as if I could get away from what hurt me." He laughed bitterly.

Richard came to the Everetts' almost every day. He was working hard as a partner in Mr. Everett's ranch company, and also managing his own land, but he still looked lost and dazed.

About that time, Mrs. Everett had offered me a salary if I would stay on with her for a few months as a paid companion. I didn't give her an answer right away, even though I knew what I wanted to do.

It was summer, and I knew that Tom would be working very hard until late fall. Why can't we set the date for our wedding then? I figured. In the meantime, I would be earning money for all of the things that Tom and I would need to fix up his house.

I was eighteen, and I didn't need my parents' permission to take a job, but I did want their approval. I went home to spend the weekend, and it was the loneliest time that I'd ever known. Somehow, I no longer felt as if I belonged in Mom and Dad's house.

When I'd told them about the job, Mom sighed. "You'll have to make your own decision. But remember that Tom loves you, Katie. He's waited a long time for you."

That night, Tom took me to a movie. At least, that was where we'd started to go. We'd ended up parked in his truck for most of the evening, arguing.

He just wouldn't try to be reasonable. "You won't be working for the Everetts," he said finally. "It won't be a real job. Maybe you don't want their money, but you do want to live the kind of life that Jolene had. You want to step into her place."

"You never loved me, or you couldn't think such a thing!" I exclaimed, shocked.

"I love you, all right. Maybe that makes me a fool. But I'm through with being the fall guy in this business," he told me grimly. "If you want to marry me, Katie, you aren't going to hire yourself out to the Everetts! You aren't going to let them pay you, while you live soft and easy. If you go back there tonight, we're through."

Having Tom talk to me that way, his voice so bitter and full of hatred, was like having the earth split open under my feet. The awful things that he'd said had made me feel so cheap. But they weren't true—they weren't!

The way that he'd laid down the law was just more than I could take. If he wanted to marry me, he'd have to apologize. I figured that if he really loved me, he'd have to make me believe that he knew I wasn't just after the Everetts' money.

Tom didn't apologize, though. I went back to the Everetts' ranch that night, but I didn't give Mrs. Everett any definite answer about whether or not I'd work for her.

My breakup with Tom had made me actually sick. We'd shared so much that was sweet, and yet, suddenly, it was all over. A few times, I'd considered giving in and going back home, but I'd told myself that I couldn't do that—not if I had any pride or self-respect

For several days, I waited for Tom to come to me, but he didn't. Finally, I'd told Mrs. Everett that I'd work for her as long as she needed me.

During that summer, Richard Grey and I developed a close friendship. At first, it was our constant talk of Jolene that drew us together.

"My other friends avoid mentioning her when they're with me," Richard said. "But, somehow, it makes me feel better to talk about her."

Late in the fall, we'd started going out together occasionally, although neither of us really thought of it as dating. We went dancing, or to concerts or movies in Middletown. We didn't talk quite so much about Jolene, and I didn't think so much about Tom.

During the winter, I'd begun to feel at peace and, yet, excited at the same time. It was a long while, though, before I'd admitted to myself that I was falling in love with Richard.

Mrs. Everett had improved a great deal, and I knew that soon, she wouldn't really need me. I knew that I should be making plans for the future, when I'd have to find some other job. And yet, I'd just seemed to drift along from one day to the next.

Then, one night when I was with Richard, I'd wondered what it would be like not to see him every day. After I'd left Mr. and Mrs. Everett, would he still keep in touch with me? I'd shivered inside, dreading life without him.

I had no idea of how Richard really felt about me. After that night, I was always wondering, always frightened, dreading the future. He was tender and protective with me, but, then, that was his way with everyone. Months after I knew I loved him, he still seemed to think of me only as a friend.

Without really planning it, I'd found myself trying to be as much like Jolene as possible in the ways that I'd thought and acted. That had seemed to draw Richard closer to me.

"Sometimes you remind me of Jolene," he told me once. "I don't mean in physical appearance, but your personality and way of thinking."

After that, I'd tried harder than ever to exhibit the qualities I'd admired in Jolene.

Mr. and Mrs. Everett had seemed pleased that Richard and I were such good friends. They still grieved for Jolene, but they had begun, at last, to make a new life for themselves without her.

It was over a year after Jolene's death when Richard kissed me for the first time. After that day, I only went through the motions of living when I wasn't with him. He was all that mattered to me.

I hadn't been really sure that he was beginning to care for me until he'd brought me a charm bracelet with tiny miniatures of objects to remind us of things that we'd shared. There was a little jeweled tennis racket for the day he'd taught me how to play. There was a pair of ballet slippers, because he'd promised me that, someday, he'd take me to the ballet. A little enamel rose was exactly like the first real one I'd ever had in my life—one that he'd given me.

It was my telling him that I felt I had to leave the Everetts and get some other job that had made Richard realize that he wanted to marry me. The sweetness of the moment when he asked me to be his wife was all I'd ever dreamed it could be.

What I hadn't counted on was that I'd remember the night when I'd gotten engaged to Tom. I couldn't help but think about the half-wild way we'd kissed, and the intense longing that we'd felt.

But I was wrong about Tom. It had only been physical attraction between us. I hadn't even seen him since we'd broken up. He'd made no attempt to see me. The fact that he'd stayed away had made it plain that he thought I'd preferred my easy life with the Everetts to him. A deep bitterness stirred inside of me—almost like hurt. He couldn't have loved me and believed that about me, I thought. I told myself that it didn't matter anymore.

"I'll make you happy," I promised Richard, and I'd meant it so much that I'd almost cried.

"Darling, that's my line," he teased. "All you have to do is to be yourself." His hunger for my lips, his impatience for us to be married, thrilled me.

It was when he'd brought me my ring that I'd remembered the one that Jolene had worn on a chain. Mine was a different ring, of course—a diamond set in an entirely different way. As Richard put it on my finger, though, I had a sudden sense of guilt, as if I were taking something that was Jolene's.

Then I told myself to be reasonable. Jolene had been dead for almost two years. She would want Richard to have a normal, happy life.

I'd seen less and less of my own family since I'd been Mrs. Everett's paid companion. Suddenly, I'd longed for them to share my happiness. When you'd grown up in a big, close-knit family, you wanted them to be a part of everything that you did.

When I'd told my parents about Richard and me, they'd both wished me happiness, but I couldn't help feeling that an invisible wall was separating us, and it hurt and disappointed me.

My sister Cassie, at least, had let me know exactly how she'd felt. When I'd asked her to be my bridesmaid, she'd turned me down.

"No," she said firmly. "I won't have anything to do with you hurting Tom more than you already have."

Mom had tried to smooth things over. "Cassie is very loyal," she told me. "Forgive her, Katie. She's seen how Tom has suffered since you broke off with him."

"He broke off with me!" I exclaimed. "Anyway, that's all over now. I'm in love with Richard. Can't you understand that?"

"Are you sure, honey?" Mom asked. "Would you want to marry him if he were poor?"

I was so hurt by her question that I'd lashed out to hurt her in return. "You don't like Richard because he has money," I said coldly. "Maybe you'd hate anyone who was better off than you!"

Mom didn't answer me. I knew I'd hurt her, but she'd certainly hurt me, too.

I'd stayed on at the Everetts' until my marriage a few weeks later. My wedding was like the vision in my little-girl dreams. I wore a white dress and veil, and there were white candles and flowers on the altar.

As I'd walked up the aisle to Richard, my heart had swelled with more than happiness. I'd felt almost a sense of relief—as if we'd come to that moment in spite of terrible obstacles. At the same time, I could hardly believe the miracle that was happening to me.

As we spoke our wedding vows, Richard's eyes seemed to say over and over again: "Katie, I love you."

My mother and father and sisters and brothers all came to see me married, of course, and they were sweet to me, and wished me happiness. Cassie did act as my bridesmaid, after all. Even so, the old closeness that I'd had with my family was gone.

Another thing that had hurt me badly was my memory of Tom. He'd said terrible things to me—believed terrible things about me. Yet, I'd wished that we hadn't parted in such bitterness. I wished, too, that I could forget what his kisses once had meant to me.

Richard and I spent our honeymoon in the Caribbean, in a luxurious bungalow at a beautiful new beach resort. Richard had planned everything about that first month so perfectly that it seemed almost unreal when I'd thought of it later. He was so sweet to me—so tender. Everywhere we went, I sensed that other women envied me, not just because he was attractive, well dressed, and successful, but because he was so attentive.

Our honeymoon was an awakening to me in many ways. I'd known that Richard loved me, of course, but I hadn't realized just how intense his love was. I hadn't understood that he wasn't completely sure of me.

Richard wanted to be with me constantly. He had to know where I was, and he didn't even like for me to go and have my hair done, or to go shopping, without him.

"I like to look at you," he'd say, half teasing, when I'd told him that he worried too much about me. "I have to keep reminding myself that you're real."

One morning I woke up early and heard the surf crashing on the beach. Richard was still sleeping. On impulse, I put on a bathing suit and went out for an early-morning swim.

I didn't swim after all, because the surf was rougher than I'd expected. Instead, I'd gone for a walk up the beach. I'd enjoyed being alone for those few minutes, but I'd also felt ashamed and guilty about my happiness. It seemed so wrong to feel that way about being alone on my honeymoon.

When I'd gotten back to our bungalow, I'd found Richard struggling into his clothes. His face was pale. When he saw me, he held me tightly to him, as if I'd been lost or missing for hours.

"Never do that to me again, Katie!" he pleaded. "When I woke up and you were gone, I was afraid that something had happened to you. I don't know what I thought. Oh, Katie! So many times in my life, I've lost the people that I've loved."

I knew it was unreasonable that my going out for a short while should have upset him so badly. But, I had also begun to realize that he needed to feel more sure of me.

"You'll never lose me," I promised. "I'll stay so close to you that you'll think I'm a pest."

At first, I wasn't too worried when I didn't thrill to our lovemaking as much as I'd imagined I would. Before our wedding, I'd read a book about married life, and it had said that sometimes a couple had to wait several months before they adjusted to their new lives together.

But Richard had worried about it so much that I'd gotten tense. "Katie, do I frighten you?" he kept asking. "If you'll only tell me, I'll try to change."

Sometimes I'd felt restless, wishing that I didn't have to answer his questions. And yet, I was deeply in love with him.

The times when both of us were the most truly happy on our honeymoon were when we'd pictured our future life together. We'd talked about having a big family. Actually, I hadn't thought much about children, even though I knew that Richard wanted them. We'd just never talked about it much. But after we were married, Richard never tired of picturing what our family life would be like, and I'd enjoyed dreaming of it, too.

"One thing I'm sure of is that our kids aren't going to be torn to pieces because of divorce," he often said. The longer I was married to him, the more I realized how deeply he'd suffered because his own family had broken up.

We'd decided that four children would be just about right for us. "At least, for a start," Richard would tease. I loved him so much— especially when he was in a laughing mood. Sometimes, though, he was so serious that I worried about him.

When we'd headed back home after a month, I'd felt a burning excitement inside of me because, finally, our marriage was really beginning. On the plane, I thought: When we have our family, it won't matter that the rest of it isn't as exciting as I expected.

I was startled to have thought such a thing, but I'd made myself face the truth. The fact was, physically, I still didn't enjoy being married to Richard, and I was beginning to feel as though I never would. Because I'd hated to hurt his feelings, I was learning to pretend to be thrilled, even when I really wasn't. I figured that children would fill my life and make up for the emotional ecstasy I hadn't found.

Maybe all brides have to learn that making love isn't the most important thing in a marriage, I told myself.

Richard and I were going to live in the beautiful house that his father had built several years before on their ranch. It had never been completely furnished. Richard had been staying in an apartment that had been intended as servants' quarters.

He told me that it would be my job to supervise the decorating and furnishing of our home, and he enjoyed my pleasure in making plans. Later, when I'd worried that some of my ideas might not turn out well, he'd laughed.

"Anything that you don't like, you can change later, honey," he assured me.

I'd known Richard was wealthy, but the amount in the checking account that he'd opened for me overwhelmed me.

He was as eager to get back to work, running his ranch, as I was to set up our home. It was never easy to keep good employees on a big ranch, and three of his best men had quit while we were away. Richard had to find replacements for them, as well as solve a lot of other problems.

Those first months were even happier and more exciting than I'd imagined they would be. There was so much to do that I hardly had time to think. I was so grateful, because Mrs. Everett gave me help and advice in deciding on colors and furniture for the house. Without her, I didn't know how I'd have gotten everything in order—the perfect way I'd dreamed of having it for Richard.

Sometimes, I'd felt as though Mrs. Everett was more of a mother to me than my own mother. Because no matter how hard I tried, I still couldn't seem to get as close to Mom and the rest of my family as I'd been before I'd met Jolene.

Not that we ever argued, though. We'd all acted friendly toward one another when we were together. It was just that I'd longed to buy clothes for my sisters and brothers, and I wanted to buy things for the house. Mom wouldn't let me. Maybe it was because I'd once accused her of being jealous of anyone who had money. I'd known at the time I'd said it that it wasn't true—I'd known in my heart that I was being cruel. I'd apologized to Mom several times since. Why couldn't she forget it, just as I'd forgotten a few mean things that she'd said to me?

My family was the first guests that Richard and I entertained in our home after it was furnished and ready. I'd served a beautiful buffet supper out on the terrace by the swimming pool. Nobody ever really let down their guard and relaxed at that dinner party, though. At least, no one in my family relaxed. Only Richard had acted as if he were having a good time.

"You'll get close to them again," he insisted. "Your folks are wonderful people, Katie. They're just shy and proud, and they still feel strange around me. They would act that way around any new son-in-law."

I'd hoped that he was right, but I didn't really believe that he was. I supposed, next to Mom, I'd missed Cassie most. She was almost seventeen, and I'd longed for us to be like other grown-up sisters— confiding in each other, and enjoying each other's company.

A few weeks after they'd had dinner with us, Richard and I were invited to Sunday dinner at Mom and Dad's. It was on that day that I saw Tom again, for the first time since we'd broken up.

Tom hadn't been invited to dinner. In fact, Mom had told me earlier that Tom had gone to Middletown to see another man on business.

We'd gotten to talking about him when we were alone in the kitchen. "Tom took your marriage very hard," Mom confided. "He's been a different person ever since. He never laughs. As far as I know, he hasn't dated any other girls. I wish he would, though. It would take his mind off his troubles. He's had a bad year. He lost all the money he put into the turkeys, and he couldn't get pickers for his tomatoes in time. There was an early rain, and most of his crop was ruined."

I wished that Mom hadn't brought up his name. Why should I have cared how Tom was getting along?

It was later, while we were eating dinner, that he'd walked into Mom's big kitchen, looking pale and troubled in his old work clothes.

"Tom!" Dad greeted him. "You should have gotten here earlier, son. But there's plenty of food left. Cassie, set a place for him."

"I can't stay," Tom said. "I didn't get to Middletown. My truck broke down. I've been working on it. If you could lend me your fuel pump, maybe that would help."

"Sure. I'll take you over and help you with the repairs," Dad offered. "Tom, do you know Katie's husband, Richard Grey?" he asked.

Tom nodded. When Richard held out his hand, Tom took it. Then he'd turned to me. "I guess I never did wish you happiness and good luck, Katie. I want you to know that I do want those things for you." I could tell that he'd meant every word.

After he had gone, I'd had sharp chest pains—the kind you got from running too fast. I'd been afraid that he'd make trouble, I told myself, and finally, I was relieved. I didn't like being enemies with anyone—most of all with Tom.

If Richard had noticed anything unusual about my reaction to Tom, he didn't mention it. He knew that we'd been engaged—although he didn't know the real reason why we'd broken up. I'd told him that Tom and I had simply outgrown each other, which was certainly true.

That winter, I'd begun to feel restless again. All the work of furnishing our house was finished. We spent a lot of time talking about the family that we were going to have, but so far, it was just a dream.

When we had been married a year, I still wasn't pregnant. Again and again, month after month, we'd faced the same familiar disappointment.

Suddenly, it had seemed to be more and more important to have children. Other things had begun to matter less and less. Richard kept reminding me that we had to be patient, even though I knew he was just as anxious as I was.

Mrs. Everett knew how worried I was. "Maybe you're rushing things, Katie," she said soothingly. "Anyway, you haven't been married long enough to settle down to being parents. You're too serious about it. Why don't you make a point of getting acquainted with more young people? You could help Richard a lot in business—entertaining for him. It would fill your time." She smiled. "You know, even a young couple in love need friends."

I'd decided to take her advice and learn how to give parties. Richard was pleased with the idea. "If you really enjoy being a hostess, I'm all for it," he told me. "I love showing you off to people. But I've always believed that a man shouldn't bring home his business associates unless his wife really enjoys meeting them."

"I haven't had any experience," I kept reminding him, "and I have a lot to learn. Maybe I won't even be a success. But at least it will give me something to do with my time, until the babies start coming."

The first parties that I'd planned were very simple, but Richard seemed to be pleased, and that was what I'd wanted. Yet, as the months had dragged on and I still hadn't gotten pregnant, I began to get sick of the parties. I felt sort of panicked all the time—as if something awful might happen to us if we didn't have a baby soon.

To celebrate our second anniversary, Richard had taken me on my first trip to Los Angeles. We'd spent two weeks there at a famous hotel, sightseeing, going to restaurants and clubs, and shopping.

In a fancy toy store, we'd bought some dolls and a model of a ranch with perfect little carved wooden animals.

"Those kids of ours can't hold out much longer," Richard said, smiling the way he had long ago. His smile didn't fool me, though. For all his outward assurance, Richard was a quiet, lonely man, and being married to me hadn't made him any less so.

It was during that same winter, the second year of our marriage, that I'd noticed that Richard was drinking more than he should. Not that he ever got drunk, of course—because he didn't. But he'd lost weight, and his color wasn't good.

We got into the habit of going dancing or out to dinner on weekends. We did a lot of dancing and met a lot of people, but none of the things we did ever really took my mind completely off of my longing for a baby.

I had often asked our doctor why I hadn't gotten pregnant, but he'd always assured me that it was too soon to worry. He'd insisted that I had plenty of time. In spite of his assurances, though, I'd begun to fear that something was wrong with me. I was worried that I'd never have children.

After our third anniversary, I'd decided that I just had to know for sure—even if I faced a terrible disappointment. When I took the tests, Richard had an examination, too.

"We might as well do this up right," he joked.

A few days later, Dr. Sullivan had the test results for us. I was apparently completely normal and could have children, but he'd learned that Richard could never father a child. Not even surgery would help him.

I was almost overwhelmed by disappointment, but I'd tried not to let Richard know. All his confidence in himself as a man seemed shaken.

"Katie, I'll give you a divorce," he told me. "I'll never try to hold you. I love you too much to hurt you, or to keep you from happiness."

"Richard, what kind of person do you think I am?" I asked. "I didn't marry you just to have children. I love you."

He'd searched my face, as if he wasn't sure I was telling the truth. Then, suddenly, his own features had contorted in pain, and I was afraid that he was going to cry. I'd wanted to say something to help him, but I couldn't think of any words at all.

Finally, he'd held me so tightly that I'd almost cried out. "Katie, I'm not a real man if I can't father a child," he said sadly. "But I don't want to lose you. I couldn't stand that!"

I'd tried in every way I could think of to prove to Richard that it didn't matter to me whether we had children or not. Dr. Sullivan had assured me that Richard would finally adjust to the situation and accept it. But, instead, weeks passed and he'd seemed to grow more and more unhappy, and less sure of himself.

Sometimes, he would wake me in the night. "Katie, are you sure it doesn't matter?" he'd ask.

"I swear to you," I'd insist. "It doesn't matter."

When he had to go away on business, I went with him and stayed with him as much as possible.

One afternoon when he was at a meeting of a ranchers' association, I went to the park across the street from our hotel. I was sitting on a bench in the sun when a little girl about three years old ran across the grass in front of me, chasing a pigeon. She'd stumbled and fallen, and I'd picked her up.

After she'd run back to her mother, I couldn't forget how her firm little body had felt in my arms. It was while I'd tried to wipe the memory out of my mind that I'd realized fully how awful it was going to be never to have a baby of my own. I didn't think I'd quite understood before. I'd been too worried about Richard's suffering. Suddenly, though, the fear had almost choked me—the terror of all the years ahead of me, when Richard and I were going to be alone.

Again and again, I had sworn to him that it didn't matter if he couldn't give me a child. I'd insisted that nothing had changed between us. And, when I'd said the words, I'd meant them with all my heart. I knew now that it did matter, though. I dreaded our life together, if it was always going to be so empty.

There must be more than this, I thought, and then I was ashamed. I knew the tragedy was greater for Richard, who blamed himself, than it was for me.

A few days after we'd gotten home to the ranch, I'd had a surge of hope. "We can adopt a child," I told Richard excitedly. "Even if we have to wait a while until we can find one, we'll have something to look forward to. We can even take more than one child."

But Richard had refused to consider adoption. The idea had only seemed to make him more conscious of the fact that he could never father a child himself.

"I wanted so much to make you happy," he told me. "But the one thing you want most and need most, I can't give you."

After that, Richard drank more and more often, and usually alone. He'd begun to start every morning with a stiff drink, and he drank whenever he felt depressed. I began to be afraid that he might become an alcoholic. I'd hated to keep after him not to drink, because it sounded like nagging, but I just couldn't give up.

Another thing was plaguing me, too. Our physical relationship was changing. Richard had always seemed to need and want a great deal of love from me, but suddenly, he'd no longer seemed interested.

I'd felt I just had to talk to someone about what was happening to us. And so, I'd gone to my mother, longing to pour out my story to her. I was afraid that something awful was happening to Richard and me—something much worse than not having children.

The afternoon I went to see Mom, all my sisters and brothers, except little Liam, were out. The younger ones were in school, and Cassie was working. I'd sat in the kitchen with Mom while she'd scalded and peeled tomatoes for canning. I'd wanted to help her, but she wouldn't let me.

"You can't work in a dress like that, and you'd get your hands stained," she said.

It was then I'd realized that I couldn't talk to her, after all. It really hurt that she still treated me like—well, like company. I was just a visitor, not family.

Jolene had been dead close to five years, and I hadn't thought of her in months, when, suddenly, one day something happened that brought her vividly to my mind. Or, had it really happened? I couldn't forget the incident afterward, though—whether I'd imagined it or not.

I had shopped in Middletown until the stores had closed that evening, and then, I'd had dinner and gone to a movie alone. Richard was away on business, and I didn't expect him home for several days.

When I'd gotten back to the ranch, though, his car was in the driveway. I was sorry that I hadn't been in the house to welcome him.

My heart sank when I thought that he might have started drinking while he'd waited for me.

Recently, Richard had been sleeping in his study, so I'd looked for him there when I couldn't find him anywhere else. When I'd opened the door, there was a heavy smell of liquor in the air.

In the dim light, I'd seen him sprawled on a chair. There was a bottle beside him on a table, and his breathing was heavy and uneven, the way it always was when he'd had too much to drink.

I was just going to get a blanket for him when I was startled by the weird feeling that he wasn't alone in the study. Even more weird was my sensation that I was an intruder. It was so strong that I couldn't move for a second. I'd stood there, frozen, while the sense of someone else besides Richard and me being in the room grew even stronger. Suddenly, I'd thought of Jolene. I was sure that she was there, guarding Richard.

At last, sick with fright, I'd run to the bedroom that Richard never shared with me anymore. After a minute or two, I'd begun to relax, and I'd told myself that I'd been a fool. My imagination had simply played a trick on me.

I didn't go back to the study that night, and I'd avoided it whenever I could in the following days. Richard had continued to sleep there, though.

We no longer gave parties, or went to restaurants or clubs. Richard neglected his work, and gradually, our friends drifted away, mainly because Richard didn't want to see them. We were alone most of the time. Mr. and Mrs. Everett had gone on a world cruise that winter, and my own family never came to see us without a special invitation.

In a way, I was glad that we were alone so much. I didn't want people to know about Richard's drinking problem. He still refused to seek any kind of help. He insisted that his problem wasn't serious, and that he could stop drinking any time he chose. Actually, he would go for several days without touching liquor. Then he would become depressed, and within a few hours, he'd be really drunk, shut up in his study.

A few months later, several of the men who worked on the ranch had quit without giving notice, including the foreman. It was just before planting time, and I knew that we'd be in serious trouble if we didn't hire new help right away. Even if Richard had been well, he couldn't have done all the work on our ranch himself.

At first, it had seemed as though the crisis had been a good thing for Richard. He didn't drink for more than a week, as far as I knew. Every morning, he went into Middletown to try to find help.

Then, one day I'd walked into his study and found Tom sitting there with him. It had been a long time since I'd seen Tom. He seemed older, thinner, and more weathered.

71

"Katie," Richard explained, "Tom is going to take over as temporary foreman for us—just until I can get someone on a permanent basis."

"I can't leave my own place for long," Tom added. "I've got my own work to do."

I knew without being told why Tom was taking the job. He needed the money. His shirt was patched and his jeans were nearly worn through.

Just being in the same room with Tom reminded me of how it had been when I was a girl back home, with Tom and me out in Mom's garden, clinging to each other. A thrill had shot through me, and then shame. I'd looked away, afraid that Tom could read my mind.

"It's nice that Tom can help us, Richard," I murmured. "I'm sure that he can use the money. He always has a hard time on that farm of his."

The minute I'd said the words, I was ashamed. I'd sounded so snobbish. I'd simply wanted to hurt Tom—to cut him with words. But what did Tom or his opinion of me matter? What did anything matter—except that Richard and I save our marriage?

After that day, I'd begun to try again to convince Richard that we should adopt children. His answer was always the same.

"Katie, every time I looked at an adopted child, I'd be reminded that I'm not really a man. I'd remember that I couldn't give my wife what she wanted most."

I began trying to make him feel masculine in as many ways as I could. It had been months since Richard had shown any desire for me, and now, for his sake, I did everything I could to make him want me.

One night I'd even thought I had succeeded, because he'd come back to our room. For a while, he'd seemed to want me as much as he once had.

I didn't know what happened—what went wrong. All I knew was that, suddenly, it wasn't any good, and there was nothing that I could do or say to lessen Richard's terrible humiliation.

"Don't make excuses for me!" he snapped when I tried to tell him that he was just tired.

After that night, Richard drank even more when he was at home, and he made more and longer business trips. He never wanted me to go with him, and he usually stayed several days at a time. He said he had business matters to attend to, but I was sure that he was simply going away to get drunk.

Often when Richard wasn't home, Tom had had to ask me about things on the ranch. Since he was working for Richard only as a temporary foreman, there were many details he didn't know about. I had to sign all the checks, too—when he paid the workmen, or bought supplies.

I knew that it didn't make sense for me to feel that way, but every meeting I had with him was an ordeal for me. We never spoke about anything personal, but sometimes, I thought I could see pity in Tom's eyes. It was almost as if he understood my loneliness and worry, and was sorry for me. I'd hated having his sympathy. Once I'd almost told him that the way I lived, and my feelings, were none of his business.

Then, one night when Richard was away, I'd dreamed that Tom was making love to me. The dream became a nightmare, because in the dream, I'd hungered for Tom's love and wanted him desperately.

There are many things that you could run away from, but a dream like that wasn't one of them. It haunted me, and I was so ashamed that I'd felt sick. Because of that dream, I was constantly aware of Tom. I always knew where he was on the ranch, at any given time of day.

I'd even found myself worrying because he'd looked thin and tired. I knew that he was working too hard. Mom had told me he was working late every night on his own land, trying to get his crops in after his day's work for Richard.

Some days when Tom was at the ranch, I would be so nervous I'd get out my car and just drive aimlessly. One afternoon, I drove over a hundred miles, to the city where Richard was staying on business. On impulse, I'd decided I'd ask him to take me to dinner. But there had been no answer when I'd called his hotel room.

Finally, I'd started back to the ranch, feeling exhausted from my own mixed-up emotions. About a mile away from Oakdale, my car had stalled. I'd managed to coast it off the highway, but I couldn't get the engine started again, and none of the cars speeding past would stop for me.

There was nothing that I could do but walk to Oakdale, where there was a restaurant, and two or three service stations. It was nearly midnight, though, and there were no mechanics on duty to see what was wrong with my car.

There were several garages that I could have called in Middletown. Instead, I'd called Tom and asked him to come for me.

"I'll bring my truck. I may have to tow you." That was all he'd said.

An hour later, he'd picked me up at the restaurant where I was waiting. He'd helped me up into the seat of his old truck—the way he used to do when we'd ride into town on Saturday nights to go to dances. For that brief second, time blurred, and I'd felt as if I were seventeen again. I was just me, Katie, living at home with a noisy, warm, close family. I hadn't met Jolene Everett.

During the dark, quiet ride back to my car, Tom didn't say anything at all, but I became more and more conscious of him. I began to wish that the night would never end—that we could go on forever, driving through the darkness.

Finally, though, Tom had reached the spot where I had turned off. He'd stopped his truck.

"I'll fasten the tow line on your car," he said. "You'll have to steer, and it may be tricky on this grade."

He'd started to lift me out of the high truck seat. When he touched me, I knew the real reason why I hadn't called a garage to send someone to help me. It had nothing to do with the fact that Tom worked for my husband. It had been because I wanted to be alone with him—because I had never forgotten the thrill of being in his arms. I still longed for him. I'd hidden that truth, even from myself, for a long time, but I couldn't hide it any longer.

Uncontrollable trembling shook me, and I swayed toward Tom and clung to him. "Oh, Tom," I whispered.

He didn't respond to me. He didn't try to kiss me, or to hold me. He'd simply set me down and walked away. In the light from the truck dashboard, I'd seen his face, and I'd read pity and disgust in his expression.

The following Saturday, Cassie came to see me. She had never been at our ranch before without the rest of the family, when they'd come to dinner at my invitation. I'd tried so hard to get closer to her. She was almost twenty, and I'd longed for her friendship. It seemed as if I'd needed it now more than I ever had.

"Cassie, how wonderful to see you!" I exclaimed when she came out onto the terrace where I was having lunch alone. "I'll have a place set for you."

Cassie shook her head. "I haven't got time, Katie, but thanks. I just dropped in because I have something to tell you."

Almost shyly, she'd held her left hand out to me. There was a tiny diamond ring on the third finger. "I've had it for a week," she said.

"You're engaged!" I was surprised and happy for her. "Who is he, Cassie? Someone you knew in school? You'll have to bring him to meet Richard and me. We'll have a party here. I hope you'll wear my veil and dress," I said, picturing the wedding.

Cassie shook her head. "Tom and I won't have a big wedding. It'll be a small one—at home."

My sister was marrying Tom! The news caught me completely off guard, and, at first, I couldn't seem to take it in. Then, gradually, the full meaning of her words had dawned on me. Tom had been engaged to Cassie when I'd called him to come and get me—when I'd wanted him to kiss me. It made what I'd done that crazy night seem ten thousand times more humiliating.

"Cassie, don't rush into anything," I said, without thinking. "Wait until fall, at least. Think about it a while."

Cassie's eyes filled with her old resentment of me. "So you want

Tom, too, is that it? Isn't Richard enough for you?"

I couldn't remember what I'd answered. Maybe I hadn't said anything at all. After she had gone, my whole body seemed to cramp with pain, and I could hardly breathe. Cassie had been right: Richard wasn't enough for me. Not as long as Tom was in the world.

Somehow, you go on living, even when you don't dare to examine your own thoughts. It was that way for me during the next few weeks.

One thing made it a little easier, though. Richard finally found a permanent foreman, and Tom no longer worked at the ranch.

Then one day, Richard told me that he had decided I was right—that we should adopt a child. Not just one child, but two or three, if possible.

"I've been a fool," he insisted, and in that moment, his face seemed firm and strong, instead of thin and dissipated. "I've thought it all out, and I know now that children are what we need—even if we can't have one of our own."

Even though I was glad, I didn't feel the deep happiness I'd once expected to feel if Richard came around to my way of thinking. It seemed wrong that we hadn't made the decision together.

Just the same, I'd grasped frantically at the hope that we could still save our marriage. I'd begun to think of the future again—to make plans. I was almost able to convince myself that the feeling I'd had for Tom that night had been a result of my unhappiness. When Richard and I had our family, I would be able to forget about the shame that haunted me.

Richard and I had filled out our applications to the adoption agencies and endured what had seemed like endless interviews with different officials and social workers. They'd asked hundreds of questions.

We'd grown impatient and restless because it was taking so long to get things settled. As Richard told Mrs. Rowland, who was in charge of our case, we had so much to offer a child—every financial advantage—that it seemed a shame to waste time in delays.

At last, we were told that we would be notified when our application had been fully considered.

During the nearly eight weeks that we'd waited, Richard had worked hard. He'd seemed more interested in ranching and his other business affairs than he had been since the first days I'd known him. Most wonderful of all, he'd stopped drinking. He hadn't had even a glass of wine since he'd decided that we'd adopt a child. I was so grateful for that.

I'd prepared a nursery and a playroom where I hoped the new member of our family would feel happy and at home. Richard and I had talked endlessly, wondering whether we'd be given a boy or a girl.

During those days of waiting, I supposed I must have deliberately pushed all thought of my sister's approaching marriage out of my mind. Then, finally, I'd had to face the cold facts. Cassie had sent Richard and me an invitation to her wedding, which was to take place in ten days.

I was plunged into a state of panic, wondering how I could face her and Tom at the ceremony. Yet, I couldn't think of any real excuse that I could give for not going.

The date was still a week away when Richard and I were called to the office of the adoption board.

"This is it," Richard said when we started the drive into town. "We're about to become parents, Katie. A real family."

We were so close then—like two people who had been saved from disaster and heartbreak. We were going to have our family, and nothing could hurt us now.

It had never occurred to us that our request for a child might be rejected. Maybe we'd wanted a child so much that we just hadn't admitted that such a thing could happen. But it did.

Mrs. Rowland was kind but honest with us. "We can't give you a child now—or at any time in the future. We're terribly sorry," she said sympathetically. "Our investigation was very thorough. We know that Mr. Grey drinks heavily in private. He has improved recently, but there is no assurance that the improvement is permanent. We are inclined to believe that any unusual trouble or worry would trigger his drinking again."

I couldn't look at Richard. I just couldn't bear to see the expression on his face. My disappointment was deeper than any I'd ever known, but I was sure that Richard's was worse. He'd blamed himself because we couldn't have a child of our own, and now, the rejection we'd suffered would be more guilt for him to bear. I wanted to hold him in my arms and comfort him, but I was afraid to hurt his pride by showing my pity.

"The most important reason we can't approve your application," Mrs. Rowland continued, "is that you seem to want a child to hold your marriage together—to satisfy your own needs as human beings. It's just too much to ask of any child. A child needs a home that's already happy—not one that he or she must make happy."

All the way back to the ranch, Richard was silent. I'd talked, trying to give him some kind of hope.

"We'll go to some other agency. We could even get a child from another country," I told him reassuringly.

It was as though he couldn't even hear me. He didn't even answer me.

When we got home, Richard went about his work as usual. I closed the doors to the nursery and playroom.

76

That night, we had dinner at the regular time, and after that, the housekeeper went to her own apartment at the rear of the house. Richard and I talked for a while about trivial matters, and then, we watched television.

It's going to be all right, I thought. Richard's resigned to what happened. But I supposed I really knew that it wasn't true. There was something false and unnatural about that whole evening.

Richard went to bed in his study, as usual. I couldn't sleep, and I was still reading in my own room when he came to me. He'd knelt down beside the bed, his hands reaching out to me desperately. He'd been drinking, but he wasn't drunk. The anguish that tore at him came from the depths of his soul—not from drunkenness.

"Katie, love me!" he begged. "Please, love me. I don't mean that you should have sex with me, and pretend that I excite you, when you know that I don't. Love me as Jolene did—for what I am. Love me for what I can't help being."

"I do love you," I insisted. "Richard, believe me!"

I was horrified that he must have known for a long time that I'd pretended desire I didn't feel. I'd clung to him and told him over and over again that I loved him. But I knew that it wasn't really love that I felt. It was pity. I didn't love him as Jolene had, and I never would. I was sure in my heart that Richard didn't love me as he had loved Jolene, either. We were two lost and hopeless people. But Richard was the most pathetic, because for all his masculinity, he was not a strong person emotionally.

Jolene would have developed strength in him through her love. She'd known what he'd needed, even though she'd been so very young at the time of her death. But I wasn't Jolene.

When Richard left me, I'd followed him and tried to keep him from drinking, but he wouldn't listen to me. Finally, I gave up.

I didn't sleep until almost morning. When I awoke, I'd found a note on my pillow.

I didn't wake you because you had such a hard night, it read. I've gone to the city on business. I want to be alone for a few days to think. Take care. Love, Richard.

I knew that he wanted to get drunk, and my first reaction was one of relief, because he wouldn't be doing it at home. Then I was ashamed. Richard needed help.

I'd thought of following him, of trying once again to get him to be reasonable, and to seek help for his drinking problem. But I knew it wouldn't do any good. I'd already said everything that I could say to him.

During the next few days, I'd faced the truth about Richard and me. I just couldn't hide from it any longer. I could never love him as he deserved and needed to be loved. If I stayed married to him, I was afraid that I would only destroy him. Maybe some failing marriages could be saved, but not ours. Our marriage never should have happened in the first place. I should never have married Richard, because I had never loved him.

It is a terrible thing to live a lie for years and then, finally, to discover what you really are. It's like looking into a mirror and seeing a different reflection from the one you'd expected—a dark image of someone who is a frightening stranger to you.

Something that I hadn't thought of in years came back to me. The night I'd come home from spending my first weekend with Jolene Everett, Mom had said: "Don't waste your time and strength envying and wanting to live another girl's life, Katie. Make the most of your own."

And Tom had said something like that on the night we'd broken up. "Maybe you don't want the Everetts' money," he told me, "but you do want to live the kind of life Jolene would have lived. You want to step into her place!"

I'd hated him for saying such a thing, but, suddenly, I realized that he'd been right. Oh, I hadn't taken over Jolene's life consciously or deliberately. My envy had always been hidden deep beneath the surface of my friendship for her.

Probably few girls in my position would have been able to be friends with her without envying her. She'd never known what it was like to be poor. She'd always had everything that she'd needed and wanted.

The real mistake I'd made was in not understanding that material things are never a substitute for love—that, without love, they simply don't mean a thing. I'd thrown away my own chance at happiness with Tom. But what I'd done to Richard was far worse.

I'd imagined myself in love with him because to me he'd seemed to represent everything glamorous and romantic. He'd belonged to Jolene, and so, like everything else in her life, he'd been special. I'd never known him as he really was. I'd been in love with a romantic shadow. Even now, with Richard suffering so tragically, I couldn't help him, because he still seemed like a stranger to me.

After Jolene's death, I'd never given him a chance to recover from the shock of grief and to build a new life. Instead, I'd become a sort of stand-in for Jolene in his life. At first, he'd wanted to see me constantly, because he'd longed to talk about her, and to keep her memory alive. Later, I'd actually tried to be like her—to think and act as she would have. And Richard, in his loneliness, had responded to me.

Our marriage had failed because it hadn't been based on love. It hadn't failed because we couldn't have children.

Realizing that, I'd tried to make plans for our future—to find some happiness for us. In the end, I'd decided that it was impossible. The only hope for us was to get a divorce, and to try to rebuild our lives separately.

I knew that my decision would be hard on Richard, at first. But, the truth was, he had known for a long time that I didn't really love him. In fact, he'd realized it before I had. Without me, without the constant hopelessness of our life together, maybe he would be able to make a new start and find happiness. If we went on as we were, he faced only disaster.

I couldn't tell him those things in person, though. I was afraid that we'd both be so upset that I wouldn't be able to finish, or to convince him that divorce was the only way for us. That was why I wrote down my feelings as clearly as I could in a letter. I'd spent hours trying to find the right words to explain my decision—trying to be gentle, and to hurt him as little as possible. When it was finished, I'd sealed it in an envelope and left it on Richard's desk in the study.

I'd packed a bag and made a reservation at a motel in Middletown. I'd told our housekeeper where I'd be, and my address was also in the letter to Richard. I'd wanted to be alone—away from everything familiar—while I tried to plan some kind of future for myself, some way to make up for the mistakes I'd made.

All too soon, I'd found that it wasn't an easy task. I was so full of regret that I couldn't seem to think.

Then, before dawn on the fourth morning, highway patrol officers had woken me to tell me that Richard had been killed in a car accident. A truck driver had found the wreckage of his car on a side road, not far from our ranch.

Richard had come home from the city at about midnight, our housekeeper said. She'd heard him and told him that I was at the motel in Middletown. Apparently, he'd gone out again and crashed his car into a telephone pole.

Someone took me back to the ranch. I couldn't remember who it was. All I knew was that later that morning, I went to the study where I'd left the sealed letter, the letter which told my husband that I wanted a divorce. It wasn't there—or anywhere else in the room.

I knew then that Richard must have read it, and that it might have been what had sent him to his death. In the end, in trying to give him another chance at happiness and a useful life, I'd caused his death.

I'd collapsed in what my family and friends had thought was simply sorrow. In fact, it was really a combination of grief, guilt, and self-accusation. I was haunted, imagining Richard's last hour of life after he'd read my letter.

My parents and Cassie had come to the ranch as soon as they'd heard that Richard was dead. They'd tried to help and comfort me, and I honestly didn't know what I'd have done without their strength and love. I'd turned to it blindly, as if I were a child again, dependent and helpless.

At the funeral services for Richard, I'd prayed that God would reunite him with Jolene, if that were possible.

A few days later, I'd started packing away everything personal in our house. I went through the things in Richard's study last of all. In his desk, I found that last letter I had written to him. It had been put into one of the drawers and had fallen behind some papers. It had never been opened. I will never know whether Richard put it there, or if it had slipped there accidentally when the housekeeper dusted.

Words could not have expressed my relief. At least, my husband had been spared one last hurt from me. I realized then that his death had most likely been accidental.

A few days later, I'd closed the house for the last time and signed papers that released every legal claim I'd had to Richard's estate. Everything was transferred to the sister and brother he had never really known after their separation in childhood.

I'd kept only enough money to see me through the first few months of what I knew was going to be a search for myself—the real self I had thrown away when I had taken over Jolene Everett's life.

You can't take over another person's destiny. You have to live your own life as best you can, making the best of any talents you might have, and trying to overcome your faults. If God judges us, maybe He does it on the basis of what we make of the opportunities and challenges He gives us. If you try to take a place you haven't earned, you hurt everyone you touch. And, in the end, you destroy yourself.

Two months after Richard's funeral, I went to work as a salesgirl in a big department store in the city. I had rented a tiny apartment in a shabby building.

At first, it wasn't easy. I was lonely, and grief for Richard was still a raw wound inside of me. I supposed in many ways it never would heal. Gradually, as time passed, I'd realized that in spite of my sadness, I'd had a feeling that I'd never known before—a calm that was the beginning of an inner peace.

Cassie had postponed her wedding to Tom out of respect to Richard. Later, I'd tried to prepare myself for the news that she and Tom had set another date for the wedding.

Another truth I'd grown to face was that I had always loved Tom. I'd lost him through my own blindness. Now I had no right to do anything but to pray for the happiness of his marriage to Cassie. I would have to rebuild my own life without any thought of him.

But Cassie never did set another date. In the fall, she came to spend a weekend with me, and she wasn't wearing her ring.

"I gave it back to Tom a few days ago," she explained. "We postponed our wedding, at first, because of Richard. But when we both put off setting another date, we began to realize that we had never really been in love. Neither one of us wanted to hurt the other, but we had to be honest. We'd both just been lonely and eager to settle down. All my friends are married. We were both tired of waiting. But we've decided that we'd better go on waiting—for the right person."

After I'd been living for a few months in the city, I began to find again some of the closeness I'd once had with my family. We'd exchanged letters and phone calls and occasional visits. Though no one had ever actually put it into words, I'd begun to see that perhaps we'd grown apart because my family had sensed that I'd never really loved Richard. They'd known, if I hadn't, that I'd married him because I'd wanted to live Jolene's life.

At Christmas, when I went home to my parents' farm, my brothers were full of stories about a wonderful new truck that Tom had bought.

"He saved the money and paid cash," Liam said excitedly. "It isn't financed! I heard him telling Dad."

So things were better for Tom, and I was grateful. He was making a success of his life because he was a decent, honest, and good person. Once more, I'd felt the pain of knowing that I'd thrown away my chance at his love.

When Tom came to Christmas dinner, the two of us were shy and strange with each other. There had been so much bitterness, so much grief, to separate us. We'd exchanged only a few words, but all the time he was in the house, I'd burned with awareness of him.

Two days later, when I was scheduled to go back to the city, Tom came over to the house and asked if he could drive me there.

"It'll be in my truck," he said, "but it's new and very comfortable."

"Tom, I'd appreciate it very much if you'd take me," I whispered, and tears stung my eyes.

Suddenly, we were in each other's arms in Mom's steamy kitchen. It was as if all the years we'd been separated had never been—as if all the sorrow and pain I'd caused were erased in that moment with the touch of our lips.

Tom and I are going to be married within a few weeks. I am going to have my chance to make him happy—a chance to do my part in building a marriage that will be as good and as fine as my parents' marriage has been.

It is this miracle that makes me feel that perhaps God has forgiven me. I am going to try to prove that I'm worthy of forgiveness.

THE END

81

MACARONI AND CHEESE
MADE ME
A BETTER WOMAN!
It's the staple menu for single moms like me,
but little did I know that the daily grind of making
that convenient little meal would make me the
envy of the perfect woman next door. . . .

I opened the kitchen window and took a deep breath of fresh air. The whole world smelled like spring. I looked out at the parking lot of our apartment building; there were still little piles of hard, blackened snow at the edges of the lot from a late-season snowstorm, but it had been sunny all afternoon and the temperature had finally hit sixty degrees.

I heard the familiar rumbling sound of Dirk Sykes's motorcycle and smiled. Soon the weather would warm up completely and I'd hear that sound almost every night. I watched as Dirk pulled into a parking space in the lot below. I wondered if he was bringing a gift to my neighbor, Marina, because he was using one of his hands to protect something that was inside of his jacket.

You've got to get a life of your own, I told myself. Dirk was Marina's boyfriend and I didn't know either one of them all that well. How dull had my existence become, if all it took was the sound of Dirk's motorcycle to make me happy? And wasn't I just a little bit too curious about his actions?

I closed the window. Good as the outside air felt, it was late afternoon and the temperature had already fallen back down to around fifty degrees. Leaving the window open would only cause the furnace to kick on more often, and I already owed an astronomical amount of money on my heating bills.

"Mommy, Mommy! Is it dinner yet?" asked my four-year-old daughter, Kaylee. She came into the kitchen trailed by my three-year-old son, Aaron. Elijah, who was a year and a half old, had fallen asleep in his playpen in the living room.

"Can we eat now, Mommy?" asked Aaron, echoing his older sister.

"Pretty soon, guys! Dinner is almost ready."

As a matter of fact, it was probably time to drain the noodles that were boiling on the stove. I was making macaroni and cheese—again. Good thing the kids and I liked cheese-and-noodle dishes, because this was the only kind of food I could afford.

I should write a cookbook, I thought wearily. I could call it, One Thousand Variations On Macaroni and Cheese.

I drained the noodles and then added some margarine to them. I heard giggles coming from the living room and the sound of little feet running, and the sound of Aaron's toy dump truck being dragged across the floor. I heard creaking sounds that meant Elijah must be stirring in his playpen and starting to wake up. Before adding milk and cheese to the noodles, I walked into the living room.

I didn't have the heart to tell Kaylee and Aaron not to giggle so loudly, because what are children supposed to do, if not have a good time? However, I did remind them to play quietly.

"Aaron! Kaylee! You've got to stop running through this apartment. You've got to be quieter, playing with that truck. I keep telling you, it makes too much noise for the people downstairs. It sounds like a herd of elephants is walking over their heads!"

The kids always laughed when I said that. But Kaylee reminded me, as she had many times before, "Mommy, we're not elephants!"

The previous spring, just a few weeks after we'd moved into this place, there'd been a knock on our front door one afternoon. "It's Marina, your downstairs neighbor," a voice had called to me as I looked through the peephole trying to identify the woman who was standing out in the hallway. I'd opened the door, and stepped out of the apartment to talk to her.

She was about my age, but not at all like me. She was tall and willowy, with a perfection of hair and makeup that I could never achieve. She was wearing jeans and a T-shirt, just like me, but I'm short and my stomach has always tended to stick out. Of course, it stuck out worse after I'd had three children. And I always looked tired at that point in my life, because I always was tired. I've never been a classy dresser, anyway. But the woman standing before me was cool and poised and pretty.

She smiled at me. "Hi, my name is Marina Saroyan. I live in the apartment right below yours."

"Hi. I'm Jeanette Loomis."

"I don't like to complain," Marina began, smiling and blushing a little, "I mean, I've seen your kids and I think they're just adorable. But my boyfriend and I are in college, and we're both studying for finals right now, and the kids are just, well—I'm afraid they're just making too much noise. I mean, I know it's not their fault, but even when they just run across the floor in your place, it sounds really loud downstairs."

I could feel my face turning red. "I'm sorry," I told her. "I didn't know that."

She looked sorry, too. "I really hesitated about coming up

here. I don't want to be a bad neighbor or anything. Dirk—he's my boyfriend—well, it's just that he and I can't concentrate on our studies. I mean, I love kids. We both do. But that's not the problem. The reason I'm in school is because I want to be a teacher."

Well, then you'd better get used to a little noise, I thought. But I did seem to be the one in the wrong, so I figured I'd better be polite. "I'll try to keep them quiet," I told her. "I didn't realize that the kids were making too much noise."

She blushed. "Oh, like I said—I hate to complain. But Dirk and I have just got to do well on these finals." She smiled again. "It's nice to finally meet you, anyway."

I smiled in return, but I was too embarrassed by that point to have much to say to her. " 'Bye," I said as she left. She did seem to be pretty nice, but I was ashamed to think that my children had been annoying her and her boyfriend. I couldn't decide if she was being too picky. After all, kids need to play. Anyone who was studying to be a teacher ought to know that.

A few days later I saw my brother, Wayne, and I asked his opinion.

"I think your neighbor is right," he told me. "I've been the downstairs neighbor more than once; unless an apartment is really well built, the people living above you can sound really noisy doing almost anything. When they walk across the floor, your whole ceiling shakes.

"Jeanette, I can imagine that when the kids are playing hard and having a grand old time, your downstairs neighbors feel like they have a herd of elephants stampeding overhead!"

"Oh, no! I didn't realize that!"

"Hey, it's no big deal," my brother surmised, shrugging. "Just a part of apartment living. You'll get the hang of it all."

"I guess so."

"Hey," he added, "are you doing okay? Do you need any money or anything?"

"No, but thanks, Wayne."

"I'm always here for you, Jeanette."

I knew he was. I'd gotten used to apartment living during this past year. In fact, I'd gotten used to a great many things since my husband had walked out on us. Often, lately, it seemed like life was just one problem after another. Huge problems like money or the lack thereof. Little problems like finding out that you're a noisy neighbor. Feeling bad because I was on welfare. Feeling worse, in a way, about the future because my welfare eligibility was rapidly coming to an end. The kids would be in subsidized day-care while I worked, but would they be well cared for?

As it was, I hadn't gotten to know any of my neighbors very well.

Marina Saroyan was by far the closest one to me in age, but I never made a big effort to become friends with her, and it seemed like she was way too busy to socialize with me, anyway.

That's understandable, I told myself. After all, she was a self-assured, beautiful college student. She couldn't possibly have a lot in common with someone like me.

Oh, we talked occasionally, in the parking lot or standing on the steps that led from the ground floor to my apartment on the main floor above. We had never been inside each other's apartments, though, in the whole year that the kids and I had been living in this building. Basically, we were still strangers.

She did introduce me to her boyfriend, Dirk Sykes, not long after the time when she knocked on my door to complain about my noisy kids. Dirk was very handsome, and I liked seeing him pull into the parking lot on his Harley. It wasn't exactly jealously, but the thought of him got me daydreaming about having a man of my own again, a man who would love me the way Dirk seemed to love Marina.

After becoming aware of the noise problem, I'd developed the habit of analyzing—some would say overanalyzing—the normal sounds my children made. Sometimes I resented having to think about that, and I resented always having to remind them not to play the way kids are supposed to play.

Sometimes, I'd see Marina walking to or from her apartment, looking so neat and competent, and I'd wonder why my own life was such a complete and utter mess. Marina even looked classy when she went motorcycle riding with Dirk. Oh, her hair would get windblown, all right, but it would still always look stylish. If it were I, I knew my hair would be standing straight up all over my head when I stepped off that motorcycle. Sometimes, I just wished I could be a whole lot more like Marina Saroyan.

I'd even made up my own private nickname for her. In my mind, she was "The Perfect Woman," even though in my heart, I knew that this wasn't purely a compliment, and that it was, in fact, somewhat mean-spirited of me to think of her this way.

Now, even though I was trying to get done fixing dinner, I couldn't resist going back to look through my kitchen window at Dirk's motorcycle parked down below and the beautiful scenery of early springtime. It was hard to believe we'd been living in this apartment, on our own, for one whole year. With a sigh, I turned my thoughts back to suppertime.

The Christmas after Aaron was born, we had received a kids' play table with four chairs from my husband's parents. I had put the little table and three of the chairs in the kitchen of this apartment, and that's where my children ate their meals. I usually just sat near them, on a chair, with my plate of food in my lap. There was nothing very formal about our way of life.

"Kids, time to wash your hands—and be sure you help Elijah," I called to them. I wondered, as usual, if even my own voice sounded too loud to Dirk and Marina downstairs.

I set the little table for supper, giving each child a glass of apple juice to drink. I put some macaroni and cheese on each plate, with green beans for Kaylee and Aaron. Elijah wouldn't touch the beans, but he would probably eat some pieces of an apple or banana later on in the evening, along with his brother and sister. I gave Kaylee and Aaron slices of buttered white bread, and cut a piece of buttered bread into finger-sized portions for my baby. I got some homemade oatmeal cookies out of the cookie jar for dessert, but I didn't set the cookies on the table just yet.

The kids came into the room holding up their hands for me to see how clean they were. Actually, Elijah just waved his little arms in the air, imitating his brother and sister. I had to smile, looking at my three children. I was hit with the sudden, overwhelming realization that any trouble I had to go through was worth it, for their sakes. I think it's moments like this that help keep people going, and that give us the energy to face our daily struggles.

There was a beautiful sunset that evening, and I felt more relaxed than I had for quite some time. The kids were playing very quietly, for a change, on the living room floor. I was half-sitting, half-lying on the sofa, watching them, not even worrying about the sink full of unwashed dinner dishes in the kitchen. I was enjoying my children and I was enjoying the view I could see through our windows. The trees were all still bare, but the soft, orange glow of the sunset on their branches made me think of those branches coming alive soon with new, green leaves. Eventually, I started to drowse, and had to rouse myself to put the kids to bed.

They didn't fuss too much, and it was pretty easy for me to get all three of them settled down for the night. Then I lied down on the couch to watch a little TV, but before long, I had dozed off again. I was half-awakened by the sound of Dirk's motorcycle taking off. I looked out the windows at the sky, which was by now a velvety, dark blue and full of stars. Moments later, I drifted back to sleep.

I was awakened by ringing, pounding sounds. Someone was ringing my doorbell repeatedly, and for some reason, also knocking loudly on the door. I got up and walked over to the door and looked out the peephole; it was Marina. But she didn't look like her usual calm and collected self; The Perfect Woman was plainly very upset. Instantly, I dropped that sarcastic attitude and hurried to open the door to her.

"Are you okay?" I asked her immediately.

"Oh, I know it's pretty late to be bothering you," she said, "but, have you by any chance seen a gray-and-white kitten tonight?"

"A kitten?"

She looked at me intently, as if trying to read my feelings. Tears came to her eyes. "Dirk gave me the sweetest little kitten today, and I've already lost her! She must've gotten out of my apartment somehow, and I feel so bad about it!" Marina wasn't wearing a coat or even a sweater, and she rubbed her hands up and down her arms. "It's going to be so cold tonight, and the kitten is so young. She was just weaned from her mother."

"Would you like me to come outside and help you look for her?" I asked.

"Oh, no—I wouldn't want you to leave your children alone." To my dismay, she was stepping into my apartment as she talked. "I just wanted to know if you had seen or heard a kitten," she continued, "and I wanted to ask you to be on the lookout for her."

I felt very uneasy suddenly, as I wondered how bad the apartment would look to Marina. In these apartments, the kitchen area is visible to anyone standing inside the front door, and my kitchen sink was full of dirty dinner dishes. There were toys and kids' socks and shoes all over the living room floor, with Aaron's playpen, full of even more toys, right in the middle of the whole mess. And how would my worn-out, frayed furniture and ancient curtains look to Marina? The entire apartment had been furnished with mismatched, discarded items donated to us by members of my family.

I could only imagine how trendy and interesting Marina's apartment must be. I knew it had to be nicely decorated, since she was always so well appointed herself. Well, almost always. Tonight, she looked almost as unkempt and tired as I did.

"What a nice apartment you've got," Marina remarked, to my complete and utter surprise. "Our place is always full of schoolbooks and clutter—it's not homey, like this."

"Uh, thanks," was all I could manage. "Um, would you like a cup of coffee or tea or anything?"

"Oh, it's very nice of you to offer, but I think I'll just keep looking for my kitten. Her name is Baby, by the way. And, please—if you do happen to find her, could you bring her to my apartment? I don't care what time of the day or night it is."

"I will," I promised, nodding. "And if you're away at school or something, I'll just keep her here with us until you get home."

Marina had tears in her eyes again. "Thanks," she said. "You can't imagine how worried I am about that kitten. And how will this make Dirk feel, me losing Baby on the very same day he gave her to me? I can't even imagine what he'll think of me for being so careless!"

"Cats and dogs are awfully good at slipping outside, and the kitten couldn't possibly have known yet that she should stay in your apartment. And anyway, I just know you'll find her," I said. "If you don't have her back yet by tomorrow morning, I'll take the kids outside and we'll all help you look for her."

"Thanks." She sounded somewhat relieved. "And thanks for just listening. Good night, Jeanette."

"Good night," I said, as I closed the door. I said a quick prayer for Marina to find Baby, all safe and sound. I prayed the little cat wouldn't have to spend the whole night outdoors in the cold.

Then I shook my head as I admitted to myself that Marina Saroyan was not exactly the one-dimensional character I had made her out to be in my mind. I thought about how difficult it'd been for me to adjust to being a single mom; I had to stop a minute to consider whether or not I was doing okay. I wondered how much my views about people in general had been warped by my husband abandoning our children and me.

The kids were all sleeping soundly, like three beautiful little angels. I got ready for bed, but then I went back to sleep on the couch. My life was definitely informal. I seldom ate sitting at a table, and I slept on the couch much more often than in my bed. I hated sleeping alone in my bed because it reminded me of being a failure. The couch was comforting, especially with background noise coming from the TV turned down low. I closed all the curtains and turned off most of the lights. It took me about an hour to fall back asleep while trying to watch some old reruns of The Mary Tyler Moore Show.

I was awakened by what seemed to be the sound of my baby crying. He usually slept through the night, but sometimes, he'd still awaken, whimpering, and need to be rocked back to sleep.

I soon realized, though, that what I was hearing wasn't coming from Elijah's room. It couldn't be him. I strained my ears, and then I realized that I was hearing the sound of a kitten mewing. I sat up immediately; it had to be Baby, my neighbor's little lost kitten.

Quickly and quietly, I pulled on some clothes and my shoes. I made certain that the kids were all still asleep, and then I put on my jacket and got my flashlight from its hook on the kitchen wall. I left the apartment, gently closing and locking the door behind me, and went out looking for the kitten.

My apartment lets out onto a small landing with steps leading down to the parking lot, past Marina's apartment and the other ground-floor apartments. I stood out on the landing, looking and listening intently for the kitten.

The night was dark and quiet. The temperature seemed to be above freezing, but not by much. I went down the stairs and then slowly walked around in front of the apartment building, shining my flashlight in different directions.

I stood stock still when I thought I heard a small sound, and then I heard it again—it was definitely the tiny mewing of a kitten, and it seemed to be coming from a staircase on the very far corner of the building. I walked over and shined my flashlight up and down that staircase, and sure enough, I saw a very young kitten, huddled underneath the lowest step.

The little cat looked up at me with soft eyes and mewed when I carefully approached her. She seemed to be asking, Are you here to help me?

Soon the kitten was safe in my arms and then I was ringing Marina's doorbell. She was at the door almost instantly; it was clear that she'd been unable to sleep.

She threw open the door to us. "Baby!" she cried, taking the kitten from my arms and hugging it close. She looked so tired. "Oh, Jeanette—how can I ever thank you? Please—come in for a minute!"

I was stunned when I entered her apartment. Books and papers were stacked all over the place, and the couch was piled high with laundry. There were several days' worth of dishes in and around the kitchen sink, and still more dirty dishes that hadn't yet been cleared from the kitchen table. The extensive collection of expensive makeup that contributed to Marina's normally flawless looks was piled in a heap on the kitchen countertop.

"Sorry about the mess," she apologized. "It seems like all I ever do is study—not that that's any excuse for the way this place looks. Anyway, would you like a cup of coffee?"

"Well, the thing is, I don't like leaving the kids alone in the apartment for too long. . . ."

"Oh, you'd hear them if they woke up."

My head jerked up and I stared at her in hurt and disbelief.

Instantly, a horrified look came over her face. "Oh, please—I didn't mean that like it sounded—I truly didn't. It's just that, well—it's honestly true. I mean, you would definitely hear them."

We looked at each other and started laughing.

"Why don't you come upstairs and we'll have coffee at my place?" I offered. "You can bring Baby with you."

Marina was still hugging Baby when she sat down on my couch, and she was still hugging and petting Baby when I came into the living room with coffee and some of my oatmeal cookies for the both of us.

"I am so grateful to you," she told me. "I don't know what I would've told Dirk, and I felt so bad about my little Baby being out in the cold and dark. I mean, she could've been run over by a car, or just anything could've happened to her!"

"Well, she seems happy now," I said. My chair was several feet away from the couch, but even so, I could hear the kitten purring as Marina gently stroked the back of her head.

"Jeanette," Marina began suddenly, "I'm really sorry we've never gotten to know each other before this. I mean, I've always admired you so much for the way you're raising your kids. I guess I just always felt like you must be too busy, and so I hesitated to bother you."

"You're kidding!"

"What do you mean?" she asked me, confused.

"I never wanted to bother you, either! I've always admired you and your boyfriend for being in college and studying all the time. You see, I didn't go to college. I've felt like such a loser, being a single mother and all. I mean, I'm on welfare, Jeanette. I thought I was the one who didn't have the right to bother you!"

We just sat there and stared at each other. I noticed that Marina's hands were trembling suddenly, and she was using holding the kitten to steady them.

"You can't know how much I've admired you, Jeanette, for the way you're raising your children. I gave a baby boy up for adoption, back when I was in high school."

The sadness of what she'd just told me hit me like a punch in the gut. I looked at her, and the pain on her face was like another blow to me. I didn't even want to think about what it would be like for me to have to live without Kaylee and Aaron and Elijah. As it was, I was having a hard enough time just getting used to the idea of dropping them off at some day-care center for several hours each day. But Marina had to deal, on a second-by-second basis, I knew, with never seeing her only child again.

"I can't even imagine how terrible that must've been for you," I told her sadly, shaking my head.

"I was fifteen years old. I wanted my son to have a real home with a mother and a father. But I think about him every single day of my life. I worry about whether or not he's healthy and happy; I worry about whether or not he was adopted by nice, loving people. Sometimes, I just lie in my bed and imagine all kinds of horrible things happening to my little boy."

"Is there some way for you to contact him, or at least find out that he's okay?"

Marina's eyes overflowed with tears. Immediately, the little kitten started licking the tears, as if to comfort Marina, and the sight of this brought tears to my eyes, too.

"Look—Baby doesn't want me to be so sad," Marina said with a faint smile, and then she was able to continue talking about herself.

"I have this nightmare sometimes in which my son needs an organ transplant, and no one but me is the right match, but nobody tells me. I'm just so full of fears and worries about him. And yet, I've never been able to bring myself to contact him or inquire about him. He's seven years old now, and I just feel like I can't intrude on his life. I feel like it would spoil the whole reason why I gave him up in the first place, which was to give him a normal childhood and a decent chance at life.

"And maybe I'm also just scared to know anything about him. Does that make any sense to you?"

Actually, it did make sense to me—perfect sense—and I told her so. Silently, I prayed that one day, somehow, she would find it within herself to contact her child.

It took several more cups of coffee and another plateful of oatmeal cookies, but by the end of that night, Marina had told me about what it'd been like to have a baby at the age of fifteen, and I'd told her about my marriage and divorce and my ongoing struggle to live on my own with three kids to raise. Sometimes, it's strangely easier to open your heart to a stranger than it is to confide in your own family. But, then, once you open your heart to someone, you are no longer strangers.

A lasting friendship began that night, as Marina and I sat and talked well into the wee hours of the morning. Along with the priceless gift of this friendship came a lesson that I have never forgotten, about not judging anyone by his or her outward appearance or by false standards. And that includes myself.

I'd like to tell you that Marina became a wonderful teacher after she finished college. But that didn't happen. In fact, she just didn't have the temperament for teaching, and she quit the profession after just three years.

She did, however, become a wonderful mother. She and Dirk have been married for fifteen years now, and they are the parents of two daughters. Recently, Dirk finally persuaded Marina to get in contact with the son she gave up for adoption all those years ago. Dirk has always known the same thing I realized that night when I first got to know Marina: A piece of her heart has stayed broken ever since she gave away that baby boy, and being reunited with him is the only way that her heart will ever be made completely whole again.

Just a few days ago, the telephone rang, and it was Marina. She was crying so hard that she could barely talk, and I was afraid that something terrible had happened to her. Finally, though, I could make out the words she was saying:

"My son just called me. I just talked to my son!"

I am filled with joy because very soon now, they are going to finally see each other again, in person.

As for me, I eventually found "the man of my dreams," although he's not anyone I ever dreamed about. Jeff and I have been married for twelve years now. He has never owned a motorcycle, and as a matter of fact, I don't think he'd be caught dead on one. Needless to say, how bad my hair would look after riding on a motorcycle never became an issue in my life.

Jeff and I had two sons together, giving us a large and happy and very busy family. The courage it takes to be the father to five children is vastly more important to me now than whatever daring it takes to ride a motorcycle. As for myself, since I ended up raising such a big family, it's a good thing I learned not to look for too much perfection in this life!

Jeff and I are fortunate to have kept Marina and Dirk as our closest friends down through the years. Our families have shared so many good times together, and helped each other through the tough times, too. It was sad for all of us when Baby died of old age. She was a wonderful cat, and since that very first day when Dirk gave her to Marina and she got out of Marina's apartment, she was always the most special link between our two families.

Nowadays, I'll call Marina or she'll call me. Maybe we'll laugh or cry about something our children are into—or up to. I might give her the latest news about Kaylee and Aaron, the first ones to leave the nest. Soon, I know I'll be hearing all about Marina's reunion with her son. No doubt, before too long, we'll be sitting together again ourselves, drinking coffee and eating cookies and looking at photos of him.

Life is good.

THE END

Shameless Seduction
MY SISTER'S HUSBAND
WILL BE MINE

"Doesn't your sister look beautiful?" Mom said. "I guess what they say is true—pregnancy can really give a woman a glow."

"Ruth has always been pretty," I muttered, trying to sound happy.

My sister beamed and ran her hand over her belly, which didn't yet show a trace of roundness. "You might not say that in a few months when I'm twice this size," she joked playfully.

"Oh, you'll still be gorgeous," said Janine, my sister's best friend. "And your pregnancy will probably be a breeze, like everything is for you."

Everyone at the baby shower laughed. I forced a smile on my face, too, and prayed that no one could see the anger and hurt behind it.

Ruth sat in the middle of a pile of lovely baby gifts. A stack of adorable powder-blue baby clothes, given to her by her many friends, sat to her left. On her right stood a lovely new crib, a special gift from Mom and Dad. All around her lay crumpled remnants of wrapping paper, bows, and ribbons. The room was all done up in blue and white balloons and streamers. Janine, who was giving the shower, had done a wonderful job of decorating. Like most people who knew my sister, she thought Ruth was great, and she was willing to do just about anything for her.

As I sat across the room watching Ruth open her gifts, all I could think was that what Mom said was right—Ruth was gorgeous. She had perfect skin, great hair, and a flawless smile. Her figure was stunning, too. It was easy to imagine her as a model. I knew that, if things went like they usually did for Ruth, a few months after delivering the baby she'd look like she'd never given birth.

But Ruth had more than good looks. It seemed like everything in her life was perfect. Her husband, Joe, was the ideal man—very good-looking, successful, and apparently very much in love with Ruth. As Dad always put it, "That man adores Ruth, and what man wouldn't?"

Joe had a good job as an electrician, and Ruth worked in sales for a large carpet manufacturing company. She was so good at her job that when she told her employer she was leaving he'd practically begged her to come back after the baby was born. He was bitterly disappointed when she said she was going to stay home for good. Together she and Joe made enough to pay for a lovely home. Now their perfect life was getting another blessing—they were expecting a baby. As I watched Ruth open gift after gift, all I could think of was that she had everything I wanted.

When Ruth was finally finished opening the huge stack of baby presents, we had cake and punch and played some games. The afternoon seemed to take forever. It was nearly five o'clock by the time Ruth's friends began to leave one by one. I gave the cheeriest smile I could as I said good-bye to each of them. When the last of the guests had driven off, Mom and I stayed to help Janine clean up.

It was dark by the time I walked from Janine's house to the nearest bus stop. As I walked I tried not to let my spirits sink any further than they already were. But as I got on the bus and headed through the dark streets to my tiny, run-down apartment on the other side of town, I felt like the weight of all my years of jealousy and competition with Ruth were coming down on my shoulders.

It may sound like an unkind thing, but I've often wondered how different my life might've been if Ruth had never been born. I was three years old when Mom got pregnant with her. Of course I don't remember those early years, but when I see pictures of myself at that age I always seem happy and smiling. It was after Ruth came into the family that things began to change.

My earliest memory of Ruth is when she was a little over one year old. Already she was a stunning child. The beauty that would continue to blossom as she grew up was apparent in the mop of shining hair and those large, round eyes. The very first memory I have from my childhood is our relatives watching Ruth play with some blocks on the floor of our living room. I have a picture in my mind of my aunts, uncles, and older cousins and how they looked just then. Their faces were glowing with pride, and they were smiling happily as they talked about how pretty Ruth was and what a special child she was growing to be. Nobody seemed to notice me standing in the doorway by myself—it was as if I didn't exist.

This was the first time I remember feeling my horrible jealousy toward Ruth, but it was hardly the last. She soon went from a pretty baby to a really stunning little girl, and it didn't take long before I became aware that I wasn't particularly pretty. It wasn't that I was homely. But in comparison to Ruth, I was very ordinary looking, and the fact that I couldn't compare to her made me feel extremely unattractive. And the older I got, the more I learned how much attention and admiration being pretty brought her.

Ruth wasn't only beautiful—she was also a good student, popular, and involved in all sorts of activities. This also brought her a lot of attention. All I heard when I was growing up was how nice it was for Ruth to volunteer with the church youth group, how great it was that she'd won the award for best essay in English class, and how good she was in the school play.

In the meantime, I just seemed to fade into the background. Since I couldn't compare with Ruth at school, sports, or anything else, I chose not to do much of anything. I knew I couldn't do as well in school as Ruth, so I didn't even try to get good grades. I knew I couldn't win anyone's favor by being the kind of "good girl" that Ruth was, so I just stayed to myself and went around with a chip on my shoulder most of the time.

Most of my family and the people I knew at school thought I was just a shy, insecure girl who didn't have much to say. What they didn't realize was that I was really being eaten up inside. I longed to have the kind of attention that Ruth did, and it hurt badly when I didn't. My jealousy over Ruth was like a terrible sickness that I just couldn't get over.

Everything seemed to come to a head the night of my senior prom. I only had two or three dates all during high school, and as the prom grew near, I soon realized I was going to be sitting at home while other girls were going out in lovely new dresses. In the meantime, many of the boys who were in my class were calling Ruth to ask her to go with them. Even though she was only a freshman, she had her choice of dates to my senior prom, and she ended up going to it with one of the most popular boys in my class—Joe Hamilton, the man she would later marry. I'll never forget watching Ruth getting into her beautiful, shimmering blue gown and the tall, handsome Joe arriving to pick her up. As I stood watching from the top of the staircase, Joe gave her a lovely corsage, and Dad took pictures of the two of them. Everyone was talking about what a lovely couple they made. Meanwhile, I prepared for an evening of sitting at home alone feeling like I wanted to die.

But before Ruth and Joe left for the prom, something happened that made me see things in a new light. Ruth's dress had these little pearl buttons at the wrist, and just when she and Joe were about to leave, one of them popped off. Mom said she could sew it on real fast and asked Joe to sit for a few minutes while they took care of it. Dad got a phone call just then, and Mom believed it was rude to leave a guest waiting by himself, so she asked me to make conversation with Joe and offer him a soft drink.

I felt really awkward at first being left alone with Joe—especially since Ruth had been so dressed up and looking so nice and there I was in a pair of jeans and a T-shirt. All I could think of was how plain and boring I was in comparison with my lovely sister. I tried to make small talk, but I couldn't think of anything to say, so things started getting uncomfortable. Finally, I remembered that Mom had some sodas in the refrigerator, so I offered Joe one. I was relieved when he said he'd like one because it gave me a chance to get out of there for a few minutes.

But then all of a sudden, something extremely embarrassing happened. I was coming back into the living room with a glass full of soda for Joe when I tripped and the drink spilled down the front of my shirt. I was humiliated enough at having stumbled, but what was worse was that my T-shirt had gotten soaking wet and was clinging tightly to my body. Since I had nothing on underneath, you could see just about everything.

For a moment I thought I was going to die. All I could think was that Joe must be thinking how stupid I was and that he'd probably be laughing at me all the way to the prom. But when I looked over at him, I realized how wrong I was. Joe wasn't laughing at all—he was staring at me with a really sexy look on his face. I was completely unused to men giving me the once-over that way, so at first I didn't know what to do. But when I realized he was enjoying looking at me in that wet T-shirt, I suddenly felt really excited.

Instead of running out of the room in tears, like I'd been about to do, I made a joke about being in a wet T-shirt contest. To my surprise, he laughed like I'd said something extremely funny. Then he said, "Let me know when you enter one because I want to be in the first row."

Suddenly, I found myself smiling at him in a kind of seductive way. I got him another drink, and then I sat down with my wet shirt still on and started asking him about himself. I was just asking him normal questions about school and his family, but my tone of voice was definitely indicating more than that. To my surprise he answered in the same sexy tone of voice I was using, and I could tell he was a little turned on.

Finally Mom came in to say Ruth was in the bathroom and would be down in a minute. But before she could say a word about Ruth, she looked at me and gasped. "Look at you!" she exclaimed. "What did you do, spill something all over yourself?"

Normally, I would've wanted to sink through the floor if she'd said something like that in front of a guy like Joe Hamilton. But all I had to do was think of how Joe had been looking at me, and I didn't care what Mom said or thought—or Ruth, for that matter.

When Ruth came down the stairs in her beautiful dress, Joe's attention turned away from me to her. I realized that he had a completely different expression on his face when he was looking at her. It was like he appreciated how beautiful she was, but he didn't have any of the seductiveness he'd had when we were alone.

Once Joe and Ruth had left for the prom, I went up to my room and took a look at myself in the mirror. That was the first time I realized that I was sexy. I might not have been stunning like Ruth was, but if I wanted to I could be very seductive in my own way. I had a good figure and if I dressed and acted the right way, I could get men to pay attention to me. Maybe not in the way Ruth could, but in my own way.

After that night, I started working on how to attract men. I soon learned that if I paid a certain kind of attention to them, talked and walked a certain way, and dressed in a sexy manner, that I could get plenty of attention. Admittedly, it wasn't the kind of attention a lot of women want to get. But it was better than being someone who fades into the woodwork and is never noticed.

From then on, I used my womanly wiles to get dates, attention, and plenty of sex. I graduated high school that June and immediately got a job working as a cashier in a supermarket where I met tons of men. I started partying constantly and going out with whatever guy would ask me out. Before long, I had the worst reputation in town, and that got me even more dates. Maybe my self-respect wasn't the highest in the world, but that didn't matter—or at least I didn't think it did. I was determined that I would never be ignored again, and if that meant being the town slut, that was fine.

While I was living it up, Ruth had taken a completely different route. After graduation from high school, she took a job as a receptionist. At night she went to junior college for secretarial and business courses. At first she wasn't making much money at her job, and it was quite a struggle for her to get by. But she kept saying she felt she had a future at her company and that she was determined to make something of herself. I got in the habit of teasing her about it. I used to ask her why she didn't go out and have fun like I did. I'd played second fiddle to Ruth for so long that it was wonderful being the one who was having all the fun. Of course I didn't think much about the fact that Ruth was working toward something worthwhile in her life while I wasn't. I was simply trying to enjoy my freedom and finally getting all the attention I'd missed as a child. I kept on partying and dating, while Ruth struggled and worked.

For a time I managed to convince myself that Ruth's career would never go anywhere. I thought she'd had her glory days in high school and now she'd be the ordinary one, while I was enjoying my popularity. So I have to admit I was surprised when she called to say she'd been promoted to a low-level sales position. She'd finally managed to convince her boss to let her try the sales department, and she was sure that she was on her way to a great future.

With her great personality and looks, Ruth was a natural in the sales department. She was soon raking in huge amounts of money on commissions. A year and a half later, she was promoted to a senior sales position.

In the meantime, her love life was also going beautifully. Joe and Ruth had been going together ever since he asked her to my senior prom. Ruth had never been interested in another man since they'd started going out, and Joe seemed to be devoted to her. Of course, I always remembered what had happened the night of the prom, but I never took it seriously. Joe was just a kid of eighteen then, and he was just flirting a little. Now he seemed to be very much in love with Ruth.

The same year that Ruth was promoted to senior sales, Joe finished his training to become an electrician, and they announced their engagement. They soon set a date for a lovely June wedding.

At first, I tried to convince myself I didn't care that everything was going so well with Ruth. I told myself I had no reason to feel jealous now. After all, I had all the men I wanted and plenty of time to party. But the truth was that the constant partying and going from one man to the next wasn't doing a lot for me. For a while I'd enjoyed the attention, but now it just made me feel sort of empty. I knew none of the men I was with had genuine feelings for me—they were all after one thing, and they only hung around as long as I was willing to give it to them. To make matters worse, I had done nothing to improve myself or my situation in life. I paid no attention to my work at all, so I had no chance of getting ahead. I still had the same low-paying job I'd gotten right out of high school and lived in the same run-down apartment.

As Ruth moved on to better things in her life I soon realized I wanted the things she had—a marriage and a decent home. As I looked at my life in comparison to hers, it seemed shabby and empty. Suddenly I found my old jealousy rising up again. Like before, Ruth seemed to have everything while I was left with nothing. Of course, I realized that it was my fault that I didn't have more than I did, but that didn't keep me from feeling bitter and angry every time I was around my sister.

The worst part was that even if I wanted to change my life, it seemed like it was simply too late. My reputation around town was so bad that no decent guy would be seen with me—let alone marry me. And since I'd never paid much attention to my work, it was impossible to get a better job. Frankly, I was such a poor employee I was lucky my boss didn't fire me. I felt completely stuck, like nothing would ever improve for me, while Ruth's life just got better and better.

Then the worst thing I could imagine happened—Ruth got pregnant. This was the final blow. Soon Ruth would have a precious baby to care for. She would have someone to call her Mama and to toddle up to her with outstretched arms. All I had was my cramped little apartment and low-paying job and nothing else.

I tried to feel happy for Ruth, but I just couldn't. I didn't know how I'd be able to stand watching as she went through her pregnancy. I'd have to hear her stories about morning sickness and buying a bassinet. I'd have to see the look on Mom and Dad's faces as they met their first and only grandchild. And I'd have to watch Ruth with her beautiful family while I was alone. My jealousy was like a bomb ready to go off.

The day of Ruth's baby shower was one of the worst of my life. Riding back to my apartment, I could feel tears of sadness and rage sting my eyes. When I finally got back to my apartment, I collapsed onto my bed in a shower of tears. Why is Ruth always the fortunate one? I wondered, my heart aching with envy. Why is my life so unhappy?

I cried until my head ached and my eyes were sore and red. I felt so awful. I felt like I was going to explode. I knew I had to do something, anything, to get rid of this awful anger. Suddenly, it occurred to me that I had to get back at Ruth. I thought of how much better I'd feel if she were knocked down a notch or two. In my confused mind, I thought that if I could only even the score with her then everything would be okay. As I tried to get myself under control, I racked my brain to figure out what I could do.

Then my mind went back to the day of the high school prom, when Joe had leered at me in my wet T-shirt. That was when the idea came to me. This was my one and only weapon—I knew how to turn men on, how to lure them. I didn't know how to do anything else, but this one thing I could do better than any woman I knew. After all, I had plenty of practice at it. A plan formed in my head. The perfect way to get even with Ruth would be for me to sleep with Joe!

As this awful idea first came to me, I tried to push it away. I may not have been the most perfect person in the world, but I'd never done anything to deliberately hurt another person—especially my own sister. Despite my awful behavior with men, I'd always been honest. The only person I'd hurt with my running around was myself. I immediately decided that I'd never sleep with Joe, no matter how much pleasure it might give me to put Ruth in her place.

"I can't do it!" I said out loud to myself as I dried my tears and started getting ready for bed. "I can't be that cruel and underhanded."

But the more I tried to put the idea out of my mind, the more tantalizing it seemed. I pictured myself in bed with the extremely handsome Joe. I pictured Ruth innocently thinking her husband had been faithful to her while all along I'd know the truth. Every time I thought about it, it seemed more pleasurable and exciting. And nothing I said to myself could make the idea go away.

Somehow I fell asleep that night, despite being very confused and upset. When I awoke the next morning, the first thing that came into my head was the thought of seducing Joe. I looked over at the calendar hanging on my wall. It was Friday, Joe's day off. Ruth was working. She'd agreed to stay on the job until the end of the month—and so Joe would be home alone. If I waited another couple of weeks, it would be too late. Ruth would no longer be working then, so she'd be home all the time. That would make it almost impossible to get Joe alone. Suddenly I realized it was now or never. This was my one chance to get even with Ruth. I couldn't let it slip through my fingers.

I was supposed to be working that day, but I called in sick. I'd never paid much attention to being a good employee, and I didn't see any reason to start now. Before heading over to Ruth and Joe's, I spent more than an hour fixing myself up. I fixed my hair so it was slightly wild looking and put the right amount of lipstick on.

When I looked at myself in the mirror, I was struck by the fact that no matter what I did I wasn't beautiful in the way Ruth was. Seductive and sexy, yes, but only because I knew how to act a certain way. Ruth had always been the beauty in the family and always would be.

This made me all the more determined to get Joe into bed. It seemed like if I could do that, then it would prove I was as important and attractive as Ruth. I finally grabbed my purse and my sweater and marched out of my apartment as if I were going off to war.

A half-hour later, I rang the doorbell at Ruth's house. It took two rings for Joe to answer. When he did, it was obvious he'd just gotten out of bed. He had on only pajama bottoms with no shirt, and his hair was rumpled. This surprised me a little since it was almost ten o'clock.

"So, this is what you do on your day off, loaf all day?" I said in my sexiest voice.

Joe stared at me with a look of astonishment. He tried to say something, but it seemed like he was so surprised he couldn't even speak.

"Aren't you going to ask me in?" I said in a suggestive tone.

For a minute Joe didn't say a word. He had a thoughtful look, like he was thinking something over, but then his face suddenly relaxed, like he'd made a decision. "Sure," he said as he swung the door open wider and gestured me in. I walked in the sexiest way I knew, and I was sure he was watching me as I did.

Once I was in, he closed the door behind him.

"You surprised to see me?" I said in my low, raspy voice.

He smiled. Now that I was in the house, it seemed like he had few doubts about why I was there or what I was planning on doing.

"Let's just say I'm surprised to see you like this. I mean, alone with me." He ran his eyes up and down my body, and I could see his thoughts were on one thing.

I went up to him and put my arms around his neck. "Surely you aren't surprised I'm attracted to you," I said. "You must know what a hunk you are."

He didn't respond in words. He just put his arms around me and ran his hands up and down my back.

"I've been attracted to you since high school," I said, trying to use as much flattery as I could. "I finally decided it was time I did something about it."

Joe was looking at me with the most turned-on expression I'd ever seen. He pulled me to him and pressed my body against his.

This was going to be easier than I'd expected. I'd thought I was going to have to work at seducing him. I'd thought he was going to put up some resistance and tell me he couldn't do anything because he was a married man and my brother-in-law. I knew I could get through his resistance—I'd done it with many other men—but I'd thought I was going to have to work at it.

But instead, Joe seemed perfectly ready. There had been just that moment at the door when he seemed to be trying to figure something out, but once that had gone, it was as if he was more than willing. I was surprised, and a little flattered, that he was so eager. He was clearly enjoying my attentions.

The only thing I noticed besides his obvious eagerness was that there seemed to be something on his mind. It didn't seem like there was any guilt or hesitation.

Maybe he's worrying about Ruth getting back unexpectedly, I thought. But that didn't seem reasonable. Ruth hadn't missed a day of work in three years.

"How about it?" I went on. At that moment, I gave him a deep, passionate kiss, which he responded to fully. When we pulled away, I could tell he was completely turned on. So I was a little surprised when he stepped back to speak.

"Relax on the couch for just a minute," he said. "I've got something to do. I'll be right back."

I was confused by his tone. It was as if he'd suddenly remembered something he had to take care of—like an errand or a meeting. It seemed like a pretty odd time to remember something like that. But I went along with what he asked and waited impatiently while he disappeared into the bedroom.

As I waited, I thought I could hear voices. I turned in surprise and tried to figure out where they were coming from, but they were quite soft, so I couldn't tell.

Maybe there's a radio on somewhere, I thought. Or maybe I'm feeling guilty and my imagination is playing tricks on me.

Just then, Joe came back into the room. I stood up to join him, thinking we'd go into the bedroom. Then, to my complete amazement, a girl appeared behind him. My look must've been something to see. My mouth dropped open about a mile. The girl was gorgeous, and hardly more than eighteen or nineteen years old. She had a sultry, rather slutty look, and she was wearing nothing but a sheet that she had wrapped around her. The odd thing was that she didn't seem upset to see me there at all.

I tried to say something but now I was the one who couldn't find words.

"Meet Roxanne," Joe said, putting his arm around the girl's shoulders.

I stared at the girl and then at Joe, and I could feel my face flame. I didn't know whether to feel embarrassed, angry, or jealous.

"Joe, I didn't know. I thought you and Ruth—" I was going to say that I thought he and Ruth had a happy marriage and that I was shocked to find out he wasn't faithful to her. But then I realized how ridiculous that would've sounded since I'd clearly come over to seduce him. "I didn't realize you saw other women," I said weakly.

Roxanne looked at me and started to laugh. "Are you talking about Joe Hamilton?" she exclaimed. "Sweetheart, Joe has more girlfriends than any man in town. There must be six women he's juggling right this very minute. The biggest joke around town is that half the women in town have slept with Joe and the other half want to." She laughed again. "Can you blame him, though? With his looks!" She looked up into his eyes flirtatiously.

"You mean . . . you sleep around?" I said. "But what about my sister?" I couldn't believe I was saying this. Not five minutes before I'd been trying to seduce my sister's husband. Now I was offended to discover he was cheating on her. I knew it didn't make a shred of sense, but my thoughts were so confused right then that I didn't know what was up or down.

"Sleep around hardly describes it," Roxanne said. "I could tell you some stories you wouldn't believe."

"And Ruth doesn't know a thing about it?" I stammered.

Joe shrugged. "Ruth has known a long time," he said indifferently. "She's just had to learn to live with it. Just after we were married, she caught me with someone and we had a huge fight about it. She bawled like a baby and threatened to leave me, but I convinced her to stay. We must've gone through something similar five or six times before she finally realized I wasn't going to change. I finally ended up telling her if she wanted me, she'd have to accept me for what I am. She says she's determined not to get a divorce, that she's going to make this marriage work regardless. I know it hurts her, but I figure she's got to learn to deal with it because I'm going to do what I'm going to do whether she likes it or not."

"And she stands for this?" I cried. "She stays with you despite your constantly cheating on her?"

Joe's face took on a look of complete contempt. "You know Ruth," he said in a sarcastic tone. "She doesn't believe in divorce. She thinks people can work things out. So she's decided she'll put up with me, I guess." Then he laughed, as though his wife's pain was just a joke to him.

I couldn't believe what I was hearing. I couldn't even speak, I was so astonished and so upset at Joe's cruel attitude. Suddenly I was horribly ashamed of myself. I pictured Ruth, who always kept a smile on her face and never let anyone know that anything was wrong in her life. Joe had always meant the world to her, and she was utterly devoted to her marriage. I knew she'd never leave Joe, no matter what. So that meant she was stuck with a husband who treated her without a bit of respect—even when she was carrying his baby. To think that I'd almost joined in on hurting her made a sick feeling rise in the pit of my stomach.

While all of this was going through my mind, Roxanne leaned up and murmured something to Joe. "Did you ask her?" she said in his ear.

"Ask me? Ask me what?" I interjected.

Joe's smile broadened. His arm was still draped over Roxanne's shoulder. "Roxanne and I were wondering if you'd like to join us," he said.

"Join you?" At first I had no idea what he meant. I was so baffled at that moment, I actually thought he was asking me to join them for lunch or something.

"In the bedroom," Roxanne explained.

"What?" I stared at them.

"Come on," Roxanne said. "It'll be fun."

I couldn't believe they were asking me this. Maybe I had no reason to act holier-than-thou about it, but the fact was, even with all my bad behavior, I'd never done anything like that. Suddenly I felt my feelings turn upside down. I couldn't believe my brother-in-law could be such a creep. And I couldn't believe I was in my sister's house ready to seduce her husband. I didn't know what I was more horrified at—Joe's behavior or my own. All I wanted to do was get out of there.

"I certainly have not done anything like that!" I declared. "And in any case, I wouldn't have anything to do with a man like you, Joe Hamilton!" With that, I stormed out of the house in a rage. My head was swimming in anger and shame as I let the door slam closed behind me. Tears stung my eyes as I rushed away as fast as I could possibly go.

As I hurried blindly down the street, the tears of shame flooded down my cheeks. A dozen emotions were churning inside me at the same time. I felt enraged at Joe and at all the women who slept with him. I felt terribly ashamed of myself for what I had become—a woman so cheap and so eaten up with jealousy that she would destroy her own sister's happiness. But mainly, I felt sorry for Ruth. All these years, I'd thought she had everything. I pictured her having this perfect life, with everything a woman could ask for. Now it turned out that her marriage was a charade.

Living with a man like Joe must be a nightmare, I thought. Yet all this time she'd kept a brave smile on her face, never letting on how hurt she was.

Knowing how courageous Ruth had been somehow gave me strength. If Ruth could keep going despite a terrible marriage and a cruel husband, then there was no reason I couldn't face up to my problems. I vowed right then to change. From that day on, I'd start working toward having a decent life. I'd stop sleeping around. I'd concentrate on improving myself and try to get a decent job. It would take a lot of work to live down the disgusting reputation I'd built up for myself, but I would do it somehow. And maybe some day a decent guy would come along, and I'd have a happy marriage and children of my own. But the first thing I would do was to work at getting close to my sister. Without knowing it, Ruth had given me strength to handle my personal problems. Perhaps I could also give her strength to get through her difficult life.

THE END

SHE SHOT MY MAN!
Why? Why? Why?

I knelt on the floor in the kitchen, brushing coffee grounds from my hair, too humiliated to notice my swelling bottom lip, and feeling utterly helpless and hopeless. My husband, Kirk, took a step toward me, and instinctively, I scrambled backward, covering my face in case he decided to take another swing at me.

"Get up, Mindy!" Kirk bellowed. "And, clean up this mess! Why isn't my breakfast ready? Why do you always have to make me late for work? I told you not to make coffee! I hate coffee."

I cowered under the kitchen table, afraid to move or to speak. Kirk's temper was explosive, and I knew better than to try to reason with him. But, Kirk didn't wait. He grabbed my arm and pulled me out from under the table, jerking me to my feet. I fought back tears, because I knew that if he saw me crying it would unleash a fresh barrage of insults—or worse.

"I'm sorry, honey. I promise that I'll try harder," I managed to stammer, choking on the words. Numbly, I began to clean up the spilled coffee grounds, hoping that it would pacify my husband. Then, I set his place at the table, making sure to arrange things perfectly, in the order that he liked.

"See that you do," he growled as he sat down, glaring at me from across the table. I breathed a quiet sigh of relief, knowing that the worst was over—at least, that time. I waited on him hand and foot as he finished his breakfast, eager for him to leave for work. Then, I knew, I could truly relax, at least mentally.

We had just moved from the city the week before, and there was still so much unpacking to do. I was busy, but that didn't stop the loneliness from creeping in during my time alone, while Kirk was at work. I knew no one in the little town—so different from the big city that we'd come from. The neighbors in our apartment complex seemed nice enough, but I'd had no time yet to make any friends, and I knew that even if I did make friends, I'd practically have to hide them. Kirk didn't like intrusions on his time at home. I was never allowed to have friends over, or even to talk to them on the phone, as long as Kirk was home.

Kirk hadn't always been like that, though. He'd always been a little jealous, but in the beginning, I'd seen it as a sign that he loved me. I was even a little flattered by his moodiness. Now that we'd been married almost six years, not only had his jealousy and possessiveness gotten worse, but I'd realized that it wasn't motivated by love at all.

No, I'd learned that my husband needed to have someone to control, and it was no longer flattering. And, when he'd started hitting me and threatening me, I'd begun to live a life of fear and intimidation, always having to be careful not to say anything that would set him off.

My poor mother would have been turning in her grave if she'd known what a nightmare my life had become. It had been us against the world, before she'd died of heart disease a few years earlier. I believed that losing her had, perhaps, made me hold on that much harder to Kirk.

I'd never known my father. He'd left my mother when she was pregnant with me, but I'd never heard her say a bad word about him. She'd just told me that he'd done what he'd had to do, and that we would have to make our way in the world without him.

After her death, I'd found myself trying to make my way in the world without my mother, too, and I missed her so much. I knew that she would have known what to do, when Kirk had started hitting me. And, she would have known what to do then, too, when I needed her the most. Because, all of a sudden, it wasn't just Kirk and me. It was also the brand-new life that was growing inside of me.

Kirk still didn't know about our baby. I'd wanted to wait until we were settled from the move to tell him. I feared that he might not be able to handle the pressure of so much, all at once. And, after his explosion of temper at breakfast, I wondered whether I should tell him at all. I wanted so much for us to be a family, and for my baby to grow up with a loving daddy, but in my heart, I wondered if it was possible. All through the day, as I unpacked and put things away, I found myself praying, and asking my mother to help me to figure it all out.

My prayers were not answered that day, though. When my husband came home, he was in the worst mood ever. With only one week behind him at his new job, his boss had already reported him for insubordination. Kirk had always had trouble taking direction from others, and as usual, his attitude hadn't been appreciated. And, as always, he took out his anger and frustration on me.

Kirk glanced into the kitchen as he brushed past me. "I see you don't have dinner ready," he said gruffly.

"I'm sorry, honey," I murmured, trying to pacify him, "but I haven't been feeling well today and I'm a little behind on things. It won't be long, though, I promise. I have a frozen dinner ready to go in the oven, and it'll just take a few minutes."

As I began to open the freezer door, Kirk whipped around and slapped me across the back of my head so hard that my face slammed into the edge of the refrigerator. Blood spurted from my nose, my ears began ringing, and I dropped to the floor, more terrified than I'd ever been in my life.

"Why can't you just do things on time?" he screamed. "So, you weren't feeling well, huh?" he asked, mocking me. "Well, why don't you think of someone besides yourself for a change? Why do you always make me hit you? When I come home from work, I want a real meal! If you weren't so lazy, it might occur to you to learn to cook!"

My head was pounding and blood was running into my mouth. I tried to get up, but instead, I fell back down, dizzy and nauseated. Looking up at Kirk, seeing the rage on his face and the veins in his neck bulging, I was frozen in that spot and couldn't move.

"Get up! You aren't hurt!" he barked. "It's just a little blood, and you'll be lucky if I don't really hurt you! Get up!"

"I—I can't, Kirk. Please, I think I'm going to be sick," I pleaded, fighting the waves of nausea that were closing in on me.

Suddenly, I was being yanked to my feet by my hair. As I cried out in pain, Kirk threw me against the refrigerator, twisting my hair around his hand for a firmer grip, and forced me to look him in the face. His eyes were wild in a way that I'd never seen before, his face was beet red, and he held a clenched fist in front of me.

"Oh, please don't, Kirk!" I begged. "Please! I'll do anything! Just please don't hit me anymore." I was desperate. I knew that I had to find a way to make him stop. I had to find a way to reach past his fury.

Suddenly, a strange thing happened. As I stared up at my husband, his eyes seem to glaze over, and then, he loosened his grip on my hair and stepped back away from me.

"Go clean up your face," he said flatly. "You're a mess."

I didn't know what to think of the sudden change, but it frightened me and I decided to run to the bathroom, before Kirk changed his mind. Once in the bathroom, I very quietly locked the door and then turned both faucets on. When I saw my reflection in the mirror above the sink, I nearly passed out from fear and nausea. I looked like something straight out of a horror movie, with my face a mass of bruising and swelling, still covered in blood.

When I washed the blood off, my injuries were even more apparent. My nose was surely broken and both eyes were black and swollen shut. I couldn't bear to look at myself. How could he have done such a terrible thing to me?

My head was throbbing, and I began shaking uncontrollably. Tears began falling down my face and I felt oddly drained of every ounce of life. I curled up on the bathroom floor.

Time passed, and I didn't know how long I lay there, sobbing. I was jarred to attention by the sound of the front door closing, and as I staggered to my feet, I realized that the water was still running. Reaching over to turn off the faucets, I had to grab onto the sink for

107

support. The dizziness was overwhelming, but I slowly made my way out to the living room.

Kirk had left. I figured that he'd probably gone to the bar. That's where he usually went, after we'd had a fight. I sank onto the sofa, knowing that I had to do something, but not knowing what it was. I had nowhere to turn—no family, no friends. My only friends lived in the city, and I didn't want them to know what Kirk had done to me.

I felt beaten on the outside, but it was nothing, compared to feeling beaten on the inside. I knew that I had to get away from my husband. I had the baby to think about—the precious little one that I already loved more than life.

I'll keep you safe, I thought. I promise.

I had to make a plan. I didn't have much money in my wallet, but I knew that there was plenty in the bank account. I decided that I should pack a few things, get my purse, and get out of there. I didn't know how long Kirk would be gone, so I had to hurry. I pulled my overnight bag from the closet and began to throw whatever I could grab into it. After I'd gone to the bank to get money out of the cash machine, I had no idea where I would go, but I decided that I would think about that later. Kirk had taken the car, but the bank and the bus station were within walking distance. If I hurried, I could get the money and be on a bus to somewhere—anywhere—before Kirk got back.

My overnight bag was stuffed to capacity when I remembered that I couldn't leave without my photographs of my mother. They were all that I had left of her, and I wouldn't leave without them. I ran to the closet and sifted through my things, until I found the small box tied with a blue ribbon. I put it in my purse and zipped up my bag. Setting the bag down near the front door, I ran back for my jacket.

It was too late.

As I opened the front door, Kirk came storming through the living room. He was in a fury, and he lunged for me. In my panic to get out, I hadn't heard him come in through the back door in the kitchen. I screamed, and as he grabbed for me, he fell headlong over the bag. Sprawled on the floor, I saw that he was temporarily dazed.

It's now or never, I thought resolutely. I knew that it was my only chance to escape. If Kirk caught me, he would surely kill me. He would never just let me leave. As he started to get up, I bolted out the door into the chilly night air, terrified and screaming. I ran in a panic, as fast as I could. Just then, I spotted a young couple getting out of their car.

"Help me! Oh, help me, please!" I pleaded, grabbing the young woman's arm. "He's going to kill me! My husband's going to kill me!" I could hear Kirk yelling, off in the distance. "He's coming—please help me!" I begged.

The woman stepped back from me, her expression a mix of shock and fear. But, thankfully, the young man quickly took my arm and pushed me toward the car.

"Get in," he said, "and get down on the floor in back! We'll just go for a little drive. We'll take you to the police station, if you want." He started the car.

"No, please, I can't go to the police!" I cried. "It'll just make him crazier. I don't know what he'll do. Can you just take me to the bank and then, to the bus station?"

"Well, yeah, but don't you think that's where he'll look for you there first? I mean, I would. I don't want to tell you what to do, but I don't think that the bus station is a good idea. Maybe we could just drive around for awhile and then you can come back home with us and we'll figure out what to do, okay? I'm Ethan, and this is Suzanne."

"I'm Mindy. Thank you so much for helping me. I don't know what I would have done if you hadn't stopped. I'm new here and I don't know anyone. I was trying to leave my husband, but he came home before I could get out. He would have killed me if he'd caught me. I'm not a fast runner, and he'd probably have caught up to me, except that he's drunk," I explained in a rush. My legs were cramping up, crouching down there on the floor. "Do you think it's safe for me to sit up now?" I asked.

"It's okay. We're far enough away," Suzanne answered. "Look, I'm sorry about the way that I acted back there. It's just that, well, your face is a mess and it frightened for a minute. Ethan, did you see her face? What did he do to you? Did he hit you with a baseball bat? Maybe we should take you to the hospital. You might have a concussion or something."

"No, I'm okay," I told her, struggling to get off the floor. "I just need some time to figure things out."

We drove around for at least an hour. We stopped at the bank and I withdrew a few hundred dollars. Then, we stopped for something to eat. I could barely eat my chicken sandwich, my lip was so swollen and sore. I felt nauseated and would have skipped eating altogether, except that I knew I needed to eat for my baby's sake.

When we got back to their place, Suzanne immediately brought a bag filled with crushed ice to put on my forehead and nose. Then, she brought me a mirror.

"Mindy, this guy needs to be put in jail for what he's done to you," she said firmly. "I know that you don't want to call the cops, but he should be arrested. Look at your face! You look like a prizefighter!"

I pushed the mirror away, not wanting to look. I knew that I looked bad. I could feel the swelling on my forehead, and I could tell that my eyes were swelling shut. Even my teeth were hurting.

I couldn't bear to look again at what Kirk had done to me. I was already feeling very queasy, and I knew that looking at the damage on my face would just push me right over the edge. Suddenly, everything that had happened just seemed to crash down upon me. I felt tears running down my face, and my resolve to stay in control of my emotions disintegrated. I collapsed, sobbing uncontrollably.

I felt an arm around my shoulder. "Come on, Mindy. Let's get you something to wear tonight. You can stay here with us until you figure things out—however long that takes," Suzanne murmured soothingly. "Right, Ethan?"

"Absolutely! The pullout sofa's yours for as long as you want to stay," he told me reassuringly.

I was amazed at their generosity. Even though I knew that they were total strangers, it didn't seem that way anymore. They had been so kind, risking their own personal safety to help me. And, on top of everything, they were telling me that I could stay with them.

"I'll figure something out really soon," I promised as I tried to stop sobbing, "and I'll pay my way, I promise. I'll help out around here in any way that I can. I can't thank you guys enough for what you've done for me."

"Don't worry about that," Ethan said. "Besides, we couldn't have you out on the streets, scaring the good citizens, could we?"

I laughed, for the first time in weeks. I realized that I felt safe for the first time in ages. It was wonderful, not having to worry about what I said, or whether everything was in perfect order for Kirk.

"You'd better get some sleep, though. You look totally exhausted," Suzanne commented. "Here's one of Ethan's T-shirts. I hope that'll be okay for tonight. Just help yourself to anything in the kitchen. If you want to play some music, feel free. Just do whatever you want, but if you need us, call us. I know how hard it can be to sleep in a strange place. See you in the morning, okay?"

After I was sure that they'd finished with the bathroom and gone to bed, I went in and changed into the T-shirt. It was big on me, but it was comfortable. In fact, I felt as though a great weight had been lifted off my shoulders, just being there. I crawled under the blanket and lay there, feeling the cool sheets on my legs.

It was wonderful, not having Kirk groping for me in the dark. He was always so rough, and sometimes, he hurt me and didn't even seem to notice—or care. If I tried to pull away, he became even rougher, so I'd learned just to go along with it and to pretend that it was okay. That way, he would just do what he wanted and fall asleep.

I knew that it wasn't supposed to be that way with two people who loved each other, but Kirk was the only man I'd ever been with, and it had always been that way with us. I'd wondered what it would have been like if he'd been gentler. Once, I'd almost gotten the courage to ask him to try. But, in the end, I was too afraid. I knew that he would take it the wrong way, and I didn't want to get him angry.

My thoughts drifted to my mother, and I thanked God that I'd been able to grab my purse before I'd run out of the house. I still had her pictures, and that was all that mattered. There was nothing else important enough to go back to the apartment for, and there was nothing that Kirk could use to lure me back. I had everything that I truly cared about right there with me—my baby, and my pictures of my mother.

See, little one? We're safe now. And, we're going to stay safe, I promise, I thought. Your mama's going to make everything all right.

Although the sofa was comfortable, I slept fitfully. Even the pillow touching my face made it hurt, and whenever I awoke, I temporarily forgot where I was. Finally, though, I fell into a deeper sleep, probably from sheer exhaustion.

I woke the next morning to the smell of coffee brewing, and felt immediately nauseous. I loved coffee in the morning, but, because of the baby, the smell made me sick. I dashed to the bathroom, retching. I held a cool washcloth to my face, and sipped a cup of water. Then, I sat on the edge of the tub until I felt better.

Hearing a faint tap on the door, I started to get up. "Mindy? Are you okay in there? Are you sick? Can I do anything?" Suzanne asked.

I opened the door. "I'm so sorry, Suzanne. I was just feeling a little sick. Was I in here too long? I didn't mean to monopolize the bathroom. I'm okay, though."

We walked into the kitchen, and Suzanne pulled a chair out for me. "Mindy, maybe we should get you to a hospital. You shouldn't be sick like this. Maybe you do have a head injury."

"No, I'm okay, really," I promised. "It's not a head injury. I'm pregnant." I realized that I'd forgotten to mention that.

Suzanne stared at me in horror. "You mean to tell me that your husband hit you, and you're pregnant? What kind of a man is he? Ethan's right—he should be arrested!"

"Kirk doesn't know I'm pregnant," I explained hastily. "Not that I think it would have made a difference—he's too out of control. I didn't tell him because I knew that he'd go crazy. We just moved here, and he's having trouble at his new job already. And, he takes all of that out on me. The last thing that I wanted to do was to give him something else to blame me for." I nibbled on the dry toast that Suzanne had put before me. "But, I was thinking that maybe I should talk to the police. I need to figure out what to do. Maybe I could go to a shelter for battered women. I know that I need to see a lawyer."

"And a doctor," Suzanne interjected. "If you don't want to tell them what really happened, then tell them you were in an accident and hit your head. We can figure out something, but I really think that you should see a doctor. And, now that I know you're pregnant, everything is different. You should do it for the baby's sake, at least. How far along are you?"

"Almost two months, I think. But, I don't have a doctor here, so I haven't seen anyone, and I don't know for sure." I took another bite of toast. "You're right. I should go see someone so that I can get prenatal care. Do you know of a good doctor?"

"Ethan and I go to the primary care center in the next town. Dr. DeStefano is a good man. You could go there." Suzanne began clearing off the table. "Would you like some tea or something? I won't offer you coffee," she added, grinning.

"Tea sounds good," I told her, nodding. "I'll call the doctor this afternoon and make an appointment. At least I have insurance. That will help. I guess I do have a lot to think about. I need to find a lawyer, too, because I'm going to file for divorce. Maybe I could apply for some kind of assistance. I don't really have any money of my own. Kirk didn't want me working, and I really didn't have to, because he made enough to support us. Now I'll have to find a job." It all seemed so overwhelming. In fact, my head was swimming with all of the things that I had to do.

"Just remember that you're not alone," Suzanne reminded me. "Like we said last night, you can stay here as long as you need to— and, you don't have to do everything today. One thing, though. Maybe you should go back to the bank and clean out the account. Why leave him with everything? He's already getting the furniture. And, besides, you're going to need all you can get for the baby. He owes you at least that much. I can take you wherever you need to go, so don't worry about transportation."

That morning, I made appointments with the doctor and with a lawyer. I needed clothes, but once I went to the bank and withdrew all the money, I'd have that problem solved. Suzanne washed the clothes that I'd been wearing when they'd rescued me, and after lunch, we went to the bank. I was thankful that Kirk still hadn't realized that I'd withdrawn cash the night before and that the balance of the account was still available. I went into the branch and withdrew everything, except for five dollars, so I had almost a thousand dollars. It wasn't that much, but it would last for a little while.

Next, I bought three inexpensive outfits at the department store. I knew that I'd be needing maternity clothes in a few months, so there was no point in buying much. Then, we headed back to their apartment so that I could get ready for my doctor's appointment.

I was nervous about the appointment, because I looked just terrible and I knew that the doctor would ask questions. Everywhere that Suzanne and I had gone, people had stared. Even with my sunglasses on, you could tell that there were bruises on my face, and I couldn't disguise my swollen lip, not to mention the enormous purple lump on my forehead. I decided to go ahead and tell the truth about what had happened to me.

It had been easier than I'd anticipated, being honest about Kirk's abuse. The doctor and nurses at the center were wonderful and understanding, but they also advised me to go to the police and to press charges against Kirk—for my own good, and for my baby's protection. They also gave me the numbers of some social service agencies, and of a therapist who specialized in abuse cases.

Dr. DeStefano told me that I was seven weeks pregnant. The reality of it had begun to set in and I was so excited at the prospect of planning for my little one. But, as wonderful as that reality was, there was another reality that was equally frightening. That was the fact that I would be doing it alone, just like mother had done with me. And, more immediate and more frightening than that was the fact that I had to tell Kirk about my pregnancy. I definitely did not want to tell him about the baby, but I knew that it was a secret that I couldn't keep for very long.

By the time we got back from the doctor's office, Ethan was home and already had dinner cooked. It was so refreshing to know that there were still decent men in the world.

"So tell me, Suzanne, does your husband have a brother that I could borrow?" I asked jokingly.

Suzanne and Ethan both looked like as though they'd been smacked with a wet fish. Then, they both started laughing.

"Let me in on the joke! Was it something I said?" I asked curiously.

"Mindy," Suzanne answered, "Ethan and I aren't married. In fact, we're not even together, at least, not in that way. We're just friends."

"Oh!" I said, taken aback. "I just assumed—"

"Yeah, most people do," Ethan said, "but it's cool. It's a natural assumption. Especially for you, since you saw us occupy the same bedroom last night. But, you were sleeping on the pullout couch, where I usually crash, so we sort of had to."

"Oh, come on, Ethan. You know that it was just a cheap ploy to get me into bed." Suzanne grinned wickedly.

"Well, it worked, didn't it?" Ethan shot back.

"The truth is, Mindy," Suzanne said, "I'm a lesbian. Ethan and I grew up together. He was the proverbial boy next door. He's like my big brother, only nicer. My real brother can't handle my sexual orientation. In fact, no one in my family can. But, that's okay. I have Ethan!"

Ethan set the table and began serving the steak and baked potatoes.

"For the record, though, I am heterosexual—and available," he added.

"And, an excellent cook," I said. The meal he'd prepared was delicious.

"Thanks! It's in the genes!" he told me proudly.

"Is cooking a hobby, or is it a family talent that's been passed down?" I asked.

"Yes! To both, I mean. It's a good thing, too, or we'd starve. Suzanne's good at cleaning up, though," Ethan teased. "Eat up, kid—don't be shy!"

"Yeah, remember that you're eating for two now," Suzanne added.

"Cooking isn't one of my talents, either. That's one of Kirk's many complaints about me. In fact, that's why he beat me yesterday. I look like this because of a frozen dinner."

"No, Mindy, you look like that because you have a monster for a husband," Ethan corrected me. "And you're pregnant? That guy needs to be taught a lesson! I know some people who—"

"He's not serious, Mindy. He's joking. Right, Ethan? Ethan is a frustrated comedian who missed his calling." Suzanne was smiling but she shot Ethan a look that I wouldn't have wanted directed at me. "You shouldn't joke about things like that."

"Who said that I was joking? The guy does deserve a beating. Do you disagree?"

"In theory, no," Suzanne said, "but you can't just go around hurting people, and you shouldn't joke about it, anyway."

"It's okay, guys," I said. "I can take a joke. I still have a sense of humor. And, anyway, Kirk isn't going to be my problem anymore. I'm filing for divorce tomorrow. I just wish that he didn't have to know about the baby, though. That kind of scares me."

"Well, it should," Ethan said, "because the man is obviously a maniac. But, there are legal things that you can do to protect yourself against him, and I think that you should. Be sure you talk to your lawyer about that. It's going to be really hard, Mindy, so I hope that you're ready for a real fight. Kirk doesn't strike me as the kind who will just let you waltz off into the sunset. He sounds like a control freak to me, and that makes him dangerous. I'm sorry. I don't mean to scare you, but you need to know these things." His voice was serious.

That night, I couldn't sleep for fear of what Kirk might do, especially when he discovered that I'd filed for divorce. Ethan had been right—Kirk could be dangerous. I'd never been able to tell what might set him off, or how violent he might become. It was like living with a ticking bomb. That was why I had to put an end to the nightmare. I would not live my life in fear. And, I would not bring a child into a life of terror. I just had to have faith that things would work out, and that no harm would come to us.

God, please protect us, I prayed.

Morning came all too early, and there was no smell of coffee, but I still had to dash to the bathroom. When I came out, Ethan had already left for work. Suzanne was sitting alone in the kitchen and seemed completely unaware of my presence. I stood there, watching the most bizarre thing that I'd ever seen. She was wearing an oversized shirt and she had the sleeves pushed up. To my horror, she was cutting her arm with a knife. She was making perfect little incisions, right into her arm, and then, she'd watch them bleed.

From the appearance of her arms, it wasn't the first time that she'd done such a thing, either. I froze, holding my breath. I choked back the gasp that was threatening to escape from my throat. I carefully backed down the hallway to the bathroom, closing the door very quietly.

Why is she doing this? I thought. I'd heard of people such things, but I'd also heard that they were emotionally disturbed people who were filled with despair. I'd seen no signs of anything like that in my new friend. In fact, Suzanne seemed perfectly normal to me.

You don't really know these people, Mindy, I told myself, and obviously you missed something. I was confused and frightened. How was I going to go out there and act as though I'd seen nothing—as though I knew nothing?

I decided that I'd best make some noise, to make my presence known. First, I flushed the toilet and ran the faucet. Then, I made a noisy job of opening the door, coughing in the hallway as I walked to the kitchen, hoping that she would have heard it all and stopped her strange behavior.

When I walked into the kitchen, there was no sign of the knife, and Suzanne acted for all the world as though she'd been wiping the table. She looked up and smiled.

"Feeling better this morning? I thought I'd let you sleep. I just put some water on for tea," she said, motioning toward the stove. "Hungry? I can make us some toast."

I couldn't believe how masterfully she'd covered her morning's activity. "Sure, tea and toast is fine," I said, pulling out a chair. "So, what have you been up to this morning? You're already dressed!" I couldn't believe I'd asked her that, but I just didn't know what to say, and it seemed like a natural question.

"Nothing much, just cleaning up Ethan's mess. He likes a big breakfast. You know, cereal and juice, toast, eggs, bacon, fruit—the whole nine yards. He may be a great cook, but he's also great at making messes!"

She's really good at this, I thought in amazement. She must have had a lot of practice. I wonder if Ethan knows about her problem.

I watched in wonder as she casually poured the water for our tea and brought the cups to the table. "Want some sugar?" she asked.

"Sure." I poured some cream into my cup.

"Are you ready for your lawyer today? Wow, Mindy, this must be so hard for you. I can't imagine what it must be like," she told me sympathetically.

"I'm as ready as I'll ever be, I guess. It's hard, but not as hard as living with Kirk. I'm too afraid of him to do anything but leave, although this sure isn't my idea of a happy ending."

"What is your idea of a happy ending?" Suzanne looked at me inquisitively.

"I don't know. I guess it's just having someone tender and gentle, who's my partner and not my master. Someone who will love my baby and me and be good to us. That's what I'd like. But, I doubt that it will ever happen. I mean, no one's going to look at me while I'm pregnant, and then after that, no one's going to look at me with a little baby. I'll be a package deal, and I don't think there are going to be many takers."

"You'd be surprised. Ethan would. And, Mindy, so would I." Suzanne put her arm around me, then stood behind me, stroking my hair. "Do you mind that I'm doing this? You have such beautiful hair—so shiny, so soft."

I didn't know what to say or do. I liked Suzanne. She'd been so good to me—helping me, driving me everywhere, letting me stay in her house, sharing her food. And, all without any thought to her own safety. Both she and Ethan had been wonderful beyond belief. Still, I felt uneasy with what I'd seen and I was filled with a strange mix of affection, confusion, and fear. I didn't want to hurt her feelings, though, no matter what I felt.

"No, it's okay. It feels nice," I replied.

It was a beautiful day with a clear, blue sky. The air was crisp and cool as we walked into the lawyer's office. No one else was in the reception area, and I was called in immediately. A handsome man strode into the room, extending his hand.

"I'm Maxwell Whitaker," he said, grasping my hand firmly. "I'm pleased to meet you." He slid into the chair behind his desk and leaned forward, pulling forms from a file folder.

"I'm Mindy Hartman," I told him as I sat down in the chair in front of his desk.

He handed me a clipboard, pen, and about a dozen forms. "I'll need to have you fill these out before you leave. But, first let's talk about why you're here, shall we?"

"I—I want to divorce my husband," I stammered. "I just can't live with him anymore. I'm afraid of him, and I don't know what else to do."

"Well, the first thing that you need to do is to decide whether or not your marriage is truly irreparable. Are you sure that counseling wouldn't save your marriage?" He tipped his chair backward as he studied me, waiting for my answer.

I took off my sunglasses, revealing the ugly purple and black bruises around my eyes. "This is what he did to me a few days ago. It isn't the first time that he's hit me, but it is the worst. I'm pregnant and I'm afraid for myself and for my baby. I need some kind of protection from him."

"Very well, as long as you're sure. We can get an injunction against him, requiring him to stay away from you. If he violates the injunction, he can be arrested. But, I would advise you to get some counseling for yourself, Mrs. Hartman, because the road ahead will not be a smooth one. Men who beat their wives are men who must remain in control. Your filing for divorce is obviously going to threaten his control over you, and you can expect that he will fight it vigorously. You will need to be strong if you're serious about ending this marriage. Do you plan to file charges against him for beating you?"

"No, I just want to end it. Do I have to file charges?" The very thought of having him charged with assault, and going through a trial, terrified me. All I really wanted to do was to get a divorce, get away from him, and be safe.

Mr. Whitaker looked at me impatiently. "You would be better off if you went to the police and filed a complaint. That way, there will be documentation of the abuse. I cannot imagine why you would not want to do that, Mrs. Hartman, especially since you're pregnant. But, no, you don't have to file charges. Bear in mind, though, that if you don't file charges, he'll be free to beat you again. I must go on record as advising you to file a complaint."

"I understand, Mr. Whitaker, but I just can't do that. I just want a divorce. I don't want to put him in prison or anything. He's not a criminal. He just has a really bad temper."

Mr. Whitaker clearly did not approve of my decision, but he dropped the matter and we went on to discuss the terms of the divorce. I told him that I didn't care about the furniture or any of our possessions. Kirk could have everything. I believed that if I just let him have everything, there would be nothing to fight over, nothing that he could use against me. And it would also speed up the divorce—or, at least, that's what I hoped.

When the details were all worked out, I got up to leave.

"Mr. Whitaker, thank you," I said, extending my hand. "And, I will see a therapist, I promise."

"I hope so," he admonished. "For your sake, and for your baby's sake. I have to say one more thing. Spousal abuse is a crime—and that makes your husband a criminal. I hope that someday soon, you come to realize that. I will be in touch, Mrs. Hartman. Take care of yourself."

That night, Suzanne, Ethan, and I stayed up late, just talking and getting to know each other. Both of them waited on me hand and foot. We joked and laughed until my stomach hurt, and it made me realize just how much I'd been missing in my life. It was a relief not to have to deal with Kirk's moods. It felt good to have friends, to have people around me who cared about me and who didn't scream at me or berate me. Watching Suzanne laughing and smiling, I had to remind myself of what I'd seen that morning, because it just seemed so inconsistent. She hardly seemed like the same person. I'd almost convinced myself that I must have been mistaken about what I'd seen, when her sleeve pulled up just enough to reveal a thin, red mark above her wrist.

I quickly averted my gaze, so that Suzanne wouldn't see me staring at her arm.

Look at Ethan. Look at anything but her arm, I told myself. I swallowed the growing discomfort that I'd begun to feel in the pit of my stomach.

That night, stricken by insomnia, I lay awake for quite awhile, my mind going in a thousand different directions. I felt better for having taken some action about the divorce, but I was still afraid of Kirk's reaction when he learned what I'd done. Mr. Whitaker had to file the papers with the court to get the injunction, and then I would have to have Kirk served with the divorce papers. I wanted to be on another planet when that happened.

But, I told myself that the most important thing was my baby. I snuggled deeper into the blankets, thinking about the new little soul inside of me.

I know that things look pretty grim right now, little one, but everything's going to be just fine. You're going to have a wonderful life, I vowed silently.

Hushed, angry, voices stirred me from my sleep. I sat up, straining to hear. The voices grew louder.

"You don't know that she is!" Ethan whispered loudly.

"And, you don't know that she isn't. You think that just because she's married, she can't be. Well, that's no proof of anything!"

"Suzanne, get real! You're dreaming! She's married and pregnant. It's proof, all right. You just don't want to see it. You'd better be careful, or she's going to catch on and get scared off. Do you want that to happen?"

"Of course not, but you're no better. You keep looking at her like she's a meal, for goodness sake!"

"Hey, wait a minute! I can't believe that we're having this conversation. That poor girl has just been beaten half to death by her husband. She's alone and pregnant and scared. Her life has been turned upside down, and now she's living with strangers. The best thing that we can do for her is to be her friends, Suzanne. And that's what I want to be. I do not look at her like she's a meal. I care about her! I think that you just want her for yourself. Let me tell you—you'd better be careful!"

"Well, I think that she can handle it, and I also think that you don't know half of what you think you know. Mindy really likes me, I can tell. Maybe she likes me more than you think she does, Ethan! But, do you know what? I'm not sleeping in here tonight. I'm going out there! Mindy won't mind sharing the pullout sofa with me. My being in here was a bad idea from the start!"

"Suzanne, wait! Just relax. Don't go out there and wake her up. Suzanne—"

I heard the bedroom door open and close, and quickly slid down into the covers, pretending to be asleep.

Oh, no! They're fighting over me! I thought frantically. And, Suzanne wants to be my. . . . I couldn't even think the words.

Slowly pulling the blanket back, Suzanne slid into the bed with me.

"Are you awake, Mindy?" she whispered.

"Mmmm. What's the matter?" I mumbled, pretending to be groggy with sleep.

"Ethan and I had a fight. Is it okay if I sleep out here with you?"

How could I refuse? It was her home, after all. "Sure. What time is it, anyway?" I asked.

"It's late. I'm sorry that I had to wake you, but I just didn't want to climb in bed with you without an explanation. Good night."

I snuggled into the covers, moving over to give Suzanne some room. But, I couldn't get back to sleep. The argument that I'd heard played again and again in my mind. I lay there, perfectly still, not wanting Suzanne to know that I was just lying there, wide awake.

After all, if she knew that I wasn't sleeping, she might want to talk. And, I wasn't ready to deal with what I thought she might say. I wasn't ready, either, for the touch of her fingers stroking my hair, and then the back of my neck and my shoulders. The situation was beginning to become too much for me to handle.

I didn't know what to do, and I felt that I was out of my league. I knew that Suzanne thought I was asleep and that I didn't know what she was doing, so I continued to pretend. I didn't want to hurt her feelings and I didn't want to confront her, either. What I'd seen her doing earlier was still very much on my mind, and I wasn't even sure that she was mentally stable.

Eventually she fell asleep, her hand still on my shoulder. My mind was reeling. I thought that maybe I should start looking for another place to stay—a battered women's shelter, perhaps. But, I didn't want them to think I was ungrateful, that I didn't appreciate everything that they'd done for me. I wished that my mother were still alive.

Mom, if you can hear me, please help me figure out what to do, I thought.

We were all awakened the next morning by an insistent pounding on the front door. I struggled to clear my head, pulling the blankets around me, as Suzanne stumbled across the living room. As she opened the door, I was mortified to see Kirk staring into the living room. He rushed past Suzanne toward me.

"Mindy, I want to talk to you. You can't do this to me," he said. His voice was calm. "We need to talk, and you need to come home where you belong. Get your things together."

"I'm not going anywhere with you, Kirk. If we talk, we talk here. And, how—" I began.

"Did I find you?" he cut in. "I saw you come into this apartment yesterday. I knew that you couldn't have gone very far, so I watched the neighborhood. Mindy, I love you and I want you to come home. Please give me another chance. I have so much to tell you. It's going to be different from now on, I promise."

To my shock, I saw that there were tears in Kirk's eyes. I had never seen him cry in all the years that we'd been together, and I felt my resolve dwindling just a little.

"Mindy, do you want us to call the police?" Ethan stood in the hallway, glaring at Kirk.

"No, Ethan, it's okay," I answered, even though I wasn't sure that it really was okay. "Kirk just wants to talk. I think maybe we need to do that, but we're going to do it here, if that's okay."

"Of course, it's okay. Just don't go anywhere with him. We'll be right here in the kitchen if you need us," he said, casting a warning glance at Kirk.

Kirk sat down on the pullout bed beside me, taking my hand in his. "Mindy, I am so sorry for what I've done to you. I don't know what's gotten into me. When I look at your face—at the bruises—I just want to kill myself." His voice was breaking, and tears streamed down his face. "Please, Mindy, please forgive me. I can never undo what I've done to you, but it's going to be different from now on. I've gone into counseling, baby. I know that I have a problem, and I know that I have to do something about it. But, honey, we've got so much history together, and I can't stand the thought of losing you. Please, at least think about coming home. I swear to you, you won't be sorry. I've even quit drinking!"

"Kirk, I just can't. At least not right now," I answered. "I need time to think. You really hurt me, and I just can't put myself in that position again, based on promises. I have to see the changes for myself before I'll even consider thinking about coming back. Too much has happened, Kirk, for too long. I'm not sure that I even love you anymore."

Kirk looked dazed, as though he couldn't believe what he'd heard. But, he recovered quickly. "Of course you love me, honey. How can you say that? Love doesn't just disappear overnight, Mindy."

"It didn't disappear overnight—that's just my point. You've treated me like dirt for years. How can you still expect me to love you, to trust you, to want to be married to you? After everything that you've done to me? No, Kirk, I'm not going home with you. And, you can't fix this with words. I don't know if I will ever trust you again, no matter what you do. Besides, I really believe that you'd say anything right now, just to get me back."

"Do you think I'm lying to you? Look, Mindy," he said, pulling some papers from his back pocket, "look at this. These are my receipts from the counseling center. And this is from AA. Mindy, I want to change. I want to work things out. Please—" His voice trailed off.

"Kirk, the best thing that you can do for me is to leave me alone for awhile. I look in the mirror, I see what you've done to my face, and it makes me sick. I have to look at it every day until the bruises fade. But, they're nothing compared to what you've done to my heart, and I don't know if that will ever heal." I paused, surprised at my ability to say such things to Kirk—and to admit them to myself. "There's something else you should know, though. I filed for divorce yesterday, Kirk."

"You what?" Kirk looked stunned, and suddenly, his face was pale. "Mindy, you can't be serious. You have to call it off. I mean, you have to give me another chance—time to prove to you that it can be different. Please, Mindy," he pleaded.

"I won't call it off, Kirk. I have no reason to believe that you're sincere beyond this moment. What about tomorrow, or next month? I just need to let that take care of itself, and see what happens. As of right now, today, I won't call it off."

"I'm going to prove it to you, baby. I can change and I want to. I'll be good to you, honey. You'll see." He got up to leave. "I'm going to do what you asked, Mindy. But, please at least agree to see me and talk to me. How will you know that I've changed unless you at least do that? I won't ask another thing of you, I promise. I'm going to leave the decision entirely to you, because I know that you're going to change your mind."

If he hadn't been so desperate, he would have sounded arrogant. He looked like a lost puppy as he left, and watching him, I didn't feel half as strong as I'd acted. I was confused by the new turn of events. I was confused about everything in my life. I felt as though I was living in the twilight zone, and that nothing was at all what it seemed to be.

Kirk had seemed so sincere, so repentant. Was it possible that he really did want to change? I just couldn't reconcile his recent violent behavior with the man that had just left. He claimed that he was in therapy and was going to AA meetings. Didn't I owe it to myself—and to him—to give him another chance? And, didn't I owe our baby the chance to grow up with both parents, if it were at all possible? I would never know if it were indeed possible, if I didn't give Kirk a chance to prove himself.

Ethan and Suzanne came back into the living room. "We couldn't help overhearing," Ethan said, "and I know that you haven't asked for our opinions, but we're going to give them to you, anyway. We think that he's telling you what you want to hear."

"And, we also think that you should be really careful, Mindy," Suzanne added. "I know that he sounded convincing and everything, but you can't trust anything he says right now. You know that, don't you?"

"I don't know anything anymore," I admitted hopelessly. "I'm on overload. I can't even think straight."

"Just stay here and give yourself some time to figure it all out. We'll help you in any way that we can. You know that," Ethan told me as he gave me a big hug.

In the three weeks that followed, I did a lot of praying and soul-searching. Kirk came to see me every day, and he seemed so much more like his old self. He didn't know, and I didn't tell him, about the unusual living arrangement between Suzanne and Ethan. He made the assumption that they were a young married couple, as I had. Suzanne and Ethan never did resume sharing the bedroom, and Suzanne continued to share the pullout couch with me, but she didn't make any further attempts to touch me. Our friendship deepened and I pushed the arm-cutting episode that I'd witnessed to the back of my mind.

Mr. Whitaker called me to let me know the papers were ready, and he told me that he would have Kirk served, whenever I gave him the word. I asked him to hold off for the time being, telling him that Kirk and I were attempting to reconcile our differences, and that Kirk was in therapy.

I even attended sessions with him, and I was impressed by his openness and honesty with the therapist. It really did look as though he was serious about changing. He was treating me well, and it seemed as though he was losing the hard edge that he'd developed over the years. Sometimes, I could almost believe that we could work things out. But, I still hadn't told Kirk about the baby, and I decided that I could not continue deceiving my husband about it. He had a right to know about our child.

One night, I'd agreed to go out with Kirk on a "date." It had been the first time he'd taken me out somewhere in years. He'd told me to dress up because he had something special planned. Suzanne told me that she thought I was making a mistake in going out with Kirk, but she went with me to my apartment to get an outfit while Kirk was at work. To my surprise, the place was immaculate. I'd expected it to be a wreck without me being there to clean it. Kirk wasn't the essence of neatness, and had rarely picked up after himself during our marriage. He'd told me that cleaning was my job, as his wife.

"Don't let it fool you," Suzanne commented. "He's trying to impress you."

"I'd agree with you, except that he didn't have a clue that I would come here. He gave me money to go buy something new. I just decided that I should save the money, and that I'd come by here and get something else," I explained. "So, you see, he couldn't have known."

"He has you trained, Mindy," she retorted. "He knew that you'd do exactly what you're doing."

"Hey, come on—I'm not a trained seal!" I was beginning to feel annoyed by her sarcasm.

"Well, from where I sit, he's got you jumping through hoops. Mindy, can't you see what he's doing? Giving you money, taking you out, being a good little boy. For now. Just until he gets what he wants, which is you, back as his little slave. If you ask me—"

"But, I didn't ask you, Suzanne," I interrupted, placing my outfit in a plastic bag. "And, I don't want to talk about this anymore with you, okay?"

"Yeah, sure, whatever," she answered.

We walked back to Suzanne's apartment in silence. I was feeling hurt by her comments, and I supposed she was feeling righteous. After all, she'd only been trying to protect me—to be my friend.

An hour later, I was showered and dressed and almost ready. Studying my image in the mirror, I carefully applied my makeup, putting on a little extra mascara and eye shadow. The bruising on my face had faded a lot and required much less foundation. I applied my favorite shade of lipstick, and stood back to view the total picture.

It won't be long before I can't get into this outfit, I thought, noticing my thickening waistline. If all goes well, I'm going to tell Kirk about the baby tonight. If I wait any longer, I won't have to tell him at all.

Kirk picked me up at right on time. He wouldn't say a word about where we were going, hinting only that it was somewhere I'd wanted to go for quite awhile. I couldn't believe my eyes when we pulled into the parking lot of a very expensive restaurant that I had been wanting to try for months. Kirk had always refused, and I'd thought that it was a dream that was destined never to come true. And, suddenly, there we were! What amazed me even more than actually going to the restaurant was the fact that Kirk had remembered how much I'd wanted to go there.

"Mindy, you are absolutely beautiful tonight," he said, when we'd been seated. He was smiling tenderly at me. "There's just something different about you. Or, maybe there isn't. Maybe it's always been there, and I've been too much of a jerk to notice." Kirk reached over and gently stroked my cheek. "Honey, I've put you through hell, and I don't know how you can ever forgive me, but I hope that you will. I promise you that if you do, I'll never let you regret it."

I didn't know what to say. I couldn't remember a time when Kirk had been that gentle with me. I couldn't remember the last time he'd told me that I was beautiful. I was touched by the new Kirk, and at that moment, I allowed myself to hope that maybe, just maybe, we could work things out and save our marriage. If only Kirk could change, even a little, I thought that we might just have a chance. I knew it wouldn't happen overnight, and that Kirk would have to work very hard, and I vowed that I would, too. But, I had some hope for the first time since I'd left him.

"Kirk, it's going to take time," I told him, "and work. We have a lot to work out."

"No, honey," he said. "I have a lot of work to do. You've been wonderful. I've been a jerk and a tyrant, and I don't deserve you at all. I've made a mess of our lives, of our marriage—of everything that I touch. If you hadn't left me, I would have gone on that way and gotten even worse. But, losing you woke me up, and made me realize that I needed help. You did the only thing that you could do, and I know that. You did the right thing by leaving me. I'm not saying that I'm a completely different person all of a sudden, but I'm learning a lot about myself in therapy, and I want to change. And, it's not just to get you back. I want to change to get myself back. I don't like the person that I've been, and I want to be able to look in the mirror and respect the man who I see looking back at me. Even if it's too late to save us, it isn't too late to save me."

I'd never heard Kirk talk that way before. Either he was sincere, or he deserved an award for his performance. I chose to believe that he was sincere.

Kirk reached across and took my hand in his. "Mindy, this is how I should have treated you before. This is the kind of life you deserve, and I've been such a fool. I want so much to make it all up to you, but I know that you need time. I'm not going to try to talk you into coming back to me, but I want you to know that I love you. I want to work it out." There were tears in his eyes, and his voice was shaking.

"Please at least say that you'll still be my friend, even if you don't come back. I need you to be my friend, Mindy, because you're the best part of me."

I was overwhelmed with emotion, seeing Kirk in such a vulnerable light. I did love him, and I did want to work things out. Most important, we did have a baby on the way, a child who deserved the best chance in life that we could give her—or him. I knew then that I had to tell Kirk about the baby.

"Kirk—" I hesitated, not sure of quite how to tell him. "I have to tell you something. I'm pregnant." I stopped, bracing myself for whatever his reaction might be. "We're going to have a baby."

My husband's face went through a complete metamorphosis. The pained expression that he'd worn on his face a moment before gave way to the broadest smile that I had ever seen, and joy filled his eyes.

"A baby? Really? I mean, you're sure? Are you feeling okay? Did you see a doctor?" Kirk was so animated that I thought he was going to get up and dance.

"Yes, to all of the above," I reassured him. "I'm fine, and the baby is fine."

Kirk leaned back, his face a mix of happiness and surprise. "So that's what it is," he said, studying me. "You're glowing, Mindy! You're beautiful and glowing!"

"Do you really think so?" I smiled. I was enjoying all the new and positive attention from my husband.

Kirk leaned forward, taking both of my hands in his. "Yes, I really do, honey, and I think that our baby is going to have the best mother in the world. I promise you, Mindy, that I'm going to try my best to be a good father. No matter what you decide, I'll never do to our baby what my father did to me." A shadow crept over his face.

"What do you mean, Kirk?" I was alarmed. "What did your father do to you?"

"I never told you this because I was ashamed of it, but he used to beat my mother and, when he was drunk, he would beat me, too. I remember waking up in the middle of the night, hearing my mom crying. I remember hearing him as he just keep slapping her around. She wouldn't leave him, and I hated him for hurting her. I hated her for staying and then, I hated myself for hating them. I never felt safe, and there was never any peace in the house until he died. I was glad when he died, Mindy," he admitted.

"After his death, I put it out of my mind and pretended that nothing bad had ever happened. When I was a kid, I promised myself that I'd never do what my father had done, and when I began hitting you, I realized that I'm just as bad as he was. But, I can change, and I will.

I'm not going to have my child grow up the way I did. I won't have my child feeling all of the hopelessness, anger, and guilt that I did. I won't let that happen, no matter what."

I was stunned. Kirk had never talked much about his parents, and the subject had seemed off limits, so I'd never pushed. He'd told me that his father had died when he was young, but beyond that, I'd known almost nothing. For the first time, things were making some sense. Kirk had carried all of those emotions inside for so many years, and finally, they were surfacing. But, at least he was willing to admit that he had a problem—the first step to doing something about it.

"Kirk, I know you won't hurt our child, because you know that there's a problem. And, you're dealing with it. I know that you'll be able to do it. You can do anything that you set your mind to doing," I told him.

"That's my Mindy, ever the optimist. You always had confidence in me, and you still do, despite everything." Kirk smiled. "I don't want to let you down. I get scared sometimes, that I can't live up to your belief in me." He paused.

"It makes me more determined than ever, now that we're having a baby, because I want you to come home. I want us to be a family. I know I have no right to ask that of you, and I'm trying so hard not to pressure you, but I'd be a liar if I sat here and told you that it doesn't matter to me. It's everything to me, honey."

"If that's true," I said, "then you'll do it. But, Kirk, if I do come home, you have to know that if you ever hit me again, I will leave. I will press charges, and I will never, ever come back. I can't live in fear, and I won't put myself and the baby through it, ever again. We can get marriage counseling, and I'll go to your AA meetings with you and whatever else you need me to do, but I won't let you hit me, ever again. I want us to be a family, too. I think that maybe we can be, but the abuse can't ever happen again. And, I still need some more time to think about it, to be sure."

"Mindy, are you saying there's a chance you'll come home?" Kirk's eyes widened. "I mean, really? You'll seriously think about it? You'll give me another chance?"

"Yes, Kirk, there's a chance. I need more time to think, but you know that I'd never tell you that just to keep you hanging. I want things to work out between us for our sake—and, for our baby's sake."

"Oh, thank you! Thank you for giving me a chance. You deserve someone better than me. Mindy, I'm so sorry for what I've put you through, for hurting you. I just can't believe that you're giving me another chance. I love you."

Kirk smiled for the rest of the evening. We enjoyed a delicious meal, and we even danced. It was wonderful, and it was well past midnight when Kirk dropped me off at the apartment. He walked me to the door and, before I went in, kissed me so tenderly that it took my breath away. Kirk had never kissed me that way before.

When I walked in the door, Suzanne was waiting up for me. I'd hoped that she would be asleep, but I managed to mask my disappointment. I just wanted to think about the evening—and about the decision that I'd have to make. I really didn't want to have a confrontation with her just then.

"So, how'd it go with your dream date?" she asked sarcastically.

Resisting the urge to explode, I bit my lip. "I had a really nice time, Suzanne. Thanks for asking." I knew that it wasn't the answer that she'd wanted to hear, but I was trying to avoid a long discussion. Suzanne, however, was not to be put off.

"Really? I'd love to hear all about it. Was he a good little boy?" she asked snidely.

"Suzanne, please give me a break. I'm really tired, and I'd like to get some sleep. Can we talk about it in the morning? I promise that I'll tell you every detail then, okay? I had a nice time and we talked about things. But, I really don't want to get into it all tonight. Where's Ethan, anyway?"

"Ethan's out for the night, at a party. So, anyway, what did you talk about? Did you tell him how impressed you were with the clean apartment?" It was obvious that Suzanne wasn't going to let it drop. "Did you tell him that his magic act worked?"

By then, I decided that I'd had just about enough. "Suzanne, can't you just let it go? The subject of the apartment never even came up. We talked about us, about trying to work things out. He's really trying, and I think I want to give him another chance. I'm pretty sure that I want to move back home."

"You what?" Suzanne shrieked. "You can't be telling me that you're going to go back for more! Are you out of your mind?" Suzanne paced back and forth, her eyes narrow slits, her hands clenched in fists. I was frightened, and just wanted to evaporate. "How can you even think of going back to him? Do you love punishment? Do you enjoy being abused?"

"Suzanne, you're way out of line! And, I'm sorry, but it's really none of your business. I mean, I appreciate everything that you and Ethan have done for me, I really do, but I'm pregnant. I owe it to my baby to give my marriage another chance. I have to try. Can't you understand that?" I asked.

"All I understand is that he plays you for a fool and you fall for it! He doesn't love you—you know that, don't you? But, still, you're falling right into his trap. How can you be so blind that you can't tell who loves you, and who doesn't?"

"He does love me. He's got some problems you don't know anything about, and he's working them out. We can get counseling to work out our problems together. Can't you be happy for me?" I wanted so much for her to understand.

That question seemed to put her right over the edge. "Happy for you? Happy to see him pull your strings? Happy to see you walk out of here, into a nightmare? Oh, I'm real happy, can't you tell? Mindy, you can stay here with us. I've told you that. Please, don't leave." There was desperation in her voice. "Mindy, please stay. I love you, and I'm afraid of what he might do," she told me, her voice breaking with emotion.

"I love you, too. You're my friend, Suzanne. I don't know what I would have done without you. You've been great, and it means a lot to me, but I belong with Kirk."

"You don't get it, do you?" Suzanne reached out, touching my hair. "I'm in love with you, Mindy. I want you to stay because I'll go crazy, worrying about you with him—and because I'm in love with you. Stay here with me, where you'll be safe. Don't go." Tears were streaming down her face.

"I can't stay, Suzanne. Even if I didn't love Kirk and wasn't pregnant or married, it wouldn't change anything. Suzanne, I'm not a lesbian, and I don't share your feelings. I care for you as a friend, not a lover."

"How in the world would you know? Have you ever been with a woman? Don't knock it until you've tried it. Stay with me, Mindy. At least give it a fair chance. You're willing to go back to someone who abused you, and who doesn't love you? That's a lot riskier than what I'm asking. Please—"

"I'm sorry, Suzanne," I broke in. "I've made up my mind. I'm going to go back to Kirk and try to make our marriage work. I know that it's the right thing for me. I have to do this."

"Okay, sure. Whatever." Suzanne stared at me blankly, and then turned and walked down the hallway to the bedroom, closing the door behind her.

Her sudden change of demeanor alarmed me, and I tiptoed down the hall, listening at the door. There was a strange, sporadic clicking noise coming from inside the room, but I heard nothing else.

Back in the living room, I grabbed the phone and dialed Kirk's number. Whispering, I told him to pick me up first thing in the morning. I told him to park outside and wait for me. He wanted to ask questions, but I told him that I'd explain everything in the morning. I didn't want Suzanne to come out and find me plotting an escape.

Suzanne never came out of the bedroom that night, and Ethan never came home from the party, so I spent the night awake, hoping and praying that I was doing the right thing. I knew that I couldn't stay there any longer, knowing Suzanne's true feelings, even if I had wanted to. Truthfully, I was a little afraid of her, and although I cared about her, I didn't trust her completely. She seemed to change moods and attitudes like most people changed their clothes. Her unpredictability made me uneasy. Besides, I knew that my place was with Kirk and our baby.

In the morning, I gathered my things and began watching out the living room window for Kirk's car. At five minutes before seven, I spotted him coming into the driveway, and I ran out to meet him, in case he'd forgotten that I had told him to wait in the car. In my haste, I realized that I'd forgotten my things. I turned to go back after them.

"No, honey, go on and get in the car. I'll go after them, and don't worry, I won't make any noise." Kirk turned and smiled at me, and bounded up the sidewalk. As I approached the car, I turned toward the building and noticed a long, dark object sticking through the open door of Suzanne's apartment. I heard a loud noise, like the sound of a car backfiring, and watched, dazed and numb, as Kirk spun around and fell backward onto the grass.

As I ran toward my husband, Suzanne's door slammed shut. Kneeling beside Kirk, I realized that he'd been shot. There was a gaping hole in his neck, and blood poured from it as I cradled his head in my arms.

Oh, God, please don't let this be happening, I prayed.

"I'm here, baby, I'm here. Hold on," I begged. Kirk's face was a white as a sheet, but he was alive and trying to say something to me. "No, baby, don't talk. It's okay, honey. Don't talk."

"I love you," Kirk whispered. And then, he was gone.

"No, no, no!" I screamed. "Please, no!" There was no one around, no one to help me as my husband lay dead in the wet grass. I was hysterical with grief and disbelief as I cradled his head in my lap, screaming for help.

What happened next is frozen in my memory like a videotape on fast forward. I remember being surrounded by police, being pulled away from Kirk's body by one of the officers, being guided to a police car where I was asked so many questions. I couldn't form words well enough to answer. There were sirens, lights, and police everywhere. They were surrounding the apartment building. I heard a voice blaring through a bullhorn. An officer put his jacket around my shoulders to protect me from the damp chill of the morning air.

They were taking pictures of Kirk as ambulance attendants stood ready to take him away. When they were done, the attendants lifted my husband's body onto the stretcher, and blood poured onto the ground. I watched as they covered his face, put the stretcher into the ambulance, and drove away.

A familiar voice came over the bullhorn, begging Suzanne to come out of the apartment, begging her to give herself up. It was Ethan! I knew that if anyone could get her to come out, he could. Over and over, he pleaded with her, until finally, the front door slowly opened. Police were all around, their guns aimed at the opening door. Suzanne threw the gun out onto the sidewalk, and slowly stepped outside. She was immediately surrounded by the police officers. She was searched, handcuffed, and led to a police car.

Throwing down the bullhorn, Ethan pushed through the gathering crowd and ran to me. "Mindy! Are you all right?" He held me in his arms, and I clung to him, shaking and crying uncontrollably. "I'm here now, and I'll be with you every minute. You're not alone, Mindy, I'm here."

And he was there, through every agonizing moment of the days that followed. He was there through the statements to the police, and my testimony at Suzanne's arraignment. He sat with me through the empty, numbing nights before the funeral, and he helped me to make the arrangements for the service. He shielded me from the prying questions of the neighbors, and from the press—hungry for a juicy story.

After the funeral, Ethan told me that he had a few weeks of vacation time coming from work, and he took me to his family's house by the beach. He sat and held me when I cried, which was often, and he never let me be alone. We spent endless hours going over what had happened, never understanding it completely.

Suzanne had used Ethan's gun to kill Kirk. Ethan had felt partly responsible for Kirk's death, until I'd reassured him that I didn't blame him. And, he'd blamed himself for not realizing how obsessive Suzanne really was. But, as I told him, she'd been very good at hiding her true feelings.

The trial was difficult. If not for Ethan, I didn't how I would have gotten through it. We learned on each other. The two of us together were stronger than either one of us were separately. In the months following the murder, and during the trial, a deep bond was forged between us. Suzanne was found guilty of first-degree murder, and was sentenced to life in prison without parole. Her family completely abandoned her.

I can't bring myself to visit her, but Ethan has gone to see her from time to time. He says that there is almost no trace of the Suzanne that he once knew and loved. I suppose prison can do that, especially to someone like Suzanne, who has no one.

I went into therapy right after Kirk died, and it has helped me so much. Sometimes, I battle depression, but I'm healing more every day.

I often wonder what might have happened if Kirk had lived. When I think of him, I like to remember him the way he was, the night before he died—finally coming to terms with his demons. And, I think that, had he lived, we would have made it. I want to think that, and after everything, I'm entitled to believe it. But, I have moved on with my life. I believe that Kirk would have wanted me to.

Little Kirk Ethan Hartman made his appearance in the world right on schedule, and he is the light of my life. Ethan coached me in the delivery room and in the months since then, he's been his usual indispensable self. Last night, he asked me to marry him. I said yes. My mother always told me that one day, she wanted me to marry my best friend. I know that she'd approve.

THE END

I'LL BE WIFE #5
Should I marry him?

"Marissa, will you marry me?"

Jake's eyes were filled with sensitivity, intelligence, passion, and love for me. Although he was surely the man I'd been dreaming about my entire life, I hesitated. Jake loved me unconditionally, respected me, and wanted to spend the rest of his life with me. So why didn't I just leap into his arms and scream, "Yes!"

Jake and I met at the lowest time in my life. A few months earlier, I'd been dumped by my fiancé, Dalton James. I'd thought Dalton was the perfect man, but I was apparently a poor judge of character. Two months before our wedding, as we were finalizing our plans for our Hawaiian honeymoon at the travel agency, he met Cheyenne Blake, the trampy little travel agent who set her mind on snatching him away from me. Before I knew what hit me, he broke our engagement, telling me he realized he didn't want to get married after all.

So there I was, thirty-two years old and alone. Dalton and I had been together for ten years, and I felt as though I'd spent my entire adult life with him. We'd been living together in his home, with his furniture, his appliances, even his dog. I owned nothing besides my clothing and the few possessions I'd brought along when I moved in with him.

So I gathered up what was left of my pride, as well as my meager belongings and my broken heart, and moved out. I rented a tiny furnished studio apartment downtown, near my office. It wasn't much, but it matched my state of mind, which was dark and gloomy.

And then, like a hurt animal, I went into hiding to lick my wounds. My best friend, Katie, tried to pull me out of the hole I'd dug for myself, but even her love and kindness couldn't salve my bruised ego.

Every morning I woke up groggy, but I had to go to work. As a paralegal, I spent my days researching law books and journals, as well as taking notes during depositions. As I yawned uncontrollably, I'd wish I were home in my bed. But yet, when I finally left work, my home was no salvation either. I sat in front of the tiny TV screen and ate a sandwich, finally falling asleep with dreams of strolling the beach in Hawaii with Dalton. Sometimes I'd wake up sobbing for the man that didn't love me anymore.

My heart was broken, and I'd given up on love forever. Katie, the eternal optimist, tried convincing me that there was a special man out there for me, alive and breathing the same air I was, and that all I had to do was get out there and find him, but I didn't believe her.

Fortunately, Jake found me because I sure wasn't looking for him. We met in the video store, where I was renting my weekend entertainment. We both reached for the same video at the same second, and our hands collided in mid-air as we grabbed for it.

He won only because he was taller and quicker. Annoyed, I turned to look at the rude person with the long slim fingers that had snatched the prize, and instead I felt myself drowning in the most beautiful eyes I'd ever seen. I could feel them smiling at me before I even saw his face. He held the tape out toward me.

"Here, you can have it. It appears to be the last copy, but I can see it anytime."

He had a very pleasant, masculine voice, and I thought it was a very nice gesture on his part. I thanked him politely and turned away, barely glancing at his face, although I couldn't forget those eyes.

In the parking lot, I sensed someone walking behind me. In the back of my mind I wondered if it could be him. I slowed up, and sure enough it was.

He was smiling at me, and I smiled back without realizing I was doing so. I'd never been one to believe in love as first sight, but it happened to me, right in the middle of the parking lot. My legs got weak as I stared at him, taking every inch of him in and devouring him.

Besides those deliciously warm eyes, he was tall and slim, with wonderful hair, a straight nose, full sensuous lips, and a deliciously sexy smile. I had an incredible urge to kiss him, my face flaming at my strangely erotic thoughts.

"Hi, I'm Jake Spencer," he said, extending his hand.

"I'm uhhh . . . Marissa," I whispered stupidly, temporarily losing my voice as my hand reached out to meet his. As we touched, the electricity flowing between us was unmistakable, and I instantly dropped my hand as though I'd been electrocuted.

He began chatting about the video, while I listened, unable to think of one halfway intelligent thing to say. But he persevered, and eventually I found my voice and my wits. It became easier to talk with him, and before I knew what I was doing, I'd given him my phone number and accepted a dinner date with him for the following night.

Driving home, reality set in and I wondered about what I'd done. Jake Spencer was a total stranger, but yet I'd accepted a date with him. This was totally unlike me, but from the moment I met Jake it was as though I knew he was someone special.

I called Katie the second I walked in the door and told her everything.

"Marissa, that's wonderful! I knew it," she exclaimed happily. "He's the one I told you about, the man I was sure you'd meet!"

Maybe he is, I tried convincing myself, although I was afraid to admit that I was excited over a man for the first time since Dalton dumped me for Cheyenne.

Later that evening, as I rummaged through my tiny closet to find a suitable outfit to wear on my date, I decided that I had nothing but rags and needed to shop on my lunch hour the next day to find something spectacular.

I found a beautiful sky-blue suit in the first store I dashed into. The saleswoman remarked that it must've been made for me as it brought out my eyes. I bought it on the spot without even looking at the price tag. For the first time in ages, money was no object.

I was ready a half-hour early, so I called Katie for moral support. I was so nervous I could barely talk. Katie laughed and assured me that all I had to do was be myself and I'd be fine. Easy for her to say!

When Jake came to my door and smiled at me, I again marveled at how handsome he was. He handed me a perfect long-stemmed red rose and smiled, his left eyebrow arching slightly in such an endearing way it melted my heart. He told me how pretty I looked, causing me to blush like a lovesick teenager.

Over dinner at a lovely restaurant he'd chosen at the shore, Jake told me about himself. He was a high school math teacher who loved his job and his students, deriving a great deal of satisfaction when he was able to "turn on the light bulb in their minds" as he phrased it, smiling warmly at me.

His parents were retired and living down south, and his sister and her family lived in a neighboring state. He was politically active and volunteered for many charitable organizations. When we began discussing our likes and dislikes, we found several things in common, such as dancing, rock and roll, funny movies, reading, and old television sitcoms. He also had a hobby of traveling across the country, visiting offbeat museums. I laughed at his amusing stories of the weird museums he'd seen.

That night was like magic. By the time we got back to my apartment and Jake took me in his arms and kissed me gently, I melted to his touch, wanting his kiss to last forever. Jake captivated me, but the feelings I had for him scared me to death.

As soon as he left, with a promise to call me the next day, I called Katie, telling her every little thing that happened and every single word he spoke to me, including the kiss that swept me off my feet.

"Wow, Marissa, it sounds like he's really gotten under your skin," she teased, laughing happily.

I was happy, too, but I was frightened as well. Would Jake return my feelings, or would he hurt me the same way Dalton had? Fortunately, I didn't have to wait long to find out.

Jake called me bright and early the next day. He said he couldn't wait to hear my voice again. I felt the same way, and knew I'd love nothing more than to spend the rest of my life hearing his sweet voice first thing every morning, whispering words of love in my ear as he softly tickled my earlobe with his kisses.

When I got to work, I found a lovely bouquet of autumn flowers on my desk, the attached card telling me what a wonderful time he had, and hoping I would join him that night for the Fall Festival at his school.

I called him and left a message on his voice mail, happily accepting his invitation, as well as thanking him for the beautiful flowers. He returned my call at lunch hour, and his smooth voice again made my insides turn to mush.

"Marissa, you make me so very happy, you know."

Oh I knew all right, because I felt the same way. But a part of me felt like I should be cautious. Then I rationalized that we were only going to his school, and then for a bite to eat afterward. There was nothing to be afraid of.

Later, as we strolled around the gym, which was beautifully decorated for the season, he introduced me to several of his colleagues, his arm lightly surrounding my waist. Afterward, he took me to a cozy Italian restaurant for a light supper. We sat alongside each other in the booth instead of across from each other, and after giving our order to the waitress, he took my hand and held it as he gazed deeply into my eyes, turning my insides to liquid fire.

"Marissa, I don't know how to say this but I have to try. It's crazy, I know we only know each other a few days, but I feel as though I've known you my whole life. Darling, I love you. Please, you don't have to say anything, but that's how I feel about you."

Joy filled my heart at his words. It was crazy, I knew, but I imagined that sometimes love happened in the craziest ways, and I'd be the world's biggest fool if I turned it away.

"Oh, Jake, I love you, too," I blurted, my eyes filling with happy tears. He brought my hand up to his lips, kissing each fingertip tenderly, causing me to cry at the intense feelings of love that were coursing through my body.

My tears embarrassed me, but he gently wiped them away, telling me that my tears were my way of showing him my love. He was right about that. I did love him, but how could I? I hardly knew him.

We shared a salad and a gourmet pizza, feeding each other morsels from our plates, kissing and touching between bites. We were acting like giggly teenagers, but we didn't mind the amused stares we received from those around us. They didn't exist—there was nobody in the world but us.

When we got back to my apartment, I made a pot of coffee. As we sat and drank at my little table, Jake said he had something important to tell me, his face suddenly turning somber.

Here it comes. I knew it was too good to be true. My romance will be over before it has a chance to begin, I thought.

"Marissa, please, get that look off your face—it's not that terrible," he joked, smiling weakly as his eyebrow arched in that endearing way he had.

"You see darling . . . the thing is, well, I've been married a few times."

"A few times?" I blurted. "What does a few mean?"

"Well, a few means four to be exact."

My mind raced as my face fell. "Four?"

He looked stricken. "Marissa, darling, please," he said, his eyes begging me to understand, but I was suddenly struck dumb as a post, and I began rambling stupidly.

"Four times? I don't know what to say. Maybe you're fickle, or maybe you just like the feeling of being in love. I don't know, maybe you have a commitment problem with women—" I said, stopping before I made a total fool of myself.

"Let me explain, okay. Please?"

I nodded. Of course I'd listen to what he had to say. He'd have to have a logical explanation!

"Marissa, my first marriage was when I was eighteen, right out of high school. She was seventeen, and we thought we were so cool. We got married at the beach at sunrise, and she wore flowers woven into her hair. It was very hippie-ish and our parents hated every second of it, but we were madly in love."

His eyes clouded with his own private memories.

"So what happened?"

"After a while, she decided that being married to me interfered with her dating." He chuckled. "So we got a divorce after about a year."

"Oh," was all I could muster.

"Then I married my second wife when I was twenty-two, right after I graduated college," he said. "We met there, went together a few months, and moved in together. My parents loved her as much as I did, and I thought this one would last, until I found out she liked drugs a little too much."

He looked at me, and I could see the pain etched in his face. This was definitely not easy for him, but he'd offered, after all, and I had to know his past if I planned on being a part of his future.

"So we got divorced when she almost set the house on fire one night, letting her pot cigarette fall from her hand while she lay drugged out on the couch. I couldn't be a watchdog twenty-four hours a day, and she absolutely refused to get help."

My mind was trying to absorb this information as fast as he was relating it. Two wives, one too young, the next addicted to drugs.

"Angela was my third wife—she was pretty and funny and sexy and she made me feel special—the problem was that she lied to me about wanting children. I'd made it plain I wanted to have a family, and she agreed with me until after we married. I found out she'd been taking birth control pills behind my back, and then she admitted to me that she had a fear of childbirth. She said she'd never go through the agony of delivering a baby. How could I trust her after that?"

He paused as though waiting for my answer, but I remained silent.

"I tried accepting her decision because I loved her, but I no longer respected her. She'd lied to me—not exactly a small lie, either—and I couldn't get past that. We began arguing more and more, over everything else in our lives, not just the baby issue, and eventually things had deteriorated so badly, we agreed to divorce.

"Number four was Breanna," he continued. "A friend at work fixed us up, thinking we'd be perfect for each other. I wasn't very eager to get married again, as you can imagine, but I really cared for her, so I thought I'd give marriage one more chance—I thought this one would be forever. And it was my longest marriage actually, eleven years, but Breanna wasn't exactly a physical woman, nor was she affectionate—hugging and kissing made her uncomfortable. She didn't care much for sex, either. I kind of knew about her lack of passion when we got married, but I thought I'd somehow live with it, but I had needs. Do you know how difficult it is to live without physical intimacy? I felt lonely and unloved, and although I'm not proud of what I did, I had an affair with a married woman, Gabriella was her name. It wasn't planned, it just happened, and we fell in love."

His mind seemed to drift back into his memories, and I sat as still as I could until he continued.

"Gabriella was very dear to me, and the pain and heartbreak we both experienced when we stopped seeing each other was something I'll never forget. She was married and had two children, but she had no intention of breaking up her family, although she said she loved me more than life itself," he said ruefully, and I could see the sharp pain etched in his face as he told me about his loss of Gabriella.

Apparently, this was a love affair not easily forgotten. I have to admit I felt an unreasonable stab of jealousy at the love he felt for Gabriella, and I wondered if he was over her yet.

"Of course, when Breanna found out about my affair, which was inevitable because I'd taken so many risks to spend time with Gabriella, she was furious with me and threw me out. Breanna didn't give second chances, so that was the end of that."

He paused and looked searchingly into my face, causing me to burn with longing for this man I was loving more and more by the second, despite everything he was revealing to me.

"Marissa, darling, I had to tell you all of this now. I'm not proud of some of the things I've done in my past, but that's what it is, the past, and you, my sweet beautiful Marissa, are my present and hopefully my future, if you allow me to show you how much I love you."

"Oh, Jake," I said as he took me into his arms and showed me with his lips exactly how much he cared.

That night made me realize how much I loved Jake, and despite his past, and mine, I was finally willing to take a chance and allow him into my heart.

I called Katie as soon as he left. Although it was late, she was used to my late-evening "crisis calls," as she called them.

I related the story as best as I could remember it.

"Four wives? And he cheated on the last one and fell in love with his married lover? Swell, Marissa, just swell! A real winner you got there."

Her words were sarcastic, but I couldn't be angry with her because she was being honest. "Not a great track record, Marissa. You're not really considering this guy for anything permanent, are you? I mean, for a date or a quickie, that's fine."

Even though she was crude, I couldn't really argue with her. Perhaps she was seeing things the way they really were, while I was seeing Jake with stardust in my eyes, which prevented me from seeing the way things really were. And as far as permanent, who knew?

"But, Katie, I love him," I blurted as though that explained everything. "Wait and see, you'll love him, too," I added with more confidence than I felt.

I decided to take the bull by the horns and get Katie and Jake to meet, so I invited them to dinner, along with Victor, Katie's boyfriend of the day. The food turned out delicious, and by the time the evening was over, I could tell that Katie was totally captivated by Jake's delightful personality.

And two months later when Jake proposed to me, I accepted without a moment's hesitation. I was so madly in love, all I cared about was Jake. I no longer cared about a big wedding, and since Jake had already walked down the aisle four times, he was reluctant to invite more than a handful of his closest relatives and his best friend who stood up for him.

We got married in the middle of a major snowstorm in a lovely restaurant in the city. Altogether there were about twenty guests, including our parents, close friends, and a few people from work.

Although I didn't wear a long gown and veil, I wore an ivory suit trimmed in iridescent pearls and felt every inch a bride with Jake at my side.

Jake had apologized that he couldn't take me to Hawaii for our honeymoon, since it was way too expensive. But I no longer cared about Hawaii; just being married to Jake, knowing I'd spend every night in his arms, being held and loved by him, made me the happiest bride in the world.

Instead of Hawaii, we took a long weekend and went to the mountains, where we attempted to ski during the day and made wonderful exciting love at night. In our log cabin, in our large four-poster bed, while the heat from the roaring fireplace cozily warmed our bodies, Jake made love to me until I practically passed out from the intense passion he ignited in me. I knew I'd never tire of his hands and his lips roaming my body in ways I'd never imagined existed.

When we returned home, I moved into Jake's apartment, which was the entire top floor of an old Victorian house. It was bright and spacious and airy. I loved living there with him, going to bed with him and making love with him half the night, waking up in his arms. I truly loved everything about being Mrs. Jake Spencer.

Life was kind to us. I was promoted to office manager, which included a substantial raise. Although we both wanted children, we had to wait a while because money was an issue for us. Jake had several family responsibilities, which included contributing toward the tuition for his college-aged niece and nephew, as well as helping his parents financially, since they were elderly and on a fixed income. I didn't mind waiting to become pregnant anyway, because frankly, I was a little selfish and wanted Jake all to myself for a while longer before the babies and diapers interfered.

Jake was the perfect husband. Everything we did was fun. Jake made going to the laundromat a fun experience. We'd bring along a deck of cards and our CD player and talk and laugh and play gin rummy and listen to oldies, sometimes getting up to dance as our clothes tumbled in the dryer.

Even watching television in bed was fun with Jake alongside me. We'd bring food with us, sharing popcorn and soda and fruit, feeding each other and making a mess and then lying in the crumbs to make love while the television blasted away.

On weekends we'd roam the city, meandering around the various neighborhoods, going to flea markets, street fairs, museums—I'd taken the city for granted until I saw it through Jake's eyes, and then it became the most exciting place in the world.

Sometimes we'd go out with Katie and whoever she was dating at the time. I kept trying to fix her up with Jake's friends so that she could be as delirious as I was, but so far we hadn't come up with any good matches. But it didn't stop me from trying.

I marveled at how well Katie and Jake got along, especially after the way Katie tried discouraging me at the beginning. And Jake was very fond of Katie, too; they could spend hours discussing and debating local politics, a subject I knew nothing about. I was glad they had something in common because they were my two favorite people in the world, and I wanted them to be friends.

When we finally decided to become pregnant, I found it hard to conceive. We tried for several months to no avail, so I went to the doctor for a checkup. Dr. Morrison told me to relax and it would happen. We relaxed, and we tried and tried, but with each month that we failed, I became more determined, which led to more failure. I felt as though I was disappointing Jake; I knew how badly he wanted children. The story about his third wife and his childless marriage echoed in my mind. More than anything, I wanted to please him and make him glad he married me, but with each month's failure, a little part of me died.

Our third anniversary was approaching, and I wanted to be able to tell Jake I was pregnant as my gift to him, but it didn't seem likely. I became increasingly despondent. Coincidentally, Jake began coming home later and later from work. Many evenings I'd come home from work and find the apartment dark, a scribbled note on the counter telling me he had to do something or other, or he was volunteering at the school for one project or another, or he was at one of his various meetings.

We no longer danced in the laundromat, nor did we make love much, either. It seemed that Jake was always tired or preoccupied, and I was so worried about what was happening to us, I wasn't acting normal, either. Apparently, the stardust in our eyes was fading, and I had this horrible fear that our romance was fading as well.

One morning Jake told me not to bother cooking dinner, that he had a parent-teacher conference after school and then a rehearsal for the class play, and he'd pick up a quick sandwich if he was hungry. For the first time ever, I sensed he was lying to me, so when I got home, I called the school and got one of the faculty members, who informed me that he'd seen Jake leaving the school hours earlier. When I asked him about the rehearsal, he told me there was no rehearsal that night. I asked if he was sure, and he assured me he was, as the school was totally empty except for him and the custodian, who was waiting with key in hand to let him out and lock up after him.

My stomach flip-flopped with gut-wrenching anxiety, and I began to shake all over. Jake had lied to me. But why? Was it because I'd become such a miserable wife? Because he was bored with me already? Because I couldn't give him a child? Because I'd lost interest in sex? That had to be it, I was convinced! Jake was cheating on me because I was refusing him sex, just as he cheated on Breanna for the very same reason!

I was beside myself. Could he be with Gabriella, the woman he'd been so madly in love with? My stomach tightened with jealousy at the thought of him making love to the faceless, but no doubt voluptuous and exotic, Gabriella. Was history repeating itself? Or perhaps I'd driven Jake away because of my obsession to have a baby, because I didn't want him to wind up leaving me like he did his third wife, and now he was cheating on me with his ex-lover?

Katie had apparently been right about Jake. Why hadn't I listened to her warnings? How could I have married a man with such a track record?

I decided to call Katie to tell her how right she was, but I got her voice mail. I was annoyed because I needed her, and because I could've sworn she told me she'd be home all night.

I began to cry at the hopelessness of the situation. I had nobody to talk to. I felt alone and miserable, and I was convinced I'd lost Jake. He was out somewhere, probably making wild passionate love to Gabriella, while I was home alone, nursing my wounded heart.

I began pacing the apartment like a caged bear, thinking of what to do. Should I confront him about my knowledge of his lie about being at school, or should I just let it go?

When Jake came home, I pretended to be asleep to avoid a confrontation. I didn't want to have it out with him until I had more facts. When I woke up the next morning, Jake was gone, but there was a note from him, informing me he'd be late again, as he had a club meeting. He belonged to many clubs and he didn't say which club it was, so I had no way of checking up on him.

Katie finally called me back, but she was short with me, telling me she was very busy at work and couldn't talk. I told her we could talk that night, but she told me she was going out and would call me when she had time.

Again my stomach began doing those flip-flops. Something was very wrong, but I wouldn't allow myself to dwell on what I was suddenly imagining about my husband and my best friend. But that was insane! First Gabriella, and now my best friend. My imagination was working overtime and I forced the thoughts out of my head. But they were both so vague about their whereabouts!

I had to keep my mind occupied, so when I got home I prepared a dinner I couldn't eat and then began working on the afghan I was knitting as Jake's anniversary present, which was now less than two months away.

After dinner I tried calling Katie, thinking I'd catch her before her date, but I got her voice mail again. I left a sarcastic message, telling her to call me back if she could spare two minutes from her busy schedule. It had been such a long time since we'd had one decent conversation—it was now fairly obvious to me that she was avoiding me.

That night, I waited up for Jake. I hid the afghan under the table when I heard his key in the door. He entered the living room, busying himself at his desk, opening his mail without saying much to me.

"How was your club meeting?" I asked casually, staring at the newspaper without reading one word.

"The meeting? Oh, yeah, the meeting, it was fine," he replied, still playing with his mail and deliberately avoiding me, or so it appeared.

He bent over to give me a quick kiss, and for a split second I could've sworn I detected a whiff of a familiar perfume although I couldn't be a hundred percent certain. I felt sick to my stomach for what I was thinking, or maybe it was the smell of the perfume, or maybe I had an upset stomach, but whatever it was, I wanted to vomit, and I did, barely making it to the bathroom in time.

"Marissa, are you alright in there?" Jake's voice sounded worried, but I didn't care. This was entirely his fault anyway—he deserved to suffer a little bit, too.

He continued to stay out several evenings a week, always making up excuses I couldn't check up on. His alibis were evasive, like attending one of his various club meetings, or helping out a "friend" with a chore, or a conference with a parent of one of his students who was bedridden.

I finally spoke to Katie, but she was definitely hiding something from me. When I asked her what she was so busy doing, she said she'd been working crazy hours and was very involved with her new boyfriend and didn't have much time to talk anymore. I almost asked her if her new boyfriend happened to be my husband, but I held my tongue in my mouth, ashamed of my thoughts. She'd been my best friend since fourth grade. If I couldn't trust Katie, who could I trust?

I continued to feel sick, like I had the flu or something, but I attributed it to my poor eating habits and my anxiety over Jake. He and I were drifting further apart as we spent less and less time together, and it was tearing me to pieces. I was slowly losing it and didn't know what to do.

And then it was the week of our anniversary, and one morning at breakfast, Jake asked me if I'd like to do anything special that weekend to celebrate. I didn't really care. I had no gift for him; the half-crocheted afghan was rolled in a ball behind the sofa, and I had no ambition to finish it. And anyway, who cared about celebrating the anniversary of a crumbling marriage?

I told him it made no difference to me, that I was feeling under the weather anyway.

"Honey, I don't like the way you've been feeling. Shouldn't you see a doctor or something? You don't look so hot."

I wanted to punch him. I didn't look so hot? How did he expect me to look when I was ready to scream at him in anger and frustration all the time?

"I'm fine, Jake, I'm just tired, that's all." I replied in an even voice although my insides were tied in knots.

"Okay, then, how about if I make reservations at The Diamond Room for Saturday night? We can have dinner there and maybe even dance like the old days? Remember how we danced at our wedding, baby?"

With that memory, he held out his arms for me, and I reluctantly stood up and began dancing with him in the middle of the kitchen at eight o' clock in the morning. It felt so good to be held in his arms, but the thought of him dancing with another woman, or worse, making love to her—Katie or perhaps the ravishing Gabriella—turned me cold, and I pushed him away before he could see the pain in my eyes.

He looked hurt, too, but my heart was turning cold to him. I thought he had no right to look hurt when I was so miserable because of him. History was repeating itself, that was for sure. I never should've married a man who had such a past—four wives and four divorces. The way things were going I'd probably be number five.

I called Katie on my lunch hour and asked her how her new boyfriend was doing.

"Who?" she asked evasively.

"Your new boyfriend, remember?" I screeched. "You told me you had a new boyfriend and that's why you had no time for me!"

"Oh yes, my new boyfriend. Do you mean Dakota? He's fine."

The tone of Katie's voice convinced me that she was lying to me. First Jake, then Katie. Everyone I loved was turning against me, for whatever reason, I had no idea, but little by little my world was crumbling around me. Whether Jake was carrying on with Gabriella or Katie made no difference anymore. All I knew was that I'd lost him for sure, and with that thought, I became nauseous and ran to the ladies' room, where I vomited my lunch.

Saturday approached, and the thought of celebrating a doomed marriage was more than I could handle. I went through the motions with as much enthusiasm as one would have preparing for a root canal.

On Saturday morning, I awakened to find a bouquet of flowers on my nightstand and a carafe of my favorite flavored coffee.

"Happy anniversary, darling," Jake exclaimed as he entered the bedroom, a big smile decorating his handsome face. My heart twinged as I recalled seeing that smile for the first time in the video store, and now it brought tears to my eyes, knowing our marriage was over.

The rest of the day passed quickly. Jake had his usual Saturday errands, or maybe he was with Gabriella. I tortured myself thinking of this and spent the day feeling sorry for myself. I dragged myself around the apartment, puttering and doing a little ironing, sewing, and taking care of my neglected appearance to prepare for our evening out. I looked pale, thin, and unhealthy, and my hair hung in strings around my gaunt, unhappy face, but I tried my best to smile as I bathed, perfumed, fixed my hair, did my makeup, and got dressed.

Jake looked more handsome than ever. He wore a charcoal gray suit, a white shirt, and the new silk tie his parents had sent for his birthday. When he smiled at me, I thought my heart would break because I loved him so much, but I was convinced this would be our last anniversary together.

I had found a dress buried in the back of my closet. I'd never worn it because it had never fit me right. But I found it now fit me perfectly except for a slight snugness around the middle. It was blue, Jake's favorite color—the same color I'd worn on our first date—but it was a short dress, low cut in the front, and very sexy.

Jake's eyes nearly popped out of his head when I came out of the bedroom after spending hours pulling myself into shape.

"Wow, look at you! Marissa, you're gorgeous." He smiled as his eyes roamed my body hungrily.

I blushed madly but said nothing. It thrilled me that he thought I looked pretty and desired me again. Maybe there was hope yet! If only I felt as good on the inside as I looked on the outside. I was still sick to my stomach, which I completely attributed to nerves.

As we drove to the restaurant, Jake casually informed me that he'd invited Katie to our little celebration.

"Katie? Why?" I asked, my stomach turning in misery once again.

"Because Katie is your best friend, and I thought it would make you happy not having to be alone with me," he replied in a tight voice. I didn't say one more word. The evening was turning bizarre, that was for sure. Why would he invite Katie to our romantic dinner?

When we arrived at the restaurant, we were escorted to a table where Katie and a strange man were already seated. She smiled and introduced him.

"Marissa, this is Dakota. Dakota, meet Marissa—finally!"

"Dakota?" My heart leapt in joy. So there really was a Dakota!

"Nice meeting you, Marissa." He smiled, shaking my hand warmly.

He turned to Jake and smiled, clapping my husband on the back in a very friendly manner.

"Hey buddy, how's it going?"

144

"It's going great, Dakota, I hope," Jake replied, his face split in a smile like a jack-o-lantern as he gazed at me with the love in his eyes I remembered from what seemed like a million years ago.

Something very strange was going on. Dakota knew Jake, but how? And why were Katie and Dakota with us in the first place? I felt like I was in an upside down world, and I could take it no longer. My head was beginning to spin dizzily, which made me nauseous again.

"Okay, what's going on here?"

The three of them looked at each other and all began smiling at once.

Jake reached over and took my hand, the love in his eyes shining brightly, which brought immediate tears to my eyes. I was so emotional—whatever was wrong with me?

"Darling, I have so much to say to you. First of all, I'm so sorry for everything. I've been fibbing to you lately, but I have a very good reason, which you'll soon see."

I looked to the three of them, to Katie, then to Dakota, then back to Jake. And then Katie spoke to me.

"Marissa, I'm sorry, too, for avoiding you. Honey, you know how I can't keep a secret to save my life."

She began giggling nervously the way I remembered from when we were kids, and then I began giggling along with her, until we both had tears running down our cheeks as we roared hysterically.

Dakota completely cracked us up when he just smiled and said, "Hey, don't look at me, I never lied to you."

When the laughter died down, Jake took my hand and caressed it gently.

"Happy anniversary, Marissa," he said as he reached into his jacket pocket. He removed an envelope and handed it to me with a big grin on his face.

I took it with shaky hands, looking deep into his eyes, knowing this was something very special.

"Come on, honey, please open it."

I did, and I immediately began sobbing like a baby.

Inside the envelope were two airline tickets to Hawaii along with reservations for two weeks at a popular resort hotel. I looked at him, my eyes swimming with tears.

"Our second honeymoon, darling," Jake explained. "I know it was your dream honeymoon, but I couldn't afford it when we were first married. I'm so sorry."

"But how? We still can't afford it."

"Darling, that's why I was fibbing to you. I took a part-time job, and I was tutoring, too. I didn't want to tell you, because you'd ask me where the money was going. After all, you're the family accountant, so I had to make up the stories I did. I'm so sorry for doing that, but I wanted this to be a surprise. Don't be angry with me, baby, please?"

My tears were choking my throat so badly I could barely breathe, and I began babbling incoherently.

"Oh, Jake, I wish you'd have told me. I thought you were—Katie and you—and then I thought you and Gabriella—oh, I'm so sorry. I thought the very worst of you."

Then I broke into sobs, and Jake handed me his handkerchief, smiling lovingly at me.

"Hey, if anyone cares, I'm really grateful for this trip, too," Dakota said with a grin, and I was more confused than ever.

"I'm the owner of the travel agency you're using," he explained, glancing adoringly at Katie, who beamed back at him.

"This beautiful lady came in one day asking for Hawaiian brochures for her best friend, and after one look at her, I knew I was going to marry her," he said, taking Katie's hand and kissing it in the continental way.

Katie blushed, looking so happy I thought she'd burst.

"Marissa, that's the other good news. Dakota and I are engaged," she explained.

She thrust her left hand in my face to show me the diamond ring sparkling on her finger.

It was all too much for me. Everything was happening at once. Jake wasn't in love with another woman after all. We were going to Hawaii, Katie was getting married, and I was going to throw up again.

I ran to the bathroom, barely making it in time, Katie trailing behind me.

"Whatever is wrong with you? Why are you throwing up so much?"

"It's nerves," I assured her. "Or maybe it's a stomach virus."

"I'd see a doctor if I were you," she said, a worried look on her face, and I told her I'd think about it.

The rest of the evening was like a dream. When Jake and I got home, first we talked. I confronted him with all my fears and my mistrust of him because of his past. He assured me he loved me dearly and would never ever cheat on me—nor would he ever lie to me again under any circumstances, no matter what. Then we made tender, passionate love for the first time in weeks, and it was better than ever because there were no lies between us any longer.

And the first thing Monday morning, I called the doctor and was given an immediate appointment. To my utter amazement, I found out the reason for my upset stomach.

On the way home, I bought Jake a little gift. Then I took a long nap, and when I awoke I prepared a special dinner for us. By the time he got home, the table was set with candles, flowers, and our best dishes. The aroma of roast chicken and rosemary permeated the air.

"Hey, something smells great. What are we celebrating?" he asked as he lifted me in his arms for a kiss. "How do you feel?"

"We, my fantastic husband, we are celebrating our love, and I couldn't feel any better," I answered both his questions, holding him tight and kissing his lips.

I'd placed a gift-wrapped box on his plate.

"Hey, what's this for?"

"Why don't you open it and find out?"

He was like a child at Christmas, tearing at the paper. When he opened the box, I saw the tears of love fill his eyes.

He held up a tiny pair of booties and looked deeply into my eyes.

"Oh, Marissa, is this what I think it means?"

"No, they're for you to wear," I said, tears filling my eyes as I grinned with joy.

"Oh, darling, I'm so happy. Are you okay? What did the doctor say?"

"The doctor said that we're going to be parents in six and a half months, and that we'd better have a great time in Hawaii. Those were his orders."

Jake danced me around the living room, holding me in his arms tenderly, and later, after I reassured him it was okay, he made gentle, tender love to me, showing me exactly how much he adored me.

And much later, after he was asleep and I lay in his warm arms, safe and secure with my head on his chest, I made a promise that I'd never mistrust my husband again. He was the best thing that had ever happened to me, and I'd do everything in my power to make him as happy as he made me.

I came to the realization that it isn't fair to judge people by who they used to be. Today was all that mattered. Jake's past was just that, his past, and it had to remain there for us to go on with our lives. Our present included the two of us and the love we shared in anticipation of the birth of our child. And our future was the tiny life growing inside of me—the product of our love for each other. Jake was my past, my present, and my future. I loved him from the day I met him, and I'd love him for all our tomorrows.

THE END

I PUT A HEX ON MY EX
So he wouldn't remarry

I didn't know Jordan was seeing anybody. I guess I should have expected it. After all, we had been divorced for a year. I just wish I'd been warned about it before I showed up at his door that day. Instead, I dropped Bradley off for his weekend with his father and came face-to-face with my ex's beautiful girlfriend.

"I'm Tiffany," she said softly, extending a hand.

My shocked gaze went past her shoulder to the foyer in search of Jordan. He was nowhere in sight, so I had no choice but to take her hand and give it a feeble shake. Was this supposed to be some kind of joke?

"I'm Caroline," I replied. "Where is my husband?"

I called him that again. For some ungodly reason, I could never refer to Jordan as my ex, no matter how hard I tried. My parents kept correcting me. My sister told me I wasn't letting go. Even the girls at the salon where I worked said I hadn't fully accepted the divorce yet. I had, actually. Truly, I had. But, after six years of marriage, it was simply a habit to still refer to him that way. It was actually very understandable.

Large eyes scanned me up and down. Her glossed lips twitched with discomfort.

"Jordan is just getting out of the shower. Would you like to come in or just drop Bradley off?"

I glanced down at my son, who stood motionless by my side. He wasn't expecting a female greeter, either. The weekends he always spent at his dad's condo were their time together. Father and son. No women were part of the picture. Resentment began festering as I tightened my grip on Brad's hand.

"I'd like to speak with Jordan. Tell him I'm not leaving our son here until we get a chance to talk."

At least she had the decency to step aside and let us in. She was the stranger in this scenario, not Bradley and me. If anyone deserved to be kept standing out on the front stoop, it was her, not Jordan's wife and child. Ex-wife, Caroline. Get it straight for once. You've got to get used to these new labels! I told myself.

Just as we began suffering in awkward silence, Jordan came down the stairs. The sight of him always gave my heart quite a tug, but this time it was the smell that did me in. That just-showered-and-shaved smell. The one I knew so well. My mind flickered with memories of the showers we had taken together.

"Hey, Brad." He beamed, coming up and giving his boy a hug. "You remember Tiffany, right? She thought we could spend the day at her beach house again. Would you like that?"

My knees almost buckled as I looked down at Bradley. "You've met this woman before? You even went to her beach house?"

His heavy gaze dipped down to the rubber toes of his sneakers. "I didn't want to tell you. I didn't want you to get all mad."

Mad didn't even begin to cover it. Livid would have been a better description. If Jordan had a girlfriend spending time with my little boy, I had every right to know about it. He should've been the one to tell me so Brad didn't feel caught up in the middle. Such a coward, Jordan. Nothing has changed. You still can't tell the truth to save your life, I thought to myself.

"Why wasn't I informed about this?" I snapped. "You could've told me about her, Jordan. If you're taking Brad to some bimbo's house, you should've been man enough to let me know."

His eyes grazed Tiffany with care and then darted coldly to me. "I don't believe it's a part of the court order to have to report to you whom I spend time with or where I take Brad on our weekends. And for your information, Tiffany has her own pediatric practice. I hardly think a bimbo could live up to an accomplishment like that."

He knew how to zing me. One of the things I was always so sensitive about in our marriage was that I never went to college or got a degree in anything. Jordan and I got married shortly after graduating from high school because I discovered I had gotten pregnant right after our senior prom. We tried to wait until we were husband and wife, but that night was purely magical. We loved each other. We knew we'd spend our lives together, so making love under the stars in the backseat of his father's car didn't seem like such a crime. But, once we realized we had a child on the way and rushed our plans to marry, we knew my going to college would be too much.

He'd be the professional earning a good living, and I'd be a stay-at-home mom. As much as I loved devoting my life to my husband and baby, there was always a part of me that wasn't fulfilled, a part that longed to see who Caroline Winchester was apart from her marriage and her role as a mother. That stirring grew stronger as Brad got older and started spending time in preschool. Jordan and I would argue about it, arguments mostly initiated by my complaining. He'd tell me to enroll in college, that Brad was old enough to stay in preschool full-time, and if I wanted a career, I could have one. But my guilt always stopped me. It wasn't fair to our child to leave him in the hands of strangers. I settled for a course at a local beauty school and learned the art of hair design, then I worked as a stylist part-time. Nothing fantastic like a pediatrician with her own practice . . . with big boobs to boot!

"I'm sorry, Mommy," Bradley grumbled, standing between the feuding adults. "It's my fault. I should've told you last time about Tiff."

Tiff? Sounds so familiar and cozy. I counted a few silent seconds to calm my temper before I spoke. "It's not your fault, Brad. It's your father's. He's responsible for letting me know what's happening, but as usual, he keeps his true feelings all locked up inside himself."

The girlfriend shifted in her strappy sandals. "Actually, we thought about telling you, but I thought—"

"What does it matter what you thought?" I interrupted. "This is between my husband and me."

Jordan placed an arm around the curvy pediatrician and squared my hurting gaze. "I'm not your husband anymore, Caroline. I'm moving on, and you'd better accept it. I'll have Bradley back home on Sunday by five. I suggest you don't stay here and make a scene."

Was that what I was doing? I'd hoped I wasn't quite that bad. Not when she was standing so dignified and controlled with class oozing out of every perfect pore.

Besides, there was Brad, who was already feeling torn apart in opposite directions like a doll in a tug of war. It would only hurt him to see his parents fight. He had enough of that during the last two years of our marriage. That was why we finally gave in to a divorce.

Quickly, I kissed my son on the cheek and gave him a very forced smile. "Have a good time, baby. I'm sorry for all the problems. I'll see you tomorrow at five o'clock when your father drops you back home."

"You're not mad?" he asked with eyes as wide as saucers.

My heart melted as I stooped down and took his little hand. "Of course not, sweetheart. Just have a good time. All Mommy wants is for you to have fun."

"She's got a dog," he chimed in, feeling more comfortable all of a sudden. "He's one of those pug dogs with those funny, pushed-in faces. I've started to train him on how to sit and stuff."

Another whammy out of the blue. Jordan wanted to surprise Brad with a dog on his fifth birthday, but I was the heavy. I said he was too young and that dogs were too much of a responsibility. We settled for a hamster. Everything Jordan lacked in his life with me was suddenly in abundance with his lady doctor. Everything I wasn't, she certainly was.

It stabbed me how happy he seemed. But, wasn't that what I said to him after our divorce hearing last fall? I'll always care for you, Jordan. I'm so sorry this didn't work out. I hope you find your happiness. And I meant it at the time, although my heart was badly breaking. I wanted him to take care of himself, be healthy and well, continue to thrive in his architectural firm. That kind of happiness. Not latching onto centerfolds with the brains to have their own medical practice.

Then she spoke. It wasn't in a bitter voice, but in a tone of warmth and understanding, something I didn't think I deserved after that remark about her being a bimbo. "I'm sorry this wasn't handled very well. It's not an easy thing. I just hope, in time, you and I can learn to get along."

Time? You mean you're going to be hanging around a while? This thing with you and Jordan isn't a passing roll in the hay? I gulped something down that tasted sour and dry, suddenly feeling like a foolish outsider.

"Sure," was all I could manage. Then I quickly looked at Jordan before turning to go back out the door.

It was horrible how it ate me alive that night. The darkness of my bedroom swallowed me like a massive pit, smothering me in visions that I didn't want to have. Her lips on his. His body against hers. Bradley happily prancing around with a pug dog while they stole some steamy moments. It angered me how tears flowed down my cheeks onto my pillow. He wasn't worth crying about. I'd done far too much of that. Wasn't his little fling with his secretary before he moved out the proof of how wrong the relationship was?

"I know it was wrong," I could still recall him confessing. "It was a meaningless one-night stand and a selfish way to deal with my problems. But it's a symptom of a problem. A problem we've had for long time. It shows how far apart we are. I think we need to be honest with ourselves and admit that this marriage is over."

Then why didn't it feel over? Why could I still hear the sounds of him in the house, see his clothes hanging with mine in the closet? Why did the empty side of our bed still call out for the heat of his body? My hand reached out and laid gently on his pillow. How I missed simply lying there and listening to his steady breathing instead of the deafening silence.

Punctual as always, Jordan's car pulled up precisely at five. I peeked out to the driveway from our living room curtains, seeing just the two males. My son and his father gathered some things from the trunk and then walked happily together toward the front door. No bimbo. No puzzle piece that wasn't cut out to belong. Just the two men who meant the most in my world and me waiting inside to greet them.

"Mommy! Look what I found. It's a sand dollar, and it's good luck to find one that isn't all broken."

Brad held a plastic freezer bag filled with sandy shells and dug out one large sand dollar. It still had the salty smell of the beach, which was where he most likely got that whopper of a sunburn. Tiff's beach house . . . the rich and wonderful doctor. Shouldn't a pediatrician know enough to put sun block on a child before he's allowed to play out on the beach? I thought.

"That's fantastic," I said, eyeing his treasure as Jordan remained oddly quiet. "I bet you'll want to find someplace special in your room to keep it. Why don't you go put it up there safe and sound right now?"

He hugged his dad good-bye and ran up the staircase, leaving the two of us alone. It used to be so good to savor little moments of privacy, where we could kiss, whisper seductively in each other's ears, promise a session of lovemaking later on. Now, we simply looked back at each other like strangers. I was relieved when Jordan finally spoke.

"How are you?" he asked, somehow knowing how stupid that sounded. "I mean, I hope you managed to have a good weekend."

Not quite as good as yours, but what the heck. Crying over your empty pillow isn't as much fun as the action you're probably getting at that beach house.

"It was fine," I answered. "I had to work yesterday afternoon, so I kept pretty busy."

"Lots of people needing their hair done?"

"Yeah. Two perms and three cuts."

He nodded. "Good. That's good."

"Not as good as treating a case of measles in a kindergartner, though, is it?" I wanted to bite my tongue, but it was obviously too late. Tiffany was bound to come up sooner or later. I just think we were both hoping it would be later.

"I didn't know how to tell you about her," he muttered. "It was awkward. I guess I just let it slide."

"That's your style," I sarcastically quipped back. "Keep me in the dark while you do whatever you want."

His jaw muscles flinched. "I don't want to fight with you, Caroline. I was just hoping we could talk about things like civilized adults."

"Things?" I echoed, hardening with anger. "Your cheap fling with some floozy in front of our son is simply just a thing? Why can't you just save your sexual romps for weekdays when Brad doesn't have to be a part of it? I'm sure he'd like to have some time alone with you."

He shook his head in frustration. "You're way off the mark. My relationship with Tiffany is hardly just sexual. In fact, you might as well know that I've asked her to marry me. We discussed it with Bradley over the weekend."

I could still see both of his hands hanging down by his sides, but I could've sworn he just punched me in the gut. There was no air to breathe or any way to move away from him. My legs wouldn't work. My mind didn't function. I felt like I suddenly died. How could he marry someone else?

"I know you're shocked," he said apologetically. "But, even though Brad just met her last weekend, Tiff and I have been seeing each other pretty heavily for four months. When we realized this was something special, we knew Brad had to be introduced to her and they should spend some time together. They really have taken quite quickly to each other, and he seems pretty happy about the wedding. I think if you do okay with it, he'll do okay, too. A lot of how he adjusts to having Tiffany as a stepmother will have to do with you."

Words hardly came, and when they did, they sounded so far away. "You want to marry her? Do you know what you're doing? It hasn't been that long since our divorce became final."

"It's been a year," he responded firmly. "And we drifted apart long before that. I'm ready to start over and have love in my life again, Caroline. My heart tells me that Tiffany and I will be very happy."

It looked so easy for him to just pick up with someone new, looking back on our marriage as if it were dust swept under the rug.

Perhaps this was the finality that the divorce papers were supposed to make me feel, but I always had hope. I always felt that move was just a temporary solution to our marital problems. That we shared a son together and too many years of closeness to just toss away. One day we'd find our way to each other again. The arguing, the erosion of our love, the final straw of his one-night stand. It would all evaporate and our future would once again be clear. Me, Jordan, and Brad—the three Musketeers. Just the way it should be.

Tears blurred my vision as I looked at him. "I don't know what to say."

His expression softened with a combination of caring and concern. "I'd like you to say that you wish us well. That you'll accept this and we can all work together for Brad's sake."

And wasn't that the reality? Our son was in the middle and would be deeply wounded if I fought his father's new relationship with my tears, screaming, ranting, and raving, when it actually wouldn't change a thing. What could I do? It was all out of my control. There was nothing left of our marriage to hold onto.

"I'll handle it," I replied coldly. "For Brad, because he's been through enough."

His smile was faint. "Thanks, Caroline. That's all I was wanting from you."

Even after his car left our driveway, those words haunted me like a ghost. He used to want so much more, like kissing me every morning when he woke up, holding me close at night. He used to want us to watch our son grow up together. What happened to those longings? How could he want to marry someone else? Didn't he hurt the way I was hurting and hunger for me deep inside?

"It bites it, but it's time to let go," Dinah said the next day at the salon. She snapped her gum and swept a pile of hair from the floor.

"I've told you, Caroline. It's not good how you hold on and act like the divorce never happened. I mean, I love Frank and still remember the good times, but life goes on for both of us. I've got a great new guy, and Frank's married with a kid on the way. You get used to it once you accept that the past is over. You just need to find yourself someone new."

"You sound like losing a husband is like having a pet die." My tone was short and filled with resentment. I could've used some female understanding. "Just bury the old one and go out and find a new one. It isn't that easy for me."

Her giggle was misplaced and hit me like nails on a chalkboard. "I suppose it isn't that much different, now that you put it like that. It hurts a lot more to keep staring at the empty doggie dishes than it does to just get a new puppy to wag his tail and eat out of them."

Her laughter followed her all the way to the back room, but I didn't see any humor in her remarks.

The only reason her statement did have any merit was because it showed me how Jordan could replace me so fast. It opened up a door of understanding. He was never very good at being alone. Wasn't that why he needed his secretary for comfort when our marriage hit the rocks? That's what he was doing. He was covering up his pain with his new fling with Tiffany. She was the new puppy eating out of the doggie bowls so he wouldn't have to face the emptiness.

"It won't work, Jordan," I whispered into the air. "You can't run from your feelings that way."

It was my turn to lock up that night, and I was more than ready. My feet hurt from standing on them for six straight hours, clipping, cutting, and curling. I still had to pick up Bradley from my mother's and then stop at the grocery store for something to make for dinner. Microwave pizza sounded better by the minute. Just as I went to shut the lights off and lock up the front door, I saw what a mess the magazines were on the table in the lobby. Quickly, I straightened them and put them in some kind of order.

It was then that one particular magazine caught my eye. It wasn't the title so much as one of the articles. In bold letters the headline read: WOMAN ON TRIAL FOR VOODOO CURSE. I wasn't even sure I believed in such things, but I couldn't seem to look away. Soon, I had the magazine stuck in my purse so I could read it later at home.

Once Brad was tucked in bed and I had a quiet moment, I flipped to the story. It was probably just nonsense made up to sell copies of this particular magazine, but what if it wasn't? What if there really was a way to manipulate people and situations with some kind of a magic curse? I eagerly read about this woman's crime and how she controlled her twin sister with a series of voodoo spells. According to the story, she was jealous of her sibling's beauty and of her success. Her sister was a Las Vegas showgirl with a glamorous life, and she was an ordinary housewife. She began practicing black magic and put an evil curse on her sister, which ultimately led to the showgirl's demise. Now the woman was on trial for killing her with witchcraft. As impossible as it seemed, I wondered if it was true. Could a simple curse bring you the results that you wanted? If it had the power to actually kill someone, couldn't it also just break up a wedding? That's all I wanted. I just needed more time for Jordan to see that he and I could still find real happiness together. We could learn from our mistakes and go on.

It may have been a ridiculous plan, but it helped in the weeks to come. As I saw more and more of Tiffany on the weekends sharing time with my son, I kept telling myself that this wedding would never happen. I'd keep studying witchcraft and put a wrench in their plans. Nothing major, of course. Just give her a case of the flu or give Jordan a flat tire. Anything to keep them apart so their union didn't become legal. All I needed was a chance to convince Jordan our love wasn't over. If I had to go to desperate measures to prevent their wedding from happening, then so be it. It would be worth it in the end.

By the middle of June, I was more than ready. I had spent countless weeks studying the art of voodoo curses, and I knew just the one to chant on their wedding day. The only thing I needed was a lock of Tiffany's hair. For once, it was a good thing that I wasn't some hotshot career woman and was just a simple stylist. It gave me the perfect opportunity to get what I needed—the last ingredient for my spell.

"This means a lot to me," Tiffany said as I trimmed and layered her shining hair. "I thought with the wedding this afternoon, that maybe you wouldn't be there or allow Brad to be our ring bearer. I was afraid our differences would get in the way. Jordan and I kept hoping you'd somehow be supportive, but we never dreamed you'd be generous enough to offer to do my hair before the ceremony. I hope you know how much I prayed for this. Just to have you as a friend. I know Jordan means the world to both of us."

What was she, nuts? Didn't she understand that I was his wife all of those years and that I even gave birth to his child? How could she be so caring and warm toward me like this? Wasn't I as big a threat to her as she was to me? I was his past and she was his future. At least, she thought she was going to be his future.

"I've come to a place where I'm comfortable with what's happening," I told her. It was true. Just not in the way that it sounded. "I want to do my part to make sure this all turns out like it's supposed to. I know we'll all be happier in the end."

A bright smile spread across her face, revealing some perfect dimples. "God does answer prayers. I talked to Him so long about helping you get to that place where you could see me in a positive light and not hate me for being a part of Jordan's and Brad's lives. I'm not here to take anyone's place, Caroline. That was never my intention. I want you to know that and believe that I'd really like to be your friend. I know Jordan still loves you in his own special way. And Brad thinks you're the best mother in the history of the world. I can't compete with that, and I won't ever pretend to. I hope that helps put some of your fears to rest."

As I looked at her in the mirror, so sincere and beautifully selfless, I felt horrible for the underhanded things I was planning. She seemed to have a heart of gold, while mine was nothing but granite. Suddenly, I didn't feel so very good about my own somber reflection.

"You believe Jordan still loves me?" An ache rose in my throat.

Her gaze misted with a tender understanding. "I know he will always love you. You gave him years and memories that no one else could give him. You had a beautiful son with Jordan, and that will forever bond you. Even though things got difficult and your marriage didn't survive, those good times are something you'll both carry inside of you no matter what other directions your new lives will take you."

It was what I needed so badly to hear. That it wasn't all for nothing. That Jordan wasn't able to just cut me from his soul as if I never meant a thing to him at all. And once I digested what she said, I felt a flowing peace. The pain of letting go, of seeing him happy with another woman, was now more of an acceptance, a part of fate that I had to find a quiet resignation for. And if I had to be honest with the deepest part of my heart, I began to feel that this was how it was supposed to be.

She saw my tears and stood up from her chair, her plastic apron crinkling between us as we hugged. To my amazement, she was also crying softly. As she pulled back to look me in the eye, her cheeks were moist and glistening.

"I'd say you and I are very lucky women." She smiled. "Jordan is a gift in both of our lives. Let's celebrate that today, okay? Neither one of us are losing. We both have a special man and little boy in our hearts, and now we have a new friend in each other. I don't think it gets any better than that."

My heart overflowed as I drowned in her gaze. "You're really a special lady who has taught me a lot today. I'm glad Jordan's marrying someone like you. I think he'll finally really be happy."

"And you'll be happy," she playfully scolded. "You'll find that perfect fit, too. You have a lot to offer a man. I admire you a great deal."

My jaw dropped. The educated pediatrician was looking at the simple hairdresser and talking admiration?

"You do? Why?" I gaped in disbelief.

"You have the priorities my parents never had, and I know Brad treasures that greatly. You gave up your dreams to devote yourself to raising your child. He never knew what it was like to feel neglected by two career parents, to go to school functions alone, to come home to an empty house. That's how I grew up, and it hurts me to this day. It was like being successful was more important than family. You knew better. Brad is a very lucky child to be blessed with such love and dedication. Nothing in this world could mean more than being a good mother. You should be very proud of yourself."

I wasn't proud. Not proud at all, but only I knew the true reasons. Up until this day, I had planned to ruin their wedding with anything I could get my hands on. The curse I'd been practicing still echoed in my ears as I looked down at the locks of hair scattered on the floor tiles.

I began sobbing with guilt and hugged her tightly. "I'm so sorry for my jealousy and all the problems I've caused. You just don't know how out of hand things were getting. I wanted to stop this wedding at any expense. I didn't want you to have my ex-husband."

"Do you hear what you just said?" she whispered into my ear. "You called him your ex-husband. That's been hard for you. I noticed that when we met. I think God has helped you to get to the place of healing you had to be at. Without it, your anger would consume you."

I blinked back in shock. I finally did call Jordan my ex. A broad smile spread across my face. "And God's peace feels so much better than the devil's game of horrid revenge. Today isn't just the start of your new life with Jordan, but a new kind of life for me, too. I can finally move ahead and put the past behind me. How can I ever thank you for that?"

"By being at the church and sharing in the celebration. It would mean a lot to have you there."

And as I watched Jordan and Tiffany exchanging marriage vows at the altar later that day, my heart soared with happiness. For her. For Jordan. For Bradley. For me. For all that our new lives would bring us.

THE END

www.ingramcontent.com/pod-product-compliance
Lightning Source LLC
Chambersburg PA
CBHW071342170626
46811CB00003B/956